ORDINARY
MAGIC

ORDINARY MAGIC

Caitlen Rubino-Bradway

BLOOMSBURY

NEW YORK BERLIN LONDON SYDNEY

First published in the United States of America in May 2012
by Bloomsbury Books for Young Readers
www.bloomsburykids.com

Bloomsbury is a registered trademark of Bloomsbury Publishing Plc

For information about permission to reproduce selections from this book, write to
Permissions, Bloomsbury BFYR, 175 Fifth Avenue, New York, New York 10010

Library of Congress Cataloging-in-Publication Data
Rubino-Bradway, Caitlen.
Ordinary magic / by Caitlen Rubino-Bradway.
p.   cm.
Summary: In a world where everyone possesses magical abilities, powerless
twelve-year-old Abby, an ordinary, is sent to a special school to negotiate a
magical world with her unmagical "disability"—and to avoid being prey of
the kidnappers, carnivores, and goblins ready to prey upon the ords.
ISBN 978-1-59990-725-3
[1. Magic—Fiction. 2. Boarding schools—Fiction. 3. Schools—Fiction.] I. Title.
PZ7.R831328Or 2012   [Fic]—dc23   2011035100

Book design by Donna Mark
Typeset by Westchester Book Composition
Printed and bound in the U.S.A. by Thomson-Shore Inc., Dexter, Michigan
2 4 6 8 10 9 7 5 3

All papers used by Bloomsbury Publishing, Inc., are natural, recyclable products
made from wood grown in well-managed forests. The manufacturing processes
conform to the environmental regulations of the country of origin.

For Diana Lampe Siwek
for being there from the start

ORDINARY MAGIC

CHAPTER 1

The day of my Judging dawned bright and clear and hot. It was searing; the air pressed against my chest with each breath. It was Olivia's turn to look after me (to make sure my dresser cast up the right clothes, that food appeared on the table, and that the hundreds of everyday things that needed doing when you were underage got done) and with all the craziness going on, no one noticed her smuggling me up to the upstairs bathroom. Then she attacked me.

"Ow!"

"Hold still."

"It hurts."

"It hurts because you're not holding *still*. You know, we'd be done by now if I could do this *normally*." The tiles scritched together as Olivia called in magic, and the bathroom took on a funny sort of double vision, a blurry knife's edge between reality and what Olivia wanted it to be. I could see it, but I couldn't feel it—you can't when you're a kid, not until you're ready, not until after you have been Judged.

"Are you going to explain it to Mom?" I asked.

Olivia hesitated (because she has to be dramatic), then waved her hand to open a window and let the spell drift out. We both knew there was no way Mom would let magic touch her kid three seconds before Judging. Nasty stuff could happen if a kid wasn't prepared, or mature enough to handle it. Olivia shrugged it off with an exaggerated sigh. She sighed gorgeously; I'd seen one of her sighs knock a man stupid at forty paces. "Fine," she said, dragging it out. "I'm an artist. I can work with anything."

Olivia tilted my head up until I was staring directly into the light. "Now stop the drama. You know you missed this."

Which was true. I had. Olivia only just moved back home a few weeks ago after graduating, and promptly picked up her Big Sister Duties with a vengeance. I was three the last time I had a full-time big sis in the house, and it turns out it's awesome. When she doesn't lock me in the bathroom.

Speaking of big sisters . . . "Do you think Alexa's here yet?" I asked, shifting.

"Of course she is, sweets. Now stop moving."

"But she has a meeting. Another meeting," I said, my stomach slowly twisting into knots. My eldest big sister, Alexa, worked for the Department of Education, running some private school for rich kids or something in Rothermere. The way she treated it you might think she worked for National Security. She wasn't allowed to talk about what she did, and there were always Important Things popping up at the last minute.

* * *

"Oh my goodness, you listen to me—she is not going to miss the most important day of your life." Olivia swapped out blush for eye shadow. "Mom would *kill* her."

Someone pounded on the door. "Who's in there? Is that you, Abby?" Mom demanded.

Olivia held a finger to her lips, like if we stayed quiet Mom might give up and go away. She should have known better.

"I know you're in there."

"No, she's not," Olivia called.

"Girls." Mom used her "this is a warning" voice.

"Abby's totally not in here. Did you check the kitchen? You know she likes . . . food," Olivia said.

"I'm counting to three."

Olivia waved her hand at the door and it swung open. "Surprise! Wow, Mom, you're a total phoenix."

"Hi, Mom!" I echoed, peeking around Olivia. She was right. Olivia might be the knockout of the family, but our mom can really put it together when she wants to.

Olivia nudged me back into place. "If I have to tell you to hold still *one more time*, I'm *tying* you down."

Mom took in my face, then cast a long, wry look at my big sister. "What have you done to Abby?"

"I'm making her beautiful. *More* beautiful," Olivia corrected. "We're not done, you can't judge it yet."

Mom waved on the water and cast up some soap, then took Olivia by the shoulder. "You, out. Abby, wash off your face."

"She's an *adult*," Olivia protested as she squeezed by Mom and out the door.

"In name only," Mom said, pinning her with a look. "She is still twelve, and she is going to wash all of that off." When I stood up she said, "Oh, for heaven's sake—she's not even *dressed!*" She grabbed my hand and pulled me out of the room. "You are going to drive me out of my mind. We don't have time for this. We have to leave in *twenty-five* minutes!"

With Olivia tagging after us, Mom dragged me down the stairs, across the shop, up the back stairs, down the hall, and around the corner to my room, muttering to herself the whole way. I jogged beside her, the soft material of my slip plastered to my back and legs with sweat. "Not even dressed yet! What do you think you're doing? We're late already—do you think they wait forever? Do you want to miss your own *Judgment?*"

"Gil almost slept through his," I said.

"Gil is a very special boy," Mom said. "And possibly narcoleptic."

"What about me? Aren't I a special boy?"

"Very cute, young lady." But Mom was smiling as she deposited me in my room. Well, it's sorta mine. As of three weeks ago I'm sharing it with Olivia, because Mom says she and Dad have more important things to worry about than maintaining stretching spells to give us all our own rooms. To be honest, I don't really mind sharing. "Olivia, call everyone in here, then get the jewelry box from my dresser."

"I can get it," I said.

Mom plunked me into a chair in front of the mirror. "Not for another twenty-two minutes. When you're done with that," she told Olivia as she cast up a warm, damp washcloth to rub over my face, "you can change your dress."

"Why? What's wrong with this dress?" Olivia protested innocently, smoothing her skirt. To give her credit, she *was* dressed for the Guild. Her outfit wasn't quite as tight or as low cut as she usually went for.

Mom didn't answer. She didn't need to. There comes a point when you're arguing with Mom that she stops talking, and that's when you just give up and do what she wants because seriously, discussion over.

So Olivia sent out a call, then went off to get the box and change her dress. The summons whispered along the walls, and moments later they came trickling in. Aunts and cousins (I have a *lot* of both) and Grandma (just one of those) appeared, until the room was packed. No Alexa, though. They piled on the bed, smoothed out the wrinkles in the Judging dress, and started laughing and talking until the air buzzed like a nest of pixies. The room was full—full of people, full of noise, full of the scent of perfume and the clatter of jewelry, and the *shuzz* of silk skirts brushing against each other as people squeezed by. And Grandma quietly combed out my hair with wrinkled hands that were still as skilled as a Guild mage's, as soft as . . . You know, there really isn't anything in the world as soft as Gran's hands.

I glanced at the Judging dress through the mirror. The Hale Family Traditional Ceremonial Judging Dress usually hangs in a special wardrobe up in the attic, next to Mom's wedding dress and all the graduation robes we acquired over the years. It's a beautiful dress—silky and rich and deep purple and so ornate that without magic it took at least four hands and fifteen very focused minutes to put it on. I hadn't been around for Alexa's Judging, and I was only three when Olivia walked up the Guild steps, barely old enough to have memories—just a sense of something soft and purple, loud voices, and being passed from person to person. But the pictures were enough; I'd been waiting to wear that dress forever. So I wasn't really sure why nerves were starting to boil in my stomach.

Olivia returned in a rose silk dress with a very modest neckline—and absolutely no back. She was holding the jewelry box up in triumph, and wincing as protection spells crackled around her fingertips. Mom took it; I saw the magic seal fall away like petals to the ground, and there was a slight *click* as the lock opened.

Mom lifted out the amethyst necklace. It was the necklace she wore on her wedding day and each of my siblings wore when they were Judged. (Even the boys had worn it; apparently Gil had claimed, half seriously, it would be bad luck if they didn't. Jeremy said that was stupid, but when his turn came he tucked it under the high collar of his shirt just the same.) The necklace would be Alexa's, as soon as she decided to marry. Grandma held my hair up as Mom fastened it around my neck. It was light and cool, and I shivered as it touched my skin. The stones felt strange for a minute, then felt like nothing at all.

• • •

Most of the family was here, except for a couple of distant cousins who sent flowers and savings bonds. Even Jeremy, who'd been going on and on about how he'd been picked as teacher's assistant this year with all that "responsibility." ("There are meetings. I can't just skip them!") He'd just finished his sixth year at Thorten, where he was a double major and getting distinguished honors and generally making life difficult for everyone who was not that great in school. But he was too busy to come home. He'd complained, "You let Alexa skip things all the time!" Then he had a quiet talk with Dad, the kind where Dad talks and you're quiet, and he ended up arriving three days early.

Alexa appeared just as Dad and Mom called me out of the house to start the procession. She ran through the crowd, her royal red skirts streaking behind her, her hair twisted up in a formal knot that makes her look all grown up and mature and makes you forget that she's only twenty-four—which Mom and Dad insist is very young but I do not get it because she's, like, an adult. She caught me up in a tight hug, twenty pounds of dress and all, and my nervousness leaked away. It was enough just seeing her, hugging her, breathing in the scent that always clung to Alexa's clothes and skin, like fresh air and fizzy soda. "Look at you! You're so pretty! I'm so, so proud of you!" she exclaimed in between smacking kisses.

"She hasn't been Judged yet," Gil said. He looked goofy and completely un-Gil-like in his colorful formals—the high-collared shirt, the frilly neck cloth, and nothing looking rumpled or slept in. His gleaming gold hair was combed (for once) and tied back into a stubby little ponytail.

"Doesn't matter. I know she's going to be amazing. Better

7

than me, I promise," Alexa said. I laughed, and she amended it to, "Better than Gilbert, at least."

Gil rubbed his hands together, grinning. "Care to put money on it? We started a pool."

"I'll put fifty on a Level Six, minimum," Alexa said.

As we headed out, Gil punched my arm. "Don't mess anything up, Abs."

It is only a ten-minute walk to the Guild. We wound down the sandstone streets, past the light stucco buildings, and through the maze of market stalls with their brightly colored umbrellas stretching overhead. It hadn't rained in forever and we kicked up red clay as we walked. It shimmered away from everyone else's magically shielded clothes and stuck to the hem of my unprotected skirts.

As far as processions go, it was not that fancy or long. People barely stopped what they were doing to watch. Some paused to look or to wave, but most just went about their business. There are too many kids in town for one more Judging to garner interest.

The toughest part was keeping at that steady, calm, processional pace. I wanted this to be over and done with. I wanted to finally be able to do things myself, and not have to beg Mom or Dad or anyone else for help with the simplest little chore. I wanted to hitch up my skirts and flat out run—straight down the street, all the way to the Guild. The want was like an itch under my skin.

When we finally reached the Guild, four of the oldest, wrinkliest mages were standing outside on the steps, wearing deep-blue formal colors, gold skullcaps, and bored expressions. An apprentice in much less ostentatious colors rushed down the steps to meet us. He barely glanced up from the crystal hovering in his palm. "You're the ten thirty?"

"That's right," Mom said. "The name is Hale."

"Right. Hale. Perfect. This is the young lady?" he asked, hurrying toward me, his robes flapping around his skinny legs.

I nodded. My mouth had suddenly gone dry.

"Wonderful, perfect. You come right here." He dragged me forward, then jerked me to a stop on the first step. "Hands down at your sides, please, not at your hips. Stand up straight. Smile, please. Very good, very lovely. You're happy, everybody's happy." He called out to the rest of the crowd, "Everybody smile, please." Olivia flashed the apprentice a smile and he blinked, dazed, and derailed into "Wonderful . . . it's wonderful . . . I, um, I"—he cleared his throat—"everybody looks . . . wonderful." He dashed woozily up the stairs to the mages, straightened his clothes, zapped his crystal away, and nodded to Mr. Graidy, the ancient head of the Guild.

Mr. Graidy spoke in a booming voice that hurt my ears. "Who comes before us to be Judged this day? Let her come forward and be named."

We'd rehearsed everything the day before, so I knew what to do. I started walking up the steps, speaking as loud as I could. "My name is Abigail Hale. I come today to be Judged." Staying steady was an out-and-out fight now. Excitement prickled under my skin with little jumps and jolts, urging me to race right up those steps and get this started.

9

* * *

The doors behind the cluster of mages opened on cue. The Guild is a tan blob of a building, one of the oldest in Lennox. No one is sure if it was actually built from stone and brick or if it was called up straight out of the ground, like the royal palace in Rothermere. What catches your eye—first, last, always—is the doors. They are almost as tall as the building and slicked a deep, menacing brown, with big stone rivets. They're the kind of doors you expect to see guarding a secret fortress; they're only missing the skeletons and cobwebs. When these doors opened it was without a murmur, revealing nothing but pitch black beyond.

I'd seen this happen a bunch of times before, for other kids in town, and never cared, but now it felt more important. Something icy shivered down my spine.

"Enter then these portals, Abigail Hale," Mr. Graidy intoned. "So that you may be tested, so that you may be Judged, so that we here present may know your true worth."

My family burst into cheers behind me, and we all followed the mages into the Guild. The doors swung shut behind us, cutting off noise and light.

• • •

My family was served refreshments in the reception room while they waited. Not the good stuff, but I couldn't help wishing I were with them, choking down dusty peanut butter cookies, instead of stuck in a dark room with a bunch of creepy mages and a handful of candles. My eyes adjusted to the dim light, and I made out a huge stone hallway with massive carved pillars forming neat rows on either side. The hallway was much too big to be contained in that small building, but then, magic is like that. We had a similar spell at work at our house, so there's enough room for all of us to live together without driving each other crazy.

There were two pillars, much bigger than the rest, that curved together to form a strange archway. The archway had spells carved into it, and it buzzed with a funny kind of magic. This wasn't the everyday stuff your parents know and you see on the street. It made the archway move and flicker, and it was fuzzy to look at, like my eyes couldn't focus.

"Abigail Hale," Mr. Graidy announced in his "at work" voice. When I ran into him on the street, he just called me Abby, like everybody else. "Are you ready to begin this grueling test of yourself?"

"Yes, I am ready to begin," I said. Finally—*finally*—I was so ready.

"Very well, then, Abigail Hale. Your first test stands before you. You must pass through the Barrier of Fortitude!" He gestured to the archway.

I glanced at the others, but they were all watching me. I stepped up to the arch, took a deep breath (I couldn't dig that shiver out from where it had wormed down into my spine), and stepped through.

Nothing.

Okay, that was . . . strange. I expected something. I'm not sure what, but I expected *something*. For a second I wondered if it was one of those "test of character" things you read about in books—where it's not about what happens but how the hero reacts to it, which really means the author didn't want to write all the interesting stuff—only then I saw the mages talking.

They were huddled together, whispering among themselves with startled little pinpricks of sound. The apprentice was scanning his crystal furiously. They drew apart, and Mr. Graidy cleared his throat. "Would you mind, my dear—stepping through again?"

I stepped back through. Nothing. Again.

When I looked back, they were all staring at me in dumbfounded amazement. Mr. Graidy held up a hand. "Once more, please."

I did. Then again. And again. And then they had me hop back and forth on either foot, until I tripped over the long skirt of my gown and crashed into one of the mages. He squealed and bounded to his feet, swatting at his robes as if they were on fire, screaming, "She touched me! *She touched me!*"

Mr. Graidy rolled his eyes, then clapped his hands and muttered something. With a cinnamony smell, the lights came up.

I had never been this far inside the Guild before. They try to maintain an air of mystery about the place so the only people who really know it are the mages, a couple of repairmen, and the ladies who come to set up for bake sales. The sudden light revealed a large welcoming hall done in cream and beige with several potted plants and a dark floor polished like a mirror. Along one side was a row of cushioned benches under a series of portraits of serious gray-haired men and women with matching sour expressions, as if they'd all been sucking on lemons.

Mr. Graidy glared at me and pointed to the benches. "Sit," he commanded. I didn't, I couldn't (something was *wrong*), but Mr. Graidy immediately turned away and ordered the apprentice, "Please go to the reception area and get this girl's parents."

I heard Mom coming down the hall well before she charged through the door, questions pouring out of her. "What's wrong? Are you okay? You didn't blow up anything, did you? What happened? Are you hurt? You don't look hurt. What happened?" she snapped at the mages. Two jumped back and the one I had crashed into burst into tears.

Dad, on the other hand, strolled in with a cup of lemonade and a sugar cookie.

Mr. Graidy cleared his throat again. "No one was hurt." He paused for a moment. "Mr. Hale, Mrs. Hale. I fear I have some unfortunate tidings. It pains me to have to tell this to anyone, let alone to a distinguished couple such as yourselves, whom I have always regarded as pillars of our fine commun—"

"Get to the point," Mom exploded.

"She's an ord."

"Beg your pardon?" Dad asked. Only Dad could sound totally relaxed and totally serious at the same time, while eating a cookie.

"She didn't even make it past the first stage," said Mr. Graidy. "She has nothing. She *is* nothing. She's an ord."

CHAPTER 2

*O*rd. Oh no, he did not just say that. He did not. It wasn't real.

"Come here, Ab—chil—you, come here." Mr. Graidy reached out to take my arm, then stopped and just waved me toward the barrier.

I closed my eyes and took a deep breath, willing it to work this time, *please work, please.* I wasn't kidding around. My parents were watching.

I stepped through. Nothing.

I turned back, needing to see my parents' faces, yet not wanting to at all. They were holding hands, looking . . . I couldn't tell. I wanted to scream or cry or smash something. It felt like rug burn in my chest.

Then Mom said, "Oh, my baby," and stepped forward, arms out. I rushed to her, and she caught me in a hug right at the barrier. When she passed through the arch, it sparked and popped, and the air in the room rumbled against the walls like fireworks.

Mom brought me back to Dad. My parents looked at each

other, sharing the Secret Parent Look, where they kind of do this telepathic thing, even though they're not. Dad swallowed the last of his lemonade and shrugged. "Okay, now what?"

"You will have to get rid of her," Mr. Graidy said, and not nicely.

"That's ridiculous," Dad said.

"I can't even believe I'm hearing this," Mom said, her arms still tight around me. "Are you seriously saying, Martin, that we should 'get rid of' our daughter?"

"There's no use getting defensive, Mrs. Hale," Mr. Graidy said. "It is the plain truth. There are few options available to the families of ords. It is a shame there are so few, but it's not as if it can be changed." At this point he offered Mom and Dad some "literature" on the subject, reassuring them that he had several more brochures, still sealed in the boxes. It seems that, until me, there hadn't been a need to unpack them.

Mom stepped forward, face flushed, blue crackles of magic snapping around her. Dad put a hand on her shoulder and she took a hard breath, in and out.

Mr. Graidy nodded sympathetically and sent the apprentice off to get a few pamphlets. "I want you to know," he continued, "I sympathize with the frustration you must be feeling. The tragedy of realizing that one of your own is . . ." He sighed. "This must be very hard. I understand that many families experience difficulty in deciding what to do. I believe a few occasionally decide to keep their . . . their . . ."

"Children," Mom cut in.

"Their children, yes. Traveling families, that sort of thing, who don't have to live with . . . normal society. But in most cases, in situations like *yours*, well, you cannot be carried away by sentiment and emotion at such a time as this. You must consider what is best for the child, as well as what is best for you," Mr. Graidy said, his words smooth and professional.

"And what, exactly, would be best for *us*?" Dad asked. His voice was smooth too. Smooth and very quiet.

"Surely you must see, Mr. Hale," Mr. Graidy said, his face a mixture of suspicion and disbelief, "that this touches not only your family, but each and every person associated with you. The town is affected by this. The entire town—"

"Stop. Now."

"Mr. Hale—"

"I'm not going to give you another chance," Dad replied, and his tone was so hard and cold and final that Mr. Graidy stopped.

The apprentice reappeared with a few glossy pamphlets in his hand. Our fingers brushed as he passed me the bundle. His face got all tight, and he snatched his hand back and started rubbing it on his robes. He was still at it when we left.

• • •

The doors opened to the right, where my family milled around, cheerful and noisy. I passed through the door, the sun bright through the windows, and somehow I kept walking, though I didn't want to. As if my body took off on its own without even asking me first. Heat crept up my neck, and I was still walking toward everyone, half hoping that I would keep going straight out of the building, down the street, and out of the county.

I wanted to cry, but with the heat and pressure it was hard enough to breathe.

Gil noticed something was wrong first. "What's the matter, freckles? Did you get a three? A two?"

"I-I . . ."

"What is it? Did you turn Graidy into a frog? They don't penalize you for that, you know."

"I didn't do anything." I pushed the words out of my swollen throat. "I can't—I'm an ord, Gil."

Gil grinned. He looked like Mom when he did that, but like a guy version of Mom. "No, you're not."

But then he saw Mom and Dad. And then he looked frightened and very young. I kept thinking if he looked at me the way the mages did, if he looked at me like *that*, I would run screaming out of the building.

But he didn't. He smiled at me, and he looked like normal, everyday Gil. "Okay, you're an ord." He tugged on my hair, and I had to smile too. "We're still going to party, right?"

CHAPTER 3

Ords.

You only ever hear about them as kids. You only ever *hear* about them, in that whisper-down-the-lane way. Your aunt's neighbor's kid's best friend turned up ord. Just last week, the waitress at the coffee shop served a couple who had an ord with them. Everybody knows somebody who knows somebody else who met the family of an ord; the family of a kid who can't do magic.

And you only ever hear them talk about the family. Always with those sad faces, always talking about how strong they are, dealing with it, how thankfully, everybody else in their family is normal. You never hear anybody talk about the kid, unless it's to say they seemed so normal, you'd never have expected it.

Because there's only one thing you can do with an ord. Get rid of it.

• • •

Right before we left, Alexa rushed up next to me and grabbed my hand. She didn't say anything, but she didn't have that worried look in her eyes like Mom and Dad did. I clung to her, and winced as the doors opened and the sunlight poured in.

I could see the news travel through the crowd. Saw it in their faces, the way everyone's expressions changed as they heard. I could hear the whispers following us, hissing through the market. And the worst part was how they *all* stopped talking after they heard. I don't know if you have ever heard a whole street of people go completely silent before, but it's creepy.

To be fair, some of them tried to act normal. But no one would look me in the eye, and instead tried to sneak sharp little stares when my head was turned. I could feel them like pinpricks on my skin. If I looked back, they'd quickly glance away. Olivia—eyes bright, blinking rapidly—glared down the gawkers.

No one said a word. I think that was the worst part; they were all so quiet, like it was a funeral.

There was a party planned. Friends and neighbors had been invited and expected, especially the throng of boys who flocked around Olivia. In the end it was only family—bad news travels fast, I guess. I told myself I didn't care that none of my classmates, none of my *friends*, showed up. And I didn't care that Aunt Vicky went white-faced when she heard and excused herself early. Nobody liked her anyway and she gave the worst presents at Twelfth Night. (Though Mom did catch her before she could wink away and told her, "If you leave now, don't ever come back." Aunt Vicky left.)

But I did care when Alexa took Olivia—who couldn't stop

blinking, who had a hand over her mouth—by the elbow and led her around the side of the house. She did it casually, like we weren't supposed to notice. As if we couldn't hear how upset Olivia got the second she was out of sight. Gil tried to turn me around, tell me a joke, but I shrugged him off and went after them.

Alexa, her fingers still digging into Olivia's elbow, spat out fierce little whispers. "Pull yourself together, you don't want her to see—"

And Olivia scrubbed at her eyes, covered her face with her hands, even as she kept shaking her head. "She can't . . . she won't . . ." Her voice broke and she stopped.

Alexa's expression went so hard and angry I took a step back. "Yes. She will. She'll do everything, just differently. And this isn't help—"

They both looked up then, as if they sensed me watching. Before anybody could say anything, Mom and Dad came over. Mom took one look at the situation and wrapped Olivia up in a hug. Olivia buried her face in Mom's shoulder as Mom stroked her hair.

Dad put his hand on my shoulder. When I didn't move he turned me around and guided me back to the party.

"Shouldn't we discuss this?" I asked. Mom and Dad were big on discussing stuff, though half the time that meant sitting down and listening to them tell you how it was going to be. Right at that moment, I would have been okay with that. It would have been easier if I knew what was going to happen.

"Discuss later," Dad said. "Party now."

* * *

When Mom and my sisters came back, red-eyed but calm, they took me inside and ushered me up to my room. Olivia and Alexa peeled me out of the Judging dress, and Mom sat me down and unpinned my hair. With the noise of the party filtering up to us, Mom ran her fingers through the braids and brushed out my hair until it hung free and heavy down my back, and I felt like myself again.

I started to take off the amethyst necklace, but Alexa stopped me. "It doesn't count," I told her as she refastened it around my neck. "I wasn't even Judged." But Alexa shook her head, then steered me out of the room and back down to the party.

The afternoon passed in a blur. There was no moon that night. When it turned dark the lights that Mom and Dad had strung in the garden twinkled to life. Coffee and fruit came out—pears drizzled with honey, and poached oranges. Steaming mint tea swirled into our teacups. Gil picked another argument, this time with Olivia, and we all pretended to ignore Dad sneaking over to pick through the presents and set aside things to return later. I figured it was the usual stuff: dolls I wouldn't be able to make move, a charm bracelet that would end up empty, a My First Potion kit that guaranteed *Hours of Enchanting Fun!*

But that's not what I remember the most about that night. What I remember is the music, twisting up into the night like ribbons. I remember pears so soft I cut them up with a spoon, the juice and honey dribbling down my chin as I scooped them into my mouth. The way the garden lights made everything look soft and secret. And I remember Dad carrying me inside after the party ended, my head against his shoulder, sleepy, full, and safe.

. . .

I woke up the next morning alone. Which was . . . strange. There's always someone there to wake me and get everything going. To charm the blankets on the bed smooth, summon clothes out of the dresser. For a second I remembered—I was twelve now, I'd been Judged, I could . . .

Then I really remembered. Ord.

It was weird; I felt exactly the same today as I did yesterday. Shouldn't you feel different after you find out that you're, you know, totally useless? I guess not. You're born an ord, I knew that. So I'd always been useless. I just didn't know it until yesterday.

I was wondering how long I'd have to wait for someone to come get me when I noticed there was something off about the room. It felt the same, but it looked and sounded different. My furniture looked strange, like it was just wood and knobs, pillows and cushions and blankets, and nothing else. I got up and pulled my sheets straight. They lay where I left them. I tiptoed to my dresser and pulled open the drawers. Underwear, socks, and shirts sat in neatly folded piles. In my wardrobe, dresses hung still and silent. This was more than just weird. This was on purpose. Someone must have come in while I slept and drained the room dry.

I got dressed quickly, and rushed to the door. It opened when I turned the handle but stayed that way, open and lifeless. I took the stairs two at a time and hurried toward the low, serious murmur of voices in the kitchen. There was Olivia's sharp ". . . trade her away like a plate . . ." And Dad said something about "no way, not ever," and then Gil, louder, "Graidy has lost his mind if he thinks . . ."

The conversation stopped as I skidded in and everyone turned to look at me. Gil was up at the counter (it was his turn to make breakfast), cracking eggs in the air. They sizzled as they fell, and landed, fried and tasty, on the serving plate. Everyone else was clustered around the kitchen table with coffee mugs. (Except for Jeremy, because he and I are still too young for coffee. Mom and Dad won't let us touch the stuff until we're eighteen, which is fine by me because Gil snuck some to me once and it is nasty.)

It was strange to see them all there. Gil spent most of his days at the kitchen table with a notebook jotting down ideas for his books, but Mom and Olivia should have been at our family's bakery at this hour, well into the morning rush, and Dad always liked to knock off a few hours at his loom before we called him in to breakfast.

"What's going on?" I asked.

Mom came over and gave me a kiss. "Good morning, baby. How'd you sleep?"

"Awful. What's going on? What did Mr. Graidy do now?"

There was a pause. Gil hurriedly cast a bowl down from one of the shelves and snapped his fingers; cinnamon buns clamored up like popcorn popping. (I must have seen them make breakfast a thousand times. It was so normal. How could I not do something so normal?) Jeremy took a hasty, choking gulp of his juice. And Olivia raked her eyes up and down the table, her mouth half-open. I wasn't sure anyone was going to answer, when Alexa did. "The mages at the Guild offered to buy you."

My stomach twisted into a hot, heavy pit. Every kid knew what happened to ords whose families didn't want them—and most families didn't. After what Mom and Dad said to Mr. Graidy, I didn't think . . . I knew they wouldn't—probably—but for a moment I wondered if this was what the kitchen table was going to look like from now on. Without me. "How much did they offer?" I asked.

"We're not going to sell you," Dad assured me.

"I want to know what the going rate for an ord is."

"A lot," Alexa told me, lifting her arms as place settings blossomed along the table in front of everyone.

"Actually, their offer was pitiful," Gil added cheerfully. "Way below market price. We could get three or four times that for you on the black market, easy."

"That is hardly appropriate," Jeremy snipped. He gets snippy a lot, but this morning his voice had a little something extra. His glasses didn't exactly hide the dark circles under his eyes, and his face was so pale it made all his freckles stand out.

"So, what if someone offers market price?" I asked.

There was an outburst of noise and protests, and Jeremy announced I wasn't being logical, of course they wouldn't sell me, because it was *illegal*, for heaven's sake. Alexa gave him a look that said *you're not helping*, and Gil smacked him on the back of the head, and Olivia said, yes, that was the *only* reason they weren't going to sell me.

* * *

Mom sat calmly on a faded wooden kitchen chair like a queen on her throne and waited until everything died down. When it did, she pointed to the space in front of her. I scrambled over. She took my hands. "Abby, look at me." I looked at her. Her warm brown eyes were serious and steely. "We are not going to sell you to anyone."

"Then what are you going to do with me?" My voice cracked.

"Oh, my baby," Mom murmured, and she hugged me close and rocked me as if I were still a little girl. Dad pulled a chair over and tucked me on his lap, and he told me not to worry because he and Mom would always, *always* take care of me.

It was Alexa who finally answered my question. "You're going to school."

"I thought I wasn't allowed to go to school," I said, leaning into Dad.

"I don't mean normal school." She rolled her eyes and tilted her head at me. "Abby, what is my job?"

"I don't know, you never say anything about it."

"I do too."

Olivia shook her head as Gil set out the food. "No, you don't."

"You always give us that line about how you're under contract and you can't give away any details, like you're a secret agent or something," Gil said, taking a seat. "I mean, we know you work for the king, which is really cool, right? And also something with education? That's all you have ever said."

"She means a school for ords," Jeremy said, as if he couldn't believe that he had to explain something so simple to us. Which is pretty much how he talks all the time.

We all stared at him, except for Alexa, who was grinning. "Are you serious?" I said.

Jeremy sighed and counted it off on his fingers. "It's not that hard. Okay, we know she works for the king, in education, on something she's never mentioned until now. Please, think with your brain muscles, people."

Mom cleared her throat.

"Sorry," Jeremy added.

A school for ords? I turned to Alexa. "There's a school for ords?"

"We've kept it pretty quiet," she said. "Not everyone's thrilled with the idea of educating ords. Or taking them off the market. But it's a really nice place. Good kids. Small student body, but we're working on that."

A hundred questions pressed down on me. "And you're going to get me in?"

"Yes," she said.

"Just like that?"

She crossed her arms over her chest. "What's this? You doubt me?"

"No." I grinned. "Not really."

Alexa looked at Mom and added, "She will have to apply like everyone else. Consider it a formality."

There was something in the way she said it, as if it really were that simple, that made the tension seep out of the room. Smells rushed in on me, and we all seemed to remember at the same time that there was food not being eaten; platters started getting passed around. I grabbed a bun out of the bowl before Olivia zapped it over to Dad. It was warm in my hands, and I knew when I pulled it apart it would be sweet and steaming.

"The school year's almost over," Alexa continued, sipping her coffee. "So there's no good in rushing you in now. We do have kids during the summer, but that's mainly because their families don't want them back. I think it'd be best to have you start next school year, in the fall."

"Where exactly, might I ask, is this school that we're sending our baby sister to?" Jeremy asked, ignoring the eggs spooning themselves onto his plate.

"Rothermere," Alexa said.

I stopped, a forkful of eggs halfway to my mouth. Mom and Dad glanced at each other.

"Ro—Rothermere?" Jeremy repeated. "But it's a big city."

"Can you pass the salt, Gil?" I asked.

"No. You don't need any salt for those eggs," Gil said.

"They're bland," I insisted.

"I cast those eggs perfectly," Gil said, holding the salt prisoner. "Can't expect an ord to know about fine cooking."

"She'll be perfectly safe," Alexa said to Jeremy.

"But she's *twelve*. You want to send our twelve-year-old sister to Rothermere?" he asked.

I gave Olivia one of those sweet, innocent smiles you perfect when you're the baby of the family. "Can you pass the salt, Livvy?"

"Of course I will. Anything for you," Olivia cooed.

Gil stabbed at his plate with his fork and muttered that Olivia was *so* making breakfast next week.

"She's not going to be alone. It's not like we're going to give her a couple bucks and tell her to have a nice life."

"Mom! Dad!" Jeremy looked to them for intervention. "You're not serious."

Olivia laughed. "You didn't throw this much fuss when I went up there."

"That's because he likes Abby better than you," Gil told her.

Which isn't true. Not really. Jeremy's just protective. I mean, they all are—that happens when you're the baby of the family by *a lot*. Jeremy was the baby for five years before I came along, and I think he was getting a little sick of it. So when I showed up, he latched on to the big-brother role with a vengeance.

Just so you know, Rothermere's not that big a deal. It's not like I'd never been to the capital city. Actually, it's one of the few places I have been, with Alexa living there and Olivia visiting all the time, too, for school. We made pretty regular trips, including a few special girls-only, shopping-sleepover weekends.

But Rothermere was still *Rothermere*, where the Royal Court was. Where King Steve lived and ruled and judged.

Of course, there's more than just the court—though that's enough. There are living trees that tangle up anything that strays too close, swallowing them in a knot of roots and branches. There are tame wyverns and wild dragons. There are Black Ladies or Red Ladies or White Ladies, who will devour you or give you gifts, depending on their mood. (Come to think

28

of it, most of the rumors I heard about Rothermere were about either stuff you could eat, or stuff that could eat you.) There are Svar bishops and Majid traders, and coffee shops on every corner, and noise and carpets and people everywhere, all the time.

"What about the bazaar people?" Jeremy retorted. "Didn't you just tell us how certain people want to get their hands on ords? How valuable is she?"

"Not that bizarre," Gil said. "If she's worth something."

"She's worth a lot," Alexa said.

"No, not 'strange' bizarre, I mean 'festival' bazaar, the festival auction people," Jeremy sputtered.

Olivia let out a satisfied *mmmm*. "He's so *cute* when he can't talk." Fuming, Jeremy chucked a roll at her head. She froze it halfway, then pushed it out of the way as she leaned over to pinch his cheeks. "And such a *sweetie*. How is it you don't have a girlfriend?"

"*Mom!*"

"Olivia," Mom said mildly, and Olivia flashed back into her seat.

"We're talking about Abby here," Jeremy continued.

"He has a point," Alexa said.

"He does?" Olivia asked.

Gil slapped Jeremy on the back. "All right, way to go, first time."

Alexa ignored them and addressed Mom and Dad. "You are going to want to keep an eye on her, whenever anybody new comes into town. Some people don't take no for an answer."

"If you don't mind my asking," Jeremy kept going, "what is the point of sending her to this school? I mean, what's Abby going to learn there that she can't learn here? That the Guild won't be able to teach her?"

Gil started laughing. "'What's the *point*?' Jeremy, you're going to be the worst teacher ever."

"That's not what I'm saying!" Jeremy's face was going red again. "I'm saying I don't get what's wrong with Abby staying here. With *us*. She could work for the Guild, as a job, and we could protect her. Alexa, of all people, *you* should know what their lives are like. What their life expectancy is."

"Jeremy," Mom said in a harsh voice.

"If you knew anything about ords, which you don't because you live in this perfect little bubble," Alexa said, her anger making the magic in the air sizzle and the room start to creak in toward her, "you would know that life expectancy is directly related to ord lifestyle. Of course they're going to"—she glanced at me—"wear out young when they're dragged all over the place, barely fed, and forced to jump through booby-trapped hoops every day of the year. That's not what's going to happen to Abby. I won't let it."

Jeremy wasn't deterred. "She's not going to be able to do anything on her own."

"I'm right here," I said.

"Exactly," Alexa shot back, stabbing an angry finger on the table. "She needs to learn how to survive."

Alexa leaned forward and spoke very clearly. "Abby won't be

able to get an education anywhere else. What, are you going to talk Thorten into taking her? Teach her all your little sparkly tricks? I'm sure that will do her a lot of good. At this school Abby will be able to learn how to live without magic." She put her elbows on the table and rubbed her eyes. "I never thought I'd have to give this speech to my own family. I didn't mean it like that, Abby," she added quickly. "It's just frustrating hitting up against the same walls over and over again."

"That's just Jeremy," Gil said. "He's frustrating in general." He reached over and whacked Jeremy on the back of the head.

Mom smiled at Dad. "Has she really been working there four years? When did we get so old?"

"You? Never." Dad leaned in to kiss her. "You never get old," he said, kissing her again. "You're still as pretty as the day we met."

Olivia rolled her eyes dramatically, and Gil covered his face with his hands, like we all do whenever Mom and Dad start making kissy faces at each other. "Do you have to start that again?" Gil demanded. "We don't need another brother or sister. Wasn't Abby enough of a surprise?"

Dad kissed Mom again—a dipping, smacking one that had us all groaning.

Alexa waited until the embarrassing display was over, then took a deep breath. "What Abby needs to learn," she said, "is that being an ord doesn't shut you off from life. It changes the way you go about it."

Jeremy opened his mouth to start backup, but Mom cut him

off. "Enough. Your father and I will discuss all of our options and decide what is best for Abby. And you"—she turned to me—"hurry up and eat. You still have school today. Your *other* school."

CHAPTER 4

I never realized how many people said hello to me until that morning, when they didn't. People shut up when I approached, and started talking again when I passed (*you'd never guess, the rest of her family is all fine*), as if their not being able to see me prevented me from hearing them.

I got to school right ahead of our teacher. Most of the other kids were talking in a big clump in the front of class. Billy Peterson also got Judged yesterday and things turned out a lot better for him. He was giving a play-by-play, and the other kids were caught up enough that I was able to sneak over to my seat.

A moment later the bell chimed and Mrs. Andrews appeared by her desk, all sunshine and violet petals. Everyone rushed to their places. I could tell when they noticed me because the whole room went quiet. Billy Peterson froze in the aisle when he saw me. He glanced at the teacher, then squeezed past me to his seat and shoved himself as far up against the wall as he could.

"Good morning, class. And how are we all today?" Mrs.

Andrews was a short woman with frizzy hair and the kind of singsongy voice that makes your ears bleed. "I hope we are all feeling very productive today. I understand congratulations are in order for William—"

Billy stuck his hand up in the air and waved it around until it almost popped out. "Mrs. Andrews? Abby Hale came to school today."

Mrs. Andrews glanced over at me, blinked once, twice, then tilted her head to the side.

Billy Peterson raised his hand again. "Also, Mrs. Andrews? My parents sent in a note about that, just in case. They'd like you to change my seat."

Mrs. Andrews skimmed the note. "Thank you, William, but I do not think that will be necessary."

I stuck my tongue out at him.

"The ord will come here. Everyone else, it is time for your examination."

I eased to my feet and headed up to the front, not believing what I had just heard. Mrs. Andrews vanished the textbooks from the desks, replacing them with test papers and pencils while I stood waiting. When the rest of the kids were working, she turned to me. "Ord—"

"It's *Abby*."

Mrs. Andrews blinked, and I noticed her knuckles clenched white on the desk. It had come out a lot stronger than I meant. "Er . . . yes, I think you should go home now. This is an important time for you, and your family needs to reflect on what next to do."

✳ ✳ ✳

"That's all right. I'd rather be in school."

"You have been through an ordeal. You need time to rest and reflect."

"Not according to my parents," I said.

"I am sure your parents would agree with me. I will put a note in your bag." *A note to my parents?* I was being sent home with a note to my parents. "It will explain everything. I am sure they will decide what is best for you. Please clear out your things from your cubby before you leave."

"I'm not coming back? Am I getting kicked out of school?" I asked.

Mrs. Andrews stood and mimed putting an arm around my shoulders. "Come along . . . child, I will help you gather your things."

She didn't help at all. She opened the portal and called out the cubbies, then stood there watching me as I got my lunch and cleared out my shelf of old papers. Before she sent away the portal, she pulled in the rest of the shelves around my now empty one until it folded out of existence.

• • •

Two hours later I was sitting outside school with the rest of my class. We were on an impromptu recess while Mom and Dad talked to Mrs. Andrews. I was sitting in the big olive tree on the crooked branch. The other kids were spread throughout the yard, kicking up clouds of dust, well away from the shade of my tree even though the day had turned hot. One kid (Jack, who's a bit of a bully) shoved Billy Peterson toward me; Billy dug in his heels, frantically shaking his head.

I was close enough that I could see Mom and Dad and Mrs. Andrews in the empty schoolroom. "I am afraid some of the parents have expressed displeasure at the prospect of an ord being taught among the other children," Mrs. Andrews was saying. Her voice carried, clear as crystal, through the open windows.

"She's an ord," Dad replied. "She's not catching."

"I am afraid they have threatened the immediate removal of their children from this fine institution if Abigail was to continue here."

Mom laughed. It was a sharp, bitter sound. "You mean they're threatening to make their kids stupid if my daughter keeps coming to school?"

Across the yard, Jack and a couple of his partners were saying something to Billy, something that included a lot of pointing at me and poking him. Finally Billy shouted, "I am not!" and marched over to me.

He stopped a safe distance from the tree. "I got a question."

I nodded, grateful to have someone talking to me, even if it was Billy.

"I'm trying to figure out which school I wanna go to." He held up a hand to shield his eyes from the sun. "You know I did totally good when I was Judged. I reached Level Five."

"You can go to almost any school you want to," I recited. Skill levels show how much power and ability you have. That's the whole point of Judging kids, to determine how strong you are so you know whether you should go to a regular school, like Challis or Lochlora, or a hard school like Thorten or Ashtend,

36
* * *

or whether you need to go to the impossibly hard, scary ones like Wixis. Level Five was very good, just shy of impressive, and opened a lot of doors, but there were two or three schools (like the Summer Palace up in the North Inlet) that wouldn't even look at you unless you were at least an Eight. But Eights are almost as rare as ords.

"Mom wants me to apply to Wixis and Ashtend, and Dad's been talking up Byes, but that's only because he went there. I've been thinking about Thorten. What do you think?"

"Thorten's really good. You know, you should talk to my brothers. Both of them got into Thorten. Gil said they're very strict, but Jeremy loves it. He's going to try to get into the grad program early, because—"

"And I heard that they're totally snooty about who they let in too," Billy interrupted.

"They are."

"Good," Billy said. "My mom says I'm going to need the best education available."

"Jeremy will probably be teaching your classes," I boasted.

"No way," Billy scoffed. "I don't want to get infected. Besides, my mom says he's going to get expelled because of you."

"He is not," I fired back, feeling hot and sick. "He's the best student there. He going for two different degrees and . . . and he runs the school book club." I couldn't stop now. "And Gilbert, he's a Level Six. Did you know that? Remind me, is Six above or below Five?"

Billy crossed his arms, his mouth twisted up angrily.

"Above," I hurled at him. "Six is above Five."

"Like Five is above zero," Billy shot back. "Doesn't matter how high your stupid brother is, he doesn't do anything with it. No wonder you're an ord. All that power and he just writes those stupid books."

"They are not stupid, you're stupid! Gil's books are wonderful!"

Billy snorted. "I'm going to do something with my power. Necromancy, or demonology, or stuff like that. Important stuff."

Okay, fine. If he wanted me to go there, I would go there. I said, "Alexa—"

"Shut up," Billy snapped, and I grinned. Because nobody could argue with Alexa, who was—wait for it—a *Level Nine*. (Rumor has it there is a Level Ten, but it's like the Queen of the Fairies. Everyone's heard about one, but no one's ever seen it.) From what I have heard, Alexa's Judging caused more fuss than mine.

After her Judging, Mom and Dad were approached by members of the Royal Court, who arranged for Alexa to be taken to the royal family's Summer Palace to be educated by special tutors. Standard procedure, Alexa tells us; she also likes to tell us how miserable it was—there were barely any other kids, trips home were rare and under strict guidelines, and every time the royal family visited, the students were shut up in a drafty wing so they wouldn't associate. According to Alexa, the workload was murder, the teachers were brutal, and instead of encouraging their students to get along, they promoted a sense of competition that Alexa says was "really, really irresponsible with kids that powerful." From what she's told us, it's clear it was a hard, lonely eight years. I think that's why she went into education—because she loathed hers so thoroughly and wanted to make sure it didn't happen to other kids.

Mrs. Andrews burst through the door just then and called the class inside. Mom and Dad appeared next to me. Mom's face was flushed, but Dad smiled. "So, we're going to be teaching you at home for a little while."

CHAPTER
5

When we told Alexa about me getting kicked out of school, she wasn't surprised. Still, it took half a day for her to stop muttering threats under her breath. Especially after I asked her if I really was contagious.

"Of course not, don't be ridiculous. Think, Abby. If you were contagious, we'd all be ords." She stopped and visibly calmed herself down. "That's just people being scared. And ignorant."

Alexa returned to Rothermere two days later, to get back to work and clear the way for my acceptance. Before she left, she sat me down at the kitchen table (ignoring Gil's grumbles about how necessary privacy was for the creative process) and worked up a charm. It looked like a simple, flat, silver disk, but when the sunlight glinted off it you could see the spiderweb of magic woven inside.

When she finished, she threaded a chain through it and, with a flick of her fingers, popped it around my neck.

"What's this for?" I asked.

"Protection. If anything ever happens, if you need me, you break this," she said, tapping the charm at my throat, "and I'll know to come get you."

Then Alexa—who was to thank for draining the magic out of my room—took me around the house to unhex the shower so I could get clean and the doors so I could move around and a bookshelf in case I wanted to read and one cupboard so I could get something to eat if no one was around, and everything else that I needed to use every day but couldn't if someone didn't help me. I knew it was a pain for my family at first—to have to use little knobs to turn on the water in the bathroom instead of just poofing the perfect pressure and temperature, and having doors open to just one room instead of whatever room it was you wanted—but nobody said anything.

A week after she went back, Alexa called to say I was in. Turns out it was just that simple. There were a few forms and formalities to take care of, but Mom and Dad had them done inside an hour. Alexa also sent regular school supplies—a handbook, a list of school rules, tuition guidelines, that sort of thing.

After the flurry of the school-application stuff was done, I read books (I had lots of time for that), helped in the bakery, and got quizzed endlessly by Jeremy, who was now home for summer break. It pains me to say it, but he is actually great with the school stuff. He's really patient when we're going over schoolwork, and he doesn't mind if you ask questions, and he's so into the material that it's hard not to get interested yourself.

Business at our bakery hiccuped a little right after my Judging, and then continued like before. But for Dad there were days, then weeks, when no one appeared at his shop. Sure, magic carpets are a luxury, but there wasn't a family in Lennox that couldn't afford one.

It was around Midsummer when the adventurers rolled in, a pair of heroes on the hunt for an ord. They made an offer for me. By that time my parents had had so many offers it almost seemed natural.

Adventurers, or treasure seekers, or traveling heroes, whatever you call them, are actually pretty common. There's money to be made in the adventuring trade (rolling-on-a-pile-of-gold-laughing-hysterically kind of money), if you are brave enough or clever enough or just too stubborn to stop looking for whatever lost thing of untold worth someone wants. It takes money to start, but you can make it back and then some by selling things legally to museums and guilds, and even more by selling them illegally to private collectors. There are always people willing to pay for powerful objects. The kind of people who usually end up on the evening news after the Kingsmen raid their homes.

Adventuring is one thing ords are wanted and needed for, and that they are actually good at. Sure, if you are clever, or just really hard to kill, you can probably get past the maze of curses and traps, double enchantments and protection spells, to the Legendary Artifact of Whatsit that's imprisoned in the Cave of Despair and Darkness by the Dread Sorcerer Whosit. But you can save yourself a lot of time and trouble by getting an ord who can just walk past all that.

* * *

This pair said they'd heard that an ord had turned up, and, coincidentally, they were looking to replace their last one. They had "a whelp" who made it through six years of enchantments and curses and dragon's fire, only to up and fall off a cliff. Or jump, Barbarian Mike wasn't too clear on that. In any case, they were eight months without an ord and two jobs behind, so they were willing to pay any price. Or so they said.

Only Barbarian Mike introduced himself. He looked, well, exactly like you'd expect a guy called "Barbarian Mike" to look. Giant sword, furry bikini shorts, and all. He was adventurer good-looking—you know, the muscular, rugged, "I get punched in the face a lot" type. His companion was lean and wiry and tense, like a bowstring pulled too tight. She was very pretty in a fierce way: deeply red hair swept back from her face; sharp, dark eyes; strong eyebrows arched at a dramatic slant. Her face was bordering on sunburned, making it look like she might burst into flame at any moment.

They knocked on our door late in the afternoon, when Mom was taking a shower and Dad was still in his shop. Barbarian Mike took a seat, but his companion just stood by the door, scowling and not saying much. (She did snap at me to get her a glass of water, and Olivia snapped back that if she wanted water, she could get it herself, and Barbarian Mike held up his hands and muttered something to his friend about "territory.") Apparently, they were going on a mission to save the world from an evil king.

"King Steve?" Jeremy said, incredulous.

"No," Mike said.

"King Ewald, then," Olivia said. Her cheeks were red from a long, hot day at work, and she'd rolled up her sleeves and unbuttoned her neckline. Barbarian Mike kept staring at her, which made his friend glare at both of them.

"King Ewald's not that bad," Gil protested.

"It's not King Ewald," Barbarian Mike said.

"Okay, wait, how many kings are there?" Olivia asked. "There's like—what?—nine provinces in Svarga? Right?"

"They're not all kings," Jeremy informed us. "Three are duly elected regents, and currently the province of Perunovic is—"

"Do regents count?" Gil asked.

"They do *not* count. They're called regents, not kings," Jeremy said, shoving his glasses farther up his nose with a severe index finger.

Barbarian Mike's companion finally spoke. "He's not king *yet*."

My brothers and sister looked at each other.

"As a matter of fact, he's eight years old," Barbarian Mike said. "You see, there's this prophecy—"

"I'm guessing you didn't hear about King Steve's edict," Olivia said, flipping her hair back in a practiced maneuver. Barbarian Mike shook his head eagerly.

"He's forbidden any and all prophecies in the Westren Kingdom. He said they're malicious and duplicitous," Jeremy added.

"That's ridiculous," the woman snapped.

"It's the law," Jeremy said.

She rolled her eyes at that.

"What my friend means," Barbarian Mike jumped in, "is that we don't have a choice. We can't ignore this prophecy. If we want to stop this evil king—"

"The evil eight-year-old?" Olivia grinned, a quick flash that left Barbarian Mike stunned and blinking.

"Yes, the evil eight-year-old king," his companion pressed on, her eyes burning into Olivia. "We need to get an ancient artifact of untold power from a dark fortress deep in forbidden territory. Our path is fraught with countless dangers, and there are evil forces that will do anything to keep us from our goal."

Gil and Olivia studiously didn't look at each other as they struggled to keep straight faces.

I wondered what kind of evil forces. In the movies the evil forces always wear long black robes and have dramatic music cues and shout things about destiny. Those kind were a lot more fun than the guys on reality cop shows; the evil forces on TV always seemed to be skinny guys who tied up their pants with rope.

"And you figure I can stroll right into there, get this artifact, and stroll out again alive," I said. I had to admit, it was nice to hear people talking about what I *could* do for once.

And then things went downhill. Fast. When I opened my mouth Barbarian Mike and his friend exchanged a glance. For the first time since they arrived, the woman wasn't scowling. She looked surprised. "You let it speak freely?"

The question wasn't mean. It was genuine astonishment, and it was directed toward Gil and Olivia and Jeremy, who did not take it well. Olivia surged to her feet; Gil managed to catch her arms and pull her back down on the couch while Jeremy, quite calmly and for once actually sounding like a grown-up, informed our guests that they should leave.

"You're joking," the woman said. She looked from Jeremy to Gil to Olivia and back again. "You're *serious*? Really?"

"I'm not going to tell you again," Jeremy said, doing a pretty good Dad impression.

Barbarian Mike held up his hands. "Whoa, babe! Everybody, let's calm down. Now, we need an ord. We'll pay double, triple, anything you want, but we need your ord. Jobs are racking up. If we don't get an ord pretty soon we'll be losing business to the competition."

"My sister is not for sale," Olivia hissed.

"Are you even the owners?" the woman asked.

"The owners?" Gil repeated.

"The legal owners of that." She pointed at me. "The ones authorized to accept or refuse an offer of purchase. Don't you even know the regulations?"

"That would be Mom and Dad," Jeremy said. Olivia shot him a savage look. "It's true."

"It is true," Gil said before Olivia could start sputtering furiously. "But you would be wasting your time. They'll give you the exact same answer. Abby is not for sale. No ord is. According to 'regulations,' buying and selling children is illegal."

The woman shook her head, muttering something about amateurs. "Look, pretty boy, we're not leaving until—"

"We would prefer to make a formal offer to the legal

owners," Barbarian Mike interrupted. "Just to keep everything simple. We can wait here while you go get them." He smiled at me. "It will give us a chance to get to know Abby better."

Gil put a hand on my shoulder, his fingers digging in so hard it hurt. "No thank you. Abby can get our parents. We'll stay here with you." He shoved me toward the door.

• • •

Dad was in his workshop, needle flashing as he frowned over a complicated section of embroidery on a special order. "Hello, brown-eyed girl," he said without looking up. "What's up?"

"They want to make a formal offer," I finished after explaining what had been going on.

Dad set his needle down and pulled on his mustache. He has one of those dashing pirate-type mustaches, and occasionally he still swings in on chandeliers and sweeps Mom off her feet. "Whose turn is it?"

"It's Mom's, but they're not very nice—well, one of them isn't—and you know how Mom gets when people are mean. They're insisting that they have to tell you their offer."

"You want to stay here while I get rid of them?" he asked.

"No way," I said. "This is my favorite part."

"Come on, then," he said, putting his arm around me. "Why are they here again?"

"They need an artifact to fulfill a prophecy and stop an evil king."

"They need a new story. That one's getting old."

Barbarian Mike's voice carried all the way down the hall. It held an indulgent "let me explain it to you again" tone. The kind that makes you want to do the exact opposite of whatever someone tells you to do. "Look, I get that you're attached to the girl, but she's not your sister anymore. She's an ord, and ords are dangerous if you don't handle them right."

Olivia started to tell him exactly what he could handle and how he could handle it when Dad charged into the living room. "What's your offer?" The guy was huge.

"Ten—"

"No thank you. Good-bye," Dad said.

"—thousand. Ten *thousand*," Barbarian Mike said.

"No thank you. Good-bye."

"Twelve thousand. Fifteen."

"Good-bye," Dad said. My brothers and sister were grinning.

"What do you want? We'll pay anything."

"I want you to leave."

The woman threw up her hands. "You people are unbelievable. I'm going to take this up with the Guild. They told us there'd be an ord. That's our ord, we get dibs."

"Dibs?" For the first time ever, Dad sounded dangerous.

"Yeah, dibs," Barbarian Mike said. He looked at us. "You guys have an ord, how can you not know this? It's basic procedure, man. Okay, so when an ord is discovered, if the town's Guild doesn't want it, they send out a call." He pointed at me. "That's our ord. Name your price, dude."

"Ellen," Dad called. "Get the police, would you? We have trespassers."

The next moment Mom was there, her wet hair leaving damp blotches on her robe. She sized up the situation and took

48

* * *

.

hold of me so tight I had finger marks on my arm for two days after. "You're trying to buy my child. My daughter will be very interested to learn this." When they glanced at Olivia, Mom added, "My oldest daughter. Who works for the king."

The adventurers stiffened at that. Barbarian Mike looked around at all of us and then at his companion. His face was friendly, with a slightly doofy smile, but I have been around Mom and Dad long enough to know when a grown-up is saying something without saying something. His friend looked at me. Really looked—up and down and all over—when neither of them had more than glanced in my direction before. But it wasn't a personal kind of look; it was more the look you'd give a carpet you wanted to buy. It was a "you are nothing" kind of look. There wasn't anything mean about it, which made it worse.

Then she turned back to Barbarian Mike and shrugged. And Barbarian Mike smiled at us and said if that was their decision he'd have to live with it, and shook everybody's hand, and left. His friend didn't do any of that except for the leaving part, which we were fine with.

Gil waited a minute and then slipped on an invisibility spell and followed after them. He was back within twenty minutes to confirm that the adventurers were out of town, heading north. That didn't stop Mom from giving the cops a heads-up, or Olivia from burying an extra row of ward stones along the protection circle that surrounded our house.

* * *

CHAPTER 6

The rest of the summer was pretty quiet—no more offers, no more adventurers. Lots of long, sunny mornings sitting in the window seat in Dad's shop, lots of Gil muttering to himself at the kitchen table and jumping out at us when we least expected it, shouting, "Which do you like better—'furious' or 'infuriated'?"

The morning we left, it was rush-rush-rush and busy-busy-busy from the first second. Wake. Shower. Dress. ("Pants, Abby," Mom called, a warning finger pointed at me.) Jeremy was in the middle of his annual "returning to school" panic attack, fretting over not having enough potion bottles and where had he packed his grimoire and why had he sent it on ahead instead of saving it to study on the flight? (Which was surprising because Jeremy usually has his spell book welded to his hands.) Olivia whipped up waffles for breakfast.

It was as if I were a normal kid—a magic kid, that is, going to a magic school. And it's not like I was truly saying good-bye;

my family has a way of getting in each other's business, no matter the odds or the distance, which is why I didn't cry that much. Olivia—eyes fierce, voice breaking—grabbed me close until she was finally able to hiss, "I swear, Abby, if we don't hear from you every week, I'll drag you back home by your hair. I am so not kidding."

"Come on, O. It's not like we're never going to see her again," Gil said, sweeping me up in a big spinning hug. "Speaking of, Abs, can I have your half of the bedroom?" Olivia smacked him. "Ow! What? It's not like I'm trying to get rid of her memory. It's about prioritizing my work space. I need a study."

"You want to share your study with Olivia?" I asked.

"Oh no. I plan to buy her out."

"I'm not selling." Olivia sniffed, swiping at her eyes.

"And it's not your house," Dad reminded us.

"You can have my room if I can have a cut," I said.

"What? Abby? I mean, I'd expect this from Olivia because she has a black, withered pit where her heart should be, but you?" Gil put a hand on his chest and did his best to look shocked. "My baby sister. Whom I convinced Mom and Dad to keep, purely out of the goodness of my heart. They wanted to get rid of you because you were funny looking."

"That's not funny," Olivia said.

Gil ignored her. "You know, because of all the freckles. They wanted to call you Spot and donate you to the local animal shelter, but I said no. I said, let us not judge a child purely on the number of freckles—"

I threw my arms around Gil and hugged him quiet.

Dad shook out one of his oldest carpets on the front lawn, the green-and-gold one with knotted fringe that he wove back in college. It was just your straightforward, no-frills flying carpet, but it was the biggest one, which was important because we were doing a favor for Alexa.

We climbed on, Mom putting me right between her and Dad, with Jeremy behind us, so they could both get to me quickly. The carpet had spells to keep everyone's balance, and there was a shield to prevent people from falling off. For extra insurance, Dad called up the rug fibers, twisting them into a rope around my waist. If I moved too much one way or another, it tightened up like a snake and jerked me back into my seat.

Dad murmured something, and the carpet lifted up. There's always a moment of freefall with magic carpets when your body goes up but your stomach stays down. It's my favorite part. The carpet picked up speed and my head started spinning as we kept going up and up and up and then—everything was perfect. The wind was rushing all around, lifting us up until we were light as frosting and twice as weightless. The sky stretched out all around us, blue and cloudless. I could see part of one moon peeking out in front of us.

There were only a few other people flying when we took off, but as we got closer to Thorten, the airspace started filling up.

Since Mom and Dad were already planning to stop in Thorten on their way to Rothermere to drop Jeremy off at school, Alexa asked if they would mind picking up a few students who lived nearby and giving them a ride into the city. Alexa arranged to meet us and accompany us the rest of the way. "They're actually not that far from Rothermere themselves— we've got a girl coming from Glendale, and a boy in Teaneck. But I'd feel better if we escorted them ourselves." Mom raised an eyebrow at this until Alexa admitted, "I'm not sure I trust the parents to get them to Rothermere. You'd be surprised how lazy some people get once they find out they have an ord." Then she grinned. "Not every kid's lucky enough to have parents as amazing as you guys."

Dad smiled and shook his head. "Please. Go on."

Alexa was waiting for us in the clear stretches of meadow outside of town, shielding her eyes from the sun as she watched us land. She gave us each a brusque kiss on the cheek. Jeremy pulled me in for a rare hug and made me promise to let him know about the curriculum. Then Alexa guided me and Dad back on the carpet while Mom and Jeremy headed off toward campus. He had to get checked in and make sure his stuff was all set.

Below us, the place was packed—move-in day in a school town is always crazy. Stores were open, hawking crystals or dried herbs or extra-long bedsheets or anything people might have forgotten. There were so many carpets, taking off and landing, it was a struggle just to get through; we didn't even try getting close to campus, and lines of students checking in wound all the way back through the streets. Even from a distance I could hear the massive doors of Thorten's front entrance groan happily as they swung open to admit a new student.

Alexa had arranged for us to meet the other new students at the Whittleby home. Their only kid, Peter, was going to be in my class. The Whittleby house was on the edge of town, small and white and square, with decorative blue tiles around the windows and tiger lilies purring along the fence. It was a nice place if you didn't look too close: if you didn't notice the chips in the tiles, or that the paint was faded and flaking, like no one was keeping up the maintenance spells.

There was a girl waiting by the Whittlebys' gate, hugging a faded leather satchel, her cheeks pink from the sun. Surprise slapped Alexa in the face, and she jogged over. "When did they drop you off? I didn't know it was going to be this early."

The girl's response was too quiet to catch. She was a tiny apple dumpling of a girl—soft and round and dimpled—with buttercup curls and a slump to her shoulders. There were deep, dark shadows under her eyes, and her fingers were bone white as they gripped her bag. She seemed to be trying to fold in on herself and disappear.

"Why didn't you go in? Aren't the Whittlebys here?" Alexa asked.

The girl shook her head and didn't meet Alexa's eyes. "No—I mean, yes—I mean, I didn't check. I didn't want to bother them."

Alexa got that look on her face like she did when she thought we were being difficult for no reason, but she didn't get a chance to say anything else because Ms. Whittleby came out then in a blur of questions and welcomes, dragging her son behind her.

Ms. Whittleby was what my mom would call a "striking beauty"—very fair with thickly lashed eyes and lots of long dark curls piled on top of her head—but the most noticeable feature was the bruise on her forehead and a scrape on her cheek.

That was what had me gaping at her. I mean, the bruise, yes, but also what it meant. Ms. Whittleby was a *grown-up*. And if her bruises were visible, it meant she was an ord. A grown-up ord!

I wanted to hug her, which wouldn't have been appropriate because Alexa was already angrily demanding to know what had happened to her face even as Dad was asking if Ms. Whittleby was all right.

"Oh, this? It's nothing. I'm fine," Ms. Whittleby assured us, with a glance at Peter. He was glaring at the ground. "We've had adventurers stopping by to make offers for Peter ever since he was . . . confirmed. Usually we tell them no and they go on their way. We got a pair yesterday that was a little more difficult than most. Apparently Barbarian Mike and Trixie didn't want to hear no."

"Yes, we've met them too," Dad replied drily. "They came to our house and harassed Abby—"

"Her name is Trixie?" I burst in, then caught myself. "I mean, sorry. I hope you weren't hurt too badly. But *Trixie*? Like, really?" Ms. Whittleby smiled and nodded. "I wouldn't tell anyone my name, either."

Alexa's lips twitched but she stayed focused. "This is ridiculous. We can't have a pair of punch-happy lunkheads harassing every family with an ord in the kingdom. As soon as I get back to my office, I'm going to let the king know."

"You do that," Peter said. "I'm sure it will help."

Ms. Whittleby murmured for her son to behave and then turned to us. "Abby and Frances, right? This is my son, Peter. You're all going to be in the same class."

"Hi," I offered. Frances started twisting her fingers and stayed silent. Peter didn't say anything either; he just looked at me like he was trying to piece together a particularly boring puzzle.

"Where are the Randallses?" Alexa asked.

Ms. Whittleby shook her head. "I spoke with Mrs. Randalls this morning. She said they would be here. She gave me no reason not to believe her," Ms. Whittleby pointed out when Alexa lifted her eyebrows.

"Who are the Randallses?" I asked.

"A family with another student," Alexa said. "Frederick Randalls—Fred. He should be here by now. This is my fault. I knew they were going to waffle. I should have pushed harder last time I talked to that vapid—"

"Alexa, be kind," Dad reproached her.

"I will not. I'll save my kindness for her son, whom they are kicking out of the house. This isn't like Abby or Peter; on the application, the Randallses requested that Fred spend all of his vacations on campus—which is a nice way of saying they don't want him to set foot inside the house again. Frankly, I'm surprised they're sending him to school and not just selling him . . . off." Alexa stopped suddenly and looked at Ms. Whittleby. "You said the adventurers were here yesterday?"

"Yes."

"Are they still in the area? Do you know if they've left town?"

* * *

Ms. Whittleby shook her head. "You don't think—"

"I think that Mrs. Randalls has been complaining an awful lot about the cost of tuition." In a second she turned into Official Business Alexa, who worked for the king. "All right, everybody on the carpet," she ordered. "We're leaving right now." Dad unrolled the carpet in one smooth flick and we climbed on. The grown-ups called up the safety belts around us ords. "We're going to do a couple of flybys," said Alexa. "Hopefully we'll see the Randallses on the road and pick up Fred. If there's trouble, I will handle it. Everybody understand that?" she asked, yanking another knot in my belt. Dad nodded. The girl—Frances—stared at Alexa with wide eyes.

Peter glanced at his mom. Alexa caught it. "Ms. Whittleby, you stay here. If there's trouble, we might have to run for it. We're going to head straight for the city."

Ms. Whittleby threw her arms around Peter, hugging him until he was forced to make gagging noises and plead for air. They took a pretty long time, and Alexa started fidgeting and kept glancing at her watch and then the road, and then back at her watch.

Ms. Whittleby gave Peter one last kiss, and the carpet lifted and we were soaring.

✳ ✳ ✳

CHAPTER 7

Dad started on loops, small at first and then arcing out wider. This far away from the campus, the streets were mostly quiet. We zipped past a woman tending her garden, a man struggling to get his carpet to rise. Alexa told Dad that now was not the time to worry about speed limits, but Dad just shook his head and said it was better to be thorough and not miss anything.

Of course, it was pretty hard to miss Barbarian Mike. He's big as a mountain. He and Trixie were about ten blocks out, toward the very edge of town where the streets and houses faded away into rambling, mossy forests. They had a kid with them. He was kind of ordinary looking; short—really short—with a bumpy nose and big ears that stuck out through his hair.

"That's them," Alexa said, and she stepped off the carpet midair. The world magically pulled toward her, sky and earth smooshing together as she took the huge space between them in a single hop.

Dad let out a sigh and then said, "Hold on." And we dropped.

Okay, it was actually a dive; Dad knows better than to do a straight drop, but it was so steep and fast it felt like the carpet had disappeared from under us and we were falling. My stomach shot up into my throat and I couldn't help but laugh. Peter squeezed his eyes shut and gripped the fibers, and Frances desperately tried to tuck her dress under her legs.

We came to a hovering stop right by Alexa, who was saying something about "by order of the king." Coming from Alexa, that means be quiet and do what I tell you; she likes to use it when people are talking in movie theaters and at some of our louder family dinners. Barbarian Mike grabbed Trixie's arm when she opened her mouth.

"Wow." I looked at Barbarian Mike and Trixie. "You guys have really bad luck with ords."

"Not this time," Trixie sneered, tugging on the boy's arm.

"I beg to differ," Alexa replied. She'd gone red again, which meant, among other things, that she was probably going to end up filling out a lot of paperwork. "That boy has been enrolled in the Green School for months. He is not a candidate for purchase. You will hand him over at once, or you will face the penalty."

Barbarian Mike shrugged good-naturedly. "Sure. What's the fine going to be this time? Twenty bucks? I think I got that on me right now." He started patting his . . . I guess he had pockets in those furry little shorts.

Alexa's smile was rich with satisfaction. "The penalty for kidnapping a minor is imprisonment. It carries a sentence of fifteen years."

Trixie looked more surprised than when my family told her

she couldn't buy me. Barbarian Mike shook his head. "This was a legal sale."

"The sale and purchase of ords has been illegal for over two years now—"

"You're joking," Barbarian Mike insisted. "He's an ord."

"I understand that you have been traveling, but it is your responsibility to review updated legislation upon returning to a country—"

"That little changeling snakes his way onto the throne," Trixie spat out, stabbing a vicious finger at Alexa, "and the first thing he does—"

Alexa's face went as red as her dress, but she kept very still and her voice was calm. "If you find fault with His Majesty's policies, you are more than welcome to bring it up with him. He takes an audience on Thursdays. I hear that it's quite easy to file a petition from prison these days."

"Someone should—" Trixie began.

Barbarian Mike snapped a silence on her before she could finish. "Easy, Trix."

It was funny because even though Barbarian Mike's spell was still active—it made the space around Trixie's mouth and throat look hazy—I could still hear her. Not loud, it was like listening through marshmallows, but her voice was there. She was saying a lot of stuff that I wasn't sure you could get away with saying to a king's agent. Things like cheat and thief and how the crown didn't belong to him and how it was their job to right wrongs and after they were done with the little eight-year-old king they were going to come back and—then a bunch of words I'm never supposed to say. I glanced at the other kids. It was obvious from Frances's face that she had heard Trixie too.

"Please forgive my friend," Barbarian Mike said. "Sometimes her enthusiasm gets the better of her."

"She would do well to learn a little of your restraint," Alexa replied.

Barbarian Mike nodded and said they'd been out of the country, and you know how it was, living on your own, off the land, away from people, and the whole time he and Trixie were still holding on to Fred with a death grip. Alexa was eyeing the situation with increasing quiet, which is never a good sign. The funny thing was that while Barbarian Mike was going on and on about how adventuring was a solitary life and if they'd lost some of their polish it wasn't meant as an insult, that wasn't what I heard. I mean, it was, but I also heard a lower, quieter Barbarian Mike voice, a soft rumble just between him and Trixie. *You make a diversion. I'll take the boy.*

And then her reply, *Fireball?*

A little more subtle, babe.

I glanced at Peter, who was clenching and unclenching his hands into tight, white fists, and Fred, whose face was a resigned blank, and Frances, who played with the carpet fringe as if she hadn't heard. But we'd all heard. I knew it.

"Alexa?" It burst out of me before I could think. "What's a diversion?"

* * *

Now, "power" in magic doesn't just mean having a lot of strength—being able to explode forests or level cities. That's only part of it. The other part of it is control; it's technique and finesse and speed.

Alexa has both parts.

The wind stopped. Everything stopped. Barbarian Mike pulled Fred toward him slowly, as if he were moving through syrup, and I saw a slow ember flicker luxuriantly between Trixie's hands. Dad lurched forward, his hands passing through the air like they were fighting a current. Around us, trees pulled their branches back with the wind in slow, sleepy arcs. It took me a moment to realize what Alexa had done: she'd slowed down time, wrapped it through her fingers like a ribbon, and pinched it until the seconds stretched out.

Then she grabbed Fred and yanked him out of Barbarian Mike's grasp in one smooth movement, shoving him toward us so fast her dress and hair seemed to be moving in slow motion behind her. Peter and I each grabbed for an arm as Fred half climbed, half jumped onto the carpet, and Frances clambered back to give him room. He was laughing. We were all laughing, especially at the adventurers' faces as they realized that Fred had disappeared. We saw the confusion, the sense of *but he isn't magic*, and then understanding starting to dawn as time finally caught up with them. But by then Alexa had leaped onto our carpet, the hem of her skirt tearing as she moved too fast for it, poofed Dad on with her, and willed us into the air.

In the next instant time shifted again and the world around us raced forward, clouds blinking by and the carpet tassels

* * *

flapping so frantically I was surprised they didn't rip off. It was weird, watching Dad's jerky movements as he scrambled into a sitting position, hearing his squeaky, high-pitched exclamations. The ground winked into a stretch of brown and green and—

And then reality came back like thunder breaking, and the carpet snapped to a slow, easy soar. Frances moaned and clutched her stomach. Fred was still laughing, a little shaky, and he was holding on to Alexa as if he couldn't let go. Alexa threw her arms around him and grinned at us. "Everyone all right?"

"We're fine. Are you?" Dad began.

"Don't worry about me." Alexa started brushing off her sleeves and skirt with mostly steady hands.

"We should call the police," Dad said.

Alexa nodded. "Meathead and Trixie probably ran the second they saw us get away, but you're right."

"Don't mention us," Peter said. "They won't come if they think it was some fuss over ords. Tell them it was normal people."

"I'll tell them the truth," Alexa said. "And they will do their job."

Peter snorted.

Alexa kept her eyes on him as she said, "Our first priority, however, is getting you kids to Rothermere. Sorry, Peter. I'll have to get your mom up to the city one day for a proper good-bye."

He shrugged.

"What about his parents?" I asked, nodding to Fred.

"They're not—" Fred began and then stopped.

"Are they going to go to jail?" I asked.

"Abby." Dad's voice was a low warning.

"That depends," Alexa said carefully. "I could probably talk to someone, arrange something. If that's what Fred wanted."

Fred glanced at all of us, mouth half-open, and then looked at his hands.

"You don't have to decide now—" Alexa stopped, whipping her head around. The air inside the force field started vibrating with a sharp, heavy twang. "Oh, you have got to be kidding me."

CHAPTER
8

"Dad," Alexa said.

"I see them," Dad replied. The carpet pulled forward, speeding up.

Alexa quickly checked and then double-checked everyone's safety belts. She was on her third go-round when I finally saw the carpet. It was a flashy one, fast, and coming up hard behind us. It had to duck and weave around parents heading home after dropping off their kids. I saw Trixie's dark hair flaming in the wind.

"These guys are desperate," I said.

Alexa gave a grim nod.

Something whizzed around us. The carpet. It lapped us in tight, dizzying circles, so close it almost crashed into us a couple of times and Dad had to slow to a near stop.

Barbarian Mike chucked things that bounced harmlessly off the force field. On the next lap, I glimpsed Trixie pulling on a pair of long gloves. Even with the wind rushing, it was not hard to catch what they were saying. They didn't really seem the "quiet conversation" type, and I definitely heard Trixie's comment about how they'd be done by now if not for *somebody's* ord mom. But she was smiling. She smiled at Barbarian Mike and he smiled back. They were enjoying themselves.

Peter had been watching the carpet's circles intently; at that comment I saw his face go dark and hard. The next second he was on his feet, the safety ropes straining against his waist, his fist passing easily through our force field and theirs to smash into Trixie's jaw. I caught the surprise on Trixie's face before their carpet dropped down again. This time it didn't come back up.

Alexa yanked Peter down, and he crossed his arms over his chest with a stubborn look. She seemed to struggle for a few seconds, then said, "How's your hand?" He held it out and she examined it.

"That was a very foolish thing to do," Dad said.

"Foolish." Alexa nodded in agreement, then added in a low voice, "But a good punch."

"You want to punch with your whole body. Not just your hand," Dad added.

Something chimed, and Dad curved the carpet up for a few seconds before we lurched into the air. Dad and Alexa cracked their heads against the force field, but we ords flew up, straight through the barrier. There was a moment of blind terror, and then the rope around my waist jerked me back down to safety.

Barbarian Mike and Trixie were coming up beneath us. They weren't smiling anymore. They circled and dropped under us again, and Alexa made a grab for Frances and me. Her arms wrapped around us just as the adventurers smashed into us again, good and hard. Alexa managed to hold us in place, but I was starting to feel sick to my stomach.

Dad took our carpet up, then twisted us around and rocketed us back down, and started zipping in a confusing zigzag. "Dad, I need you to drop the force field," Alexa said. "I'm putting a stop to this now."

"There are a lot of people around here," Dad said as we whizzed by a crowded carpet.

"Trust me." Alexa grinned, and Dad dropped the force field. The magic barrier couldn't stop ords, but it kept Alexa and Dad in and the wind out. Without it, the wind was unbelievable. It barreled into us, the carpet fibers burning along my legs as the wind pushed us back. The safety belt cut into me so tightly I thought it was going to snap me in half.

Alexa shouted something to Dad that I couldn't hear, and he slowed down. He tried to separate us from the crowd, but there were so many people screeching and shouting as we wove past. As the adventurers got closer, Alexa stood. She looked wild and vengeful in all that wind.

"*I order you to stop, in the name of King Stephen!*" Alexa boomed, her voice doing that weird double-resonance thing it does when she's really calling in the power.

"Ord lover!" Trixie shouted, so loud we could hear her over the rushing wind. "No king of mine!"

And then Alexa got the Look. It's a lot like the look Mom

gives us when she has had *enough*, but without the compassion or restraint. When Alexa gives you the Look, you either sit down and shut up or you get the heck out of there.

Barbarian Mike and Trixie ducked around and under us—and in one quick flash Alexa leaped over us and off the carpet. For one endless second she hung in the air like a pendant, the magic around her so strong the entire world seemed drawn toward her.

And even though the adventurers' carpet was some distance away, Alexa landed neatly on it, right in between Barbarian Mike and Trixie. I saw flames building around Trixie again, but Alexa had control of the carpet now and it plummeted, spiraling toward the ground until it disappeared below us.

Dad snapped the force field back up. "What exactly . . . does your sister do?" Fred managed, staring over the edge of the carpet.

"She's in education," I said.

CHAPTER 9

Barbarian Mike and Trixie had booked it into the forest, leaving Alexa gulping ice water after swallowing one too many fireballs. The cops said they couldn't really do anything except take a report of the incident and "keep an eye out for them."

Mom was furious with us when we met up with her and explained what happened, even though it's not like we *asked* Barbarian Mike and Trixie to chase us. Still, Mom told Alexa that she'd scared us half to death and to never do it again. Alexa lied and said she wouldn't. And Dad worried that Alexa might get in trouble; authorities frown on time spinning—it's that whole "no reordering the world to suit you" thing. But Alexa basically told us that while King Steve wouldn't let her get away with murder, he pretty much gave her free rein. "If spinning a few seconds to save a kid is going to upset the court I'll take the heat. Besides, I should get some fun out of suffering through that awful Summer Palace."

Fred just kept laughing about how that was the coolest thing he'd ever seen.

"I'm sorry," I told him, then rushed on, explaining, "about your parents selling you. It stinks."

"Deeta's . . . not my mom," Fred said. "She's my stepmom."

"It still stinks," I said.

Fred shrugged, his eyes on the carpet. "I'm not surprised. I'm not. I don't know, I guess it's hard on them."

Alexa scoffed at that, and Mom elbowed her with a stern, "Alexa Eleanor."

"That's no excuse," I said.

"Well, I am an ord," Fred said.

"That still doesn't make it okay."

That got us talking about being ords, and about our Judgings. I told Fred about mine, and how it stunk, and I asked if he found out when he was Judged too. And Fred told me he had suspected it for a while but hadn't been sure. One time he and his brothers had been babysitting their young cousin while their parents were hosting a charity banquet. Apparently they started roughhousing and his older brother threw a spell at another brother and it hit Fred on the arm when it shot by.

"Arthur panicked," Fred said. "He thought he nailed me, that I was going to turn into a freak or something." Fred paused and cleared his throat. "But I was okay, so he thought . . ."

"That he hadn't hit you," I finished.

"But he did, I felt it. They got Peggy. Our cousin. They got her less than me, and *she* disappeared." He snapped his fingers. "We were still tearing up the attic, looking for her, when our parents got home. She ended up as an umbrella stand in the foyer." Fred smiled, but it looked out of place. "That was the second-worst day of my life."

He hadn't known for sure until he was Judged this past winter. They asked him to leave school right afterward, just like me, so he'd been out much longer and he was worried about classes. "I tried to read more," he said. "I went to the library a lot. They tried to keep me out but, you know, they couldn't."

"What do you mean?" I asked.

"Protective barriers. Warding spells. Force fields. None of those things work on . . . people like us."

"Ords," Peter said.

"Yes, exactly, ords, thank you," Fred said. "We can walk through all that. You mean you haven't tried it? Not even once?" I shook my head and Fred grinned. "It's kinda cool."

"It's called breaking and entering," Mom told us, "and that's illegal."

Fred nodded, chastened.

"I—" Frances paused. We looked at her. She turned pink and whispered, "I spent a lot of time at the library, also. But I haven't missed any school . . ."

I asked how long she had known.

"A month. My birthday is August first."

"So your parents really had to move fast to get you in this year."

"It was—"

"Pardon?" Fred said, leaning forward.

"It was Mrs. Eames, actually," Frances said, her eyes darting back and forth like a frightened puppy's. She had the most enormous blue eyes, they seemed to take up half her face. "My parents are very busy. They couldn't be expected to . . ."

"Who's Mrs. Eames?" I asked.

"She's our neighbor. She lives across the street. I, um, lived with her after my Judging."

"Oh," I said. There was an awkward, silent moment. I mean, everybody *knows* that's what you do with an ord. You get rid of them. But my parents had kept me, and Peter's mom kept him, and Fred—okay, his dad and stepmom had apparently tried to sell him to adventurers, but still, that meant they'd retained custody, at least.

So I said, "I'm sorry," but that didn't seem like enough either. It didn't matter; Frances had already tucked into herself again, and she didn't answer. I turned to Peter desperately. "What about you?"

Peter didn't look up from his book. "I have always known."

"How?"

It took a moment, but he answered. "My mom."

I glanced at Alexa, confused.

"Peter is an ord because his mother is an ord," Alexa explained, tucking a strand of hair behind her ear.

"I thought that wasn't tried and true," Mom said.

"It's not," Alexa said. "But it is very likely."

• • •

Originally, Rothermere was just the site of the royal palace, shaped from a single perfect garnet that the very first queen, Samira, discovered deep in the earth. Queen Samira wanted a nice place where she could host official guests for parties and hold those endless political meetings that don't really accomplish anything, as opposed to the house she had by the sea, where she could run around barefoot with her kids. It's a beautiful castle, gleaming red in the sunshine and black in the moonlight. We have been up to Rothermere a lot—Olivia went to school in the city, and later for Gil's book events. I have taken the official castle tour five times, which never gets old because the structure changes from day to day.

Of course, if you're going to have a political centerpiece, you're going to need a lot of support, and no sooner had Queen Samira opened the doors than the rest of the city exploded around it.

We arrived just after noon, when the sky was clear and the sun was soft and the city glowed like a pearl without the oyster. Dad kept us hovering above the crazy local traffic until we got close to the school, then brought us down so fast even Frances was shocked into smiling. The climate was more humid here than in Lennox, the air hot and heavy with the scent of people and clay, incense, and sausages. The streets were swamped, people jostling each other as they rushed past, checking out store windows, and vendors selling charms or incense or jewelry or—oh, pretzels, those looked good. And the *noise*—voices and shouting and music and every so often there were sirens.

Following Alexa's directions, Dad parked the carpet right in front of a large building on an unusually empty street. Well, only half-empty. The opposite side was just as busy as every other place we had seen, but the sidewalk in front of the school?

Nothing. Nobody. Carved into the paving stones was ward upon spell upon curse, until they all curled in on each other and it was impossible to pick one from another. Jeremy could probably tell the difference, but then, Jeremy was memorizing the entire spell catalog, front to back, for fun. When we climbed off the carpet, Mom winced from the force of the entry spells, and Dad took a moment to brace himself.

This was it. This was where I was going to spend the next eight years of my life. I took a good long look at the school, taking a couple steps back to see it all.

The school was square, and built out of dark-brown bricks. It was smaller than the buildings around it, only four stories tall, with a glass structure on top that gleamed so brightly under the sun it hurt to look. There was a fence all the way around the building, with bars on the first-floor windows and thick, strong shutters on the upper windows. The main entrance was barred by a sturdy gate that stretched above our heads, then arched into a short tunnel, revealing a courtyard beyond. The window bars, shutters, and front gate were all made from the same rough dark metal with a strange, muted sheen, almost like sunlight on frost. Cold iron, I realized. But that much must have cost a fortune. The most iron anybody ever needed was a few sprinklings of iron dust in the corners, to keep the fairies out. If someone had spent that much money on that much iron, then that someone had to be serious about this school.

See, cold iron isn't just cold, or hard or strong. It feeds off magic, sucks it in. It drains a normal person's magic to get even stronger and leaves you empty. It's got, well, not a mind of its

* * *

own, but an awareness. I have heard that cold iron works best on things like night fey, and Red Ladies, and all those scary creatures that are just supposed to be in bedtime tales, that kids aren't supposed to know are real.

Flowering vines climbed up the stone walls, bursting with bright, hot color. But they gave the iron a wide berth as they crawled up one side of the entrance and curved over the arch, leaves dripping down. To the right, the flowers politely arced around a shiny engraved plaque, which read:

MARGARET GREEN SCHOOL
Chartered in 1 STPN
by writ of His Royal Majesty
King Stephen I

There was another, smaller plaque on the gate with a button: RING FOR ASSISTANCE.

Alexa pushed the button, and there were three strong, clear rings in succession. It took a minute for someone to answer, and Mom's shoulders slowly tightened and Dad started shifting from foot to foot. Apparently, the iron affected them too.

"Breathe through your mouth," Alexa told them. She was standing close enough to the gate that her words fogged in the air. "It helps a little."

A woman with glasses whisked up to the gate. She was lean and wiry, with an aura of shrewd-eyed responsibility about her, as if she did a lot of babysitting. Her face was lean too. She had one of those quirked-eyebrow, thin-lipped faces that's not so much pretty as it is interesting. Her cap of short dark hair was uneven, as if she cut it herself. She was wearing a high-necked, long-sleeved jacket buttoned all the way up, scuffed leather boots, and a length of black chain around her hips like a belt. The deep, rich green of her jacket caught the light as she wrenched open the gate barehanded.

Most important, she had something—or maybe a lack of something—that reminded me of Ms. Whittleby. Of Peter, and Fred and Frances and me. The missing piece and the look in her eye that said "ord." And she was *old*. Not as old as Ms. Whittleby (this one looked like she was in her early twenties, give or take a few years, maybe around Gil's age), but still. Another one.

"You're late," she announced. Her voice was brusque but friendly. She took a good hard look at Alexa and said, "Fireballs, huh?"

Alexa grinned. "A couple."

"Looks like more than a couple. Looks like more than just fire."

Alexa shook her head. "One of these days I'm going to get used to you doing that, Becky."

The woman looked at us and then dropped down into a crouch by Alexa's hem. "Quick lesson," she said, waving us kids down next to her. "The first part is obvious. This," she said, drawing her finger along a line of thread in Alexa's skirt, "is new. It tells us something damaged her dress and it needed to repair itself. See here," she said, pointing at a trace of wavy magic clinging to the hem. "How it looks like heat off a griddle?"

"Could we step off the sidewalk for this?" Alexa asked.

"The next clue is the smell." She grabbed Alexa's hem and held it out toward us. "Go on, take a sniff." Fred glanced at us, wary, and Frances shook her head, but Peter and I leaned in and smelled. It smelled like heat, thick and almost muggy, and beyond that, the acrid shadow of smoke. "That's fire magic. There's a little more to it than that, but those are the basics—"

"Becky," Alexa said. "Could we please go inside? Before the charms in your sidewalk start eating through my nice new boots."

Becky stood, smooth as a cat, and, grinning, swung the gate wider to wave us in. "Mrs. Murphy already checked everyone else in and she's working on the dinner. Ms. Macartney's taking them on a tour now. I can get O'Hara, though."

She took us through the main entrance into the brightness of the courtyard. A middle-aged man sailed over as we entered. He had a hearty, good-natured face, and his clothes were well worn but clean, with professorly patches at the elbows. "Miss Hale!" he exclaimed, clasping Alexa's hands in his. "What a completely expected surprise. However, we expected you to surprise us much earlier. I hope there wasn't any trouble."

"Fireballs," Becky informed him.

"I thought you had the triumphant air of someone who'd just picked a fight," Mr. O'Hara remarked. "Nothing serious, I hope?"

"Adventurers," Alexa said. "A nasty pair. They got away, for the moment. I'd recommend upping security."

"Because of a pair of adventurers?" Becky sounded skeptical.

"Because they were desperate enough for an ord that they

77

chased us down and threw fireballs," Alexa said. "If one pair of adventurers are that desperate, it won't be long before they, or someone else, turn their greedy little minds to this school."

"The children are safe here," Mr. O'Hara said, more to Mom and Dad than Alexa.

"Here, yes. Absolutely. No worries. But outside?" Alexa turned to us. "I'll be saying good-bye now. I have to speak to His Majesty." She hugged me tight, twice. "I'll be back as soon as I'm finished, okay? Save me a seat at dinner." I nodded and she kissed Mom and Dad, apologizing, "I'm sorry. It's work; I can't help it."

"We understand," Mom said, planting kisses on her cheeks. "We'll see you soon." The *or else* was implied.

As Alexa rushed off, Mr. O'Hara turned to Mom and Dad. "You must be Miss Hale's parents," he said, extending his hand. "It's a pleasure to finally meet you. Miss Hale has told us quite a lot about your family, though I'm certain she's told you next to nothing of what she does here. Let me assure you, Alexa is our single greatest champion. You should be very proud of her."

"We are," Mom said. You could hear it in her voice.

He smiled down at me. "Miss Hale has told us all about you as well, Miss Abigail."

"I hope not all," I said, because I have got plenty of embarrassing stories.

"No need to worry, almost all of it was good."

Mr. O'Hara greeted Fred and Frances and Peter and welcomed us to the Margaret Green School. He said he hoped we were as excited to start the school year as they were. "If you would follow Mr. Dimitrios here"—we looked around for a Mr. Dimitrios—"he will take you to your rooms and hand out your keys. You are all on the second floor." The courtyard was open and sunny but I couldn't see anyone. I glanced at Fred, who shrugged. Peter still had his head in his book and Frances kept her eyes glued to the ground.

"They finally showed." The voice was a low, warm rasp, like gravel and sand. I jumped, and Frances let out a little squeak. Peter smiled.

Suddenly there was a mountain next to us, one with horns.

Mr. Dimitrios was a minotaur. A real minotaur; the hoofs, the horns, the tail, the nose ring, even the spear, it was all there. His horns were short, just peeking out of his floppy hair, which made him look young—well, youngish. Minotaurs don't really like people knowing things like how they age and how old they get. I had never seen a minotaur before except on those shows where they interview movie stars; huge and hulking in the background are the minotaur bodyguards. Which is probably why Mom and Dad were smiling so much as they shook Mr. Dimitrios's hand. If this school had hired a minotaur, even a young one, they were serious about security.

It also helps if you don't get weirded out easily. Minotaurs are a strange race. They're magical beings—they can interact with, or manipulate, or use magic, whatever the right word is. But they choose not to lots of times, and that freaks out some folks. I guess they think it's simpler to just punch someone in the face, the old-fashioned way.

Before we could recover from that little surprise, Becky

herded us toward the west side of the building. Mr. Dimitrios joined us, one of his strides eating up three of ours. He was big and muscular and hairy, but his fearsome beast image was ruined somewhat by his wide, lopsided smile.

Becky stopped at a door that was mostly bars and an enormous lock and hauled it open one armed.

It turns out we weren't the only people at the school—kids were here tucked away in the dorm. There were doors open all along the first-floor hall, and we heard the buzz of conversation and music, and someone complaining loudly about having to do laundry. As we climbed up a flight of stairs to a bright-white hallway, three kids raced by us going the other direction. Becky barked at them to slow down.

"Can't!" one of them yelled. "You don't know what she'll do to us if we're late!"

The second floor was empty, with all the doors standing open. Each room was exactly the same—plain and white and rectangular. Entering one was like walking along the edge of a mirror. There were two perfectly identical halves, each with a small closet alcove and a narrow single bed. On the side opposite the door, a desk ran the length of the wall. Each half had one chair, one window, and a shared set of shelves overhead. It was nice and clean, but the furniture looked barely used, and the glossy floor had a freshly polished sheen. It had none of the scuffs and bangs that make a place feel lived in.

We only had a minute to look at our rooms before Mr. O'Hara appeared and whisked us on a tour. "We have to get this done quickly so we can get ready for the welcome-back dinner." He was a big man, built like an oak tree but significantly shorter—so how did he move that fast? Up and down and around and around. He answered any questions we had, but he never slowed. We saw so many spiral staircases and white hallways I started to think that's all the school was. He rushed us by teachers' offices, the greenhouse at the very top, and the laundry at the bottom, and I'm pretty sure we stopped by some dark cave where the minotaurs lurked. Yes, I said minotaurs, because we paused long enough to see there was another one (bigger than Mr. Dimitrios, if you can believe that), and a holding cell with actual bars and locks. The classrooms were normal looking, thank goodness.

The way Mr. O'Hara ran us around, it seemed confusing, but the school was actually laid out simply enough. It was basically a giant *U*, with the dorm on one side and classrooms on the other, and everything else scrunched in between, with the courtyard in the big empty space in the middle.

• • •

Mom and Dad left after the tour. They had to leave, I knew they had to leave, but I still wasn't looking forward to it. When they left it would be final.

Mom cried a bit, and I was crying too. Dad tried to keep it cheerful, but his eyes were bright as he swooped me up off my feet for a hug. I knew I would see them again, hug them again, but I'd always had those things whenever I wanted, and after today I wouldn't. I couldn't. Even the moment in the Guild when Mr. Graidy said I was an ord hadn't seemed this huge or achy or final.

Eventually they pulled away. They said they would call and that they'd see me . . . we just didn't know exactly when. Not until Fall Fest, probably, and that was forever. Well, eight weeks.

I wasn't allowed to watch them fly away. We had to say good-bye in the courtyard, with Mr. O'Hara standing at a respectful distance until it was time to escort them out. I stood there, waving, as they stepped back onto the street, and the gates closed with a cold, solid *clunk*. Mr. O'Hara made sure the protection spells snapped properly back into place, and then stood off to the side until I had rubbed my eyes and was ready to join the others.

CHAPTER 10

There was barely time to be sad or even think after Mom and Dad left. Becky showed up the second Mr. O'Hara released us and roped me into helping out an older student who was in a rush to get his clothes put away so he could get to work. He snapped at Becky about foisting some newbie off on him instead of a kid who actually knew what she was doing, but then told me he didn't mind stuff getting shoved in drawers as long as it got done. He was reedy, with sharp, tight features and a burn scar that reached up into his hair and left a little bald patch. When I asked him why he was in such a rush, he told me he was a "kitchen rat."

"Cook Bella's special staff," he explained shortly at my confused look. "We help out in the kitchen. It's hard work, but you eat better. Not that anyone eats bad here, but the rats get special attention. Whatever it takes to eat well while you can, you know?"

I didn't, actually. I'd always eaten well.

Becky rapped on the door. "Time, Nate. If you're late, Bella's not going to ream me out over it."

"It's her fault," Nate said, shoving me out of the way of the door. "Newbies always . . ." I didn't catch the rest because he started running.

"Ignore him," Becky said, taking my arm. "Come on, you've got to get ready. You don't have colors yet, so wear nice clothes if you have 'em."

"I do."

"Good. See if you've got anything that'll fit Fran while you're at it. The poor thing's barely got a change of underwear and a pair of socks."

I had just finished getting dressed when the bell rang for dinner. Students poured down the stairs, dashing out across the sweet green-grass-smelling courtyard to the dining hall in the opposite wing. Frances, holding up the skirt of her borrowed dress so she didn't trip, couldn't stop blushing. But she didn't look as silly as Fred, who had apparently taken Becky's "nice clothes" comment way too seriously: he was decked out in a full-on formal suit, and looked completely uncomfortable and out of place.

The dining hall was one long rectangle, the walls the same dark-brown bricks as the outside. There was a bit of open space at the front, but the rest of the hall was filled with round wooden tables. Becky sat us toward the back, past groups of kids who snickered as Fred walked by, to a table with three other kids who looked about as confused and nervous as we did. There was a pair of Majid sisters who must have sailed across the sea to come here and would only speak to each other, their gorgeous language rippling quietly in the background the whole night. The other student was a boy swallowed up by an enormous high-necked shirt, and so still and quiet it would have been easy to miss him if he hadn't looked like a tent pole. The only thing that moved were his eyes; there was something about the way they darted around the room—lingering on the doors and windows—that made you want to start checking the exits too.

Standing in the open space up front was Mr. O'Hara with two other teachers I assumed were the Mrs. Murphy and Ms. Macartney that Becky mentioned earlier. I was excited to see Alexa, off to the side, in her semiformals. Becky went to join them, moving around students so quickly and smoothly it was hard to keep your eyes on her.

There were also more minotaurs, and I'm sure there were more we couldn't see, but you know what? I decided to stop being surprised by anything at that point. They were stationed around the room, with Dimitrios—as he told us to call him— by our table and a massive one with scarred horns up by the teachers. There were four teachers in all, including Becky, which I hadn't expected because she was an ord. As far as I knew, ords didn't have a lot of time to go to graduate school to get their teaching certificates.

One moment the room was buzzing and the next everyone quieted down so abruptly it took us by surprise. Fred was caught in the middle of a joke, his voice squeaking to a halt. Behind us, one of the double doors opened, revealing a huge kitchen. Heat rolled over our table in waves. There was a muffled clanging and clattering from inside, and someone hissed, "Dude, shut up, Murphy's going to talk!"

One teacher stood at the head of the room. Mrs. Murphy, I presumed. She was slim as a willow branch, with shiny, springy, silvering copper hair cut close to her head. "Well, I see you're all here. Again." Her brisk, warm voice carried through the crowd. "Now, you know I don't like to give speeches"—someone choked off a laugh—"but this is an extraordinary occasion. I could not let it go by without saying . . . how disappointed I am." Everyone at my table sat up straight, shooting quick, worried glances at each other, but all around us the other kids were smiling. "Yes, another year has started, and we have *exactly* the same number of students as last year. Not *one single student* was lost."

Amid the cheering and pounding on tables, Frances whispered, "Is that unusual?"

Mrs. Murphy held up her hands, and the room quieted down. "Wait. Wait—I'm mistaken. We don't have the same number of students. With our new Year Ones"—she inclined her head toward our table—"we have more.

"Think of all the wasted opportunities," she moaned dramatically. "The Red Lady from the other side of the river who wouldn't leave us alone if we paid her. She wouldn't leave us alone even *when* we paid her. Did any of you get eaten like good little ords? No-oo!" She pulled the word out as if it caused her pain. "You rallied together and fought her off. Then there was the chimera outbreak. Again: heroism, ingenuity, *survival*. What are we to tell the king? That his ord population is booming?"

86
✳ ✳ ✳

"She's not serious, is she?" Fred asked as someone from across the room shouted, "Hey, I broke my leg!"

"Oh, to be sure, there was one injury. We're all very impressed, Mr. Naveen. I'm not even going to mention last winter," Mrs. Murphy continued, throwing up her hands. "Don't you laugh, Mr. Dane. You have gained at least twenty pounds since you came here. What have you done to help us out, hmm? Have you gotten kidnapped? Did anyone here get kidnapped over the summer?"

"She can't be serious," Fred said, and we exchanged another nervous glance before I caught Alexa watching me. She shook her head and fought down a smile.

"I have never met a more selfish, irresponsible . . . help me out here," Mrs. Murphy called.

"Disrespectful!" someone shouted.

"Inconsiderate!"

"Ungrateful!"

"Precisely." Mrs. Murphy let out a sharp sigh, a smile struggling at the corners of her mouth. "I suppose there's nothing left to do but get through another year."

More cheering. Somebody whistled.

Mrs. Murphy raised her voice over the noise. "Oh, for—I'm not done yet, you heathens! Has no one taught you any manners? Now, before we get on with all the celebration nonsense, I would like each and every one of you to think long and hard about the trials you are putting your poor teachers through. Look at Miss Corey there. Her nerves are strained to the breaking point, watching after all of you." She gestured to Becky, who was standing calmly in the shadows with her hands clasped in front of her. "She is losing her mind."

"She never had it!" someone shouted from the back.

"*That* is beside the point," Mrs. Murphy said. "It is still tragic. As for our new students"—she looked at us, and her eyes were bright with suppressed humor—"on behalf of the entire school, which will join me, I know, we hope you have a very dull and educational year. Now, let's eat."

Behind us, kids suddenly rushed out of the kitchen doors, faces flushed and eyes focused. One student popped up over my shoulder and spun a basket of bread and a bowl of salad onto our table. Another plunked down a pitcher, water splashing around the rim and ice cubes clinking together. The teachers dispersed, each one edging a chair into one of the full tables. There was a tap on my shoulder and Alexa slid into a seat next to me. "I told you I'd come back." She laughed when I threw myself at her.

Over crusty bread and salad Frances started talking in starts and stops. She tried to slip in comments when they'd be least noticed, like when we were talking about family and she mentioned she was the third of four girls.

Fred buttered another slice of bread with a sound that might have been *hmm* or *aah* and asked which sister was her favorite.

Peter looked up in what might have almost been surprise. "You have favorites?"

"Yeah," Fred and I answered together.

"You do?" Alexa shot me a sly look. "And who, may I ask, is your favorite?"

I grinned. "You, of course."

Alexa speared a tomato in her salad. "You're a terrible liar."

Frances nibbled on a roll until she thought we weren't paying attention. "Susan. She's nice. She's the talented one. She wants to own a nursery. Plants, not babies. She, um . . . I haven't heard from her since . . ."

Then Fred asked Frances how she found out about being an ord. Frances explained (her face slowly going pink) that she had been out with her family a week before her Judging. She crossed the street a little too fast. "There was a carpet, and the driver didn't see me until the last second. He cast at me, to get me out of the way, but nothing happened. Luckily, I ducked. I didn't even realize until later what it meant that the driver's magic didn't work on me." She shrugged and offered a watery smile. "They had to call off my whole Judging."

"So you didn't get Judged?" I asked.

"No. I mean . . . there wasn't any point," she explained. "But Daddy got some of his deposit back. So it wasn't . . . it wasn't that bad."

"Then you don't know if you're an ord? Not for sure," Peter said.

"You're an ord," Becky said. She was standing just behind Peter.

"How can you be sure?" Fred asked.

"I'm sure." She came over, flicking her dark bangs out of her eyes as she crouched in front of Frances. "When you're an ord long enough, you can tell. You can see it in other people. No, that's not right," she corrected herself. "It's more like you recognize it. There's just a certain *something* that ords don't have." She took Frances's hand, rubbed it between her own. "It doesn't make us worse, Fran. Just different. Sometimes it takes a little while to figure it out, is all. It's scary, I know," Becky continued, to all of us. "But ever since King Steve took the throne, things for ords are better than they have ever been. He's done a lot for us."

Peter laughed, and looked up from his book. "Like what?"

"Like building this school," Becky returned with a bit of an edge to her voice. "Like giving us a place to stay. A safe one, where we don't have to worry about when we'll eat next," she added with a pointed look at Peter's full plate. "Like standing up for us when that fool's court starts yelling about ords being dangerous. He didn't need to stick his neck out for us, and heaven knows it'd be easier for him if he didn't. So I will not hear a word against him, Peter Whittleby. Not from you or anybody else." She stared him down until he dropped his eyes. Then Becky glanced at Alexa. "He's a good man."

"Yes," Alexa agreed. "He is."

• • •

Around the fourth course, Nate, the boy I'd helped earlier, charged over to our table. "We need some help in the kitchen with the dishes. Murphy said to recruit one of you newbies to lend a hand. Well?" he demanded before anyone could answer.

There was a brief silence when everybody looked at one another. "I will," I said.

"Great. Come on. Come *on*," he said, yanking me up out of my chair. He dumped a load of plates in my arms and pushed me through the kitchen door and into chaos—shouting and smells and people and a heat that nearly knocked me back. The place even looked like heat, with bright yellow walls and red tile floors and constant movement. There were kids wiping down counters and bending over a hot stove and slamming things into cupboards. "Hey! Watch that!" called a stout, hippy woman by the stove—Cook Bella, I guessed. She had round pink cheeks, and her hair was bound back tight and covered with a scarf. "You take those pans out and stack them again, and I'll thank you to do it nicely this time. If you don't take the time to learn, I'll make you do this whole kitchen over again."

The kid took the pans out, stacked them on the counter, and then put them back again, gently and neatly.

Nate led me to a great double sink on the other side of the room. To the right was a pile of dirty dishes, to the left a crowded drain board, where clean dishes sat drying. "Here, here, here, here." Nate splashed his dishes down into the soapy water. "You ever wash dishes before?"

I shook my head.

He rolled his eyes. "Oh, for— Okay, pay attention. You take the dirty dish, you put it into the soapy water, you take the sponge—tie your hair back, newbie, nobody wants a hair on their plate—you put the soap on it. You following me? You take the sponge, wash all the gunk off"—he demonstrated—"then under the faucet, you have to turn on the faucet first, then scrub, and into the drain board. Got that? You use hot water, got that? Always hot water. I'm going to dry and put away. Any questions?" He tossed the sponge at me, not giving me a chance to ask. "Wash."

I turned on the water ("hot water, *hot*"—he twisted the lever to the right) and poured enough soap on the sponge to turn it slick and bubbly.

After the first couple of dishes I paused to roll up my sleeves. Most of the time the gunk washed off easily, but sometimes I had to scrape and scratch bits off. Twice some kid whisked by and dumped more plates on the counter. The hot water stung my hands, turning them red, then tender, then numb. But the pile started shrinking, slowly at first, and then faster as I got the hang of it.

"Wash fast. But not too fast. If you don't do a good job, she'll make us do it all over again." Nate nodded toward Cook Bella, who was taking pans out of the oven. A warm, buttery smell drifted across the room—and for a second I was back in Mom's bakery, and the sense of home was so strong my throat clogged and my eyes stung. Across the room, Cook Bella set the pans aside to cool and turned off the oven. I inhaled again, trying to hang on to the memory of home.

"Nate, how are you two doing on those dishes?" Cook Bella called without looking up.

"Good, Chef." The words were clipped and respectful.

"Maybe I'll just come over and make sure." Wiping her hands on her apron, she worked her way over to us, tasting here, correcting there, until she poked her head between us. With a sniff, she took a plate from Nate and inspected it. He went on drying and didn't breathe. She looked at it so long I was surprised he didn't pass out.

Finally she handed it back to him. "You're learning."

Nate's shoulders sagged in relief.

Cook Bella took a wet dish from the rack. Another careful inspection. She handed it to Nate and turned to me, eyes narrowing in scrutiny. "What's your name?"

"Abby—" A pot slipped out of my hands and splashed back into the water, splattering bubbles on my face. "Abby Hale."

"You ever wash before?"

"It's her first time," Nate said.

Cook Bella pinned him with a look. "Did I ask you?"

"No, Chef." He focused on his dishes.

She turned back to me. "This your first time washing dishes?"

"Yes, uh, Chef," I said.

She looked me up and down. "You're a Year One, all right." Before I could answer, recognition lit her face. "Hale. Wait. You're our watchdog's sister."

"Watchdog?" I repeated. Nate elbowed me; I ignored him.

"I hear your family likes you," Cook Bella continued as if I hadn't spoken. She took my hands abruptly, and turned them over, back and forth. She didn't seem to care that they were soaking wet and a dull, buzzing red. "Never had a day's work in your life."

Um, no, Chef was probably a safer answer than *I guess that depends on what you mean by "work."*

"You ever even set foot in a kitchen before?"

"Yes, Chef. At home." That didn't seem to be what she

93

wanted to hear, and I caught myself adding, "Also, my mom owns a bakery. I help out sometimes, but it's a normal bakery."

"Did Nate here volunteer you?"

"He asked. He said he needed help; I said I'd help him."

Cook Bella glanced at Nate, who nodded. She smirked and let go of my hands. "A normal bakery doesn't count."

"Yes, it *does*," I snapped on a surge of protectiveness.

Cook Bella raised her eyebrows. Nate elbowed me again; I ignored him again. The entire kitchen had gone quiet. "Normal bakeries—magic folk? They don't really cook. They *cast*. Same bland little muffins and tarts as everyone else."

I said, "My mom makes shortcake." Which is not what I wanted to say, but Cook Bella was a grown-up, and you're supposed to show respect to grown-ups, even if they don't know what they're talking about.

"Shortbread," Nate jabbed under his breath.

"No, short*cake*," I told him. "Shortbread's like a cookie; Cook Bella just made shortcake."

Cook Bella looked straight at me. Her eyes were hazel, which I'd always thought was a soft, pleasant color until now. Slow and steady as a snake, she went over to her baking pan, cut off a corner of the cake, and tossed it at me. I had to drop the sponge to catch it. "What else?"

The fragrant golden square burned my hands like a challenge.

Okay, it probably was not my smartest moment. But it wasn't fair, it wasn't right, her saying Mom didn't really cook. I mean, she made this exact same thing. I should know, I spent enough time watching Mom cast and conjure, and playing official taster for her. Shortcake was one of Mom's specialties: soft, a little spongy; and the bakery would have that toasted, buttery smell all day.

Then I forgot to be angry for a second because I was picking up another scent. Something faint and floral and silky, something that wasn't supposed to be there. I took a cautious bite. "Roses. You used rosewater?" I said, surprised. "That's not right. That's not in the spell."

Cook Bella looked me over, her expression bland. "Ords don't follow spells. And everyone needs to get back to work," she added, moving off to check the dishes and the dessert.

I caught Nate watching me. "You'd better like washing dishes."

"Most fun I've had in my life." My back was starting to ache.

Noise came from the dining hall, the strings and horns and drumbeats of a band tuning up. Kids perked up, and Cook Bella started barking orders about almond cream and raspberries.

By the time I rinsed out the last cup and shut off the faucet, my fingers were prunes and my hair was falling out. (Falling out of its tie, that is; I wasn't going bald.) Nate tossed me a towel, and we got the last of the dishes dry and put away. By that time, the music was in full swing, and Cook Bella was setting plates out on the island. The kitchen kids gathered around, and Nate inched over and said something to Cook Bella. She looked at me and shook her head, murmuring something about "not one of us yet."

So while the rest of the kids bellied up to the island and dove into raspberry tarts, I headed toward the door.

"Work's not over yet," Cook Bella called in a carrying voice. "There's still dishes to be washed when dessert's done."

I stopped and glanced around. The kids were still sitting at the island, focused on their food, studiously *not* paying attention to me. I had said I would help, so I went back and stood by the sink.

In between the clink of spoons and *mmms*, there were snatches of talk. One kid mentioned she had "Macartney first thing tomorrow morning." It set off a round of sympathetic murmurs.

"It's best to get it over and done with right away," one of the kids replied around a mouthful. "Like pulling off a bandage, you know? Then you're not freaking out for the rest of the day."

Cook Bella clapped her hands and immediately the room quieted down. The sounds from the dining hall continued to filter in—a bouncing song and a singer with a rough voice, plus feet stomping and laughter and people shouting above the music. "All right, servers, dessert out. Dinner dishes back in. Do it quick and do it right, and then we'll have a bit of fun."

I made sure my hair was tied back and sleeves rolled up and apron secure before starting in on the dinner dishes. The music thrummed through the floor and up my legs. I made myself go steady, check that each dish was really clean before handing it to Nate. After a while, there was only me and Nate left, and Cook Bella standing in the doorway, listening to the music.

When we finally finished, Nate raced for the exit.

"Make sure you're back here for the dessert dishes," Cook Bella said, holding the door open.

The dining room was hot and loud. Most of the kids were up at the front dancing. A band played away in a corner. The kids still in their seats laughed and shouted at one another and dove into their plates of fruity wonderfulness. Up front they'd pushed chairs aside and tables back until the space had doubled. How could there only be fifty kids here? It seemed like hundreds, thousands, everywhere at once. Everywhere except at our table; for some reason the other kids were giving us a wide berth.

I slid into my seat as one song ended. The music started again right away, and there was a race to find partners and places. Alexa asked Peter to dance; he got up and followed her without a word. Fred glanced at me and Frances, then straightened up (I think his heels even clicked together) and held out a hand. "Would either of you, I mean, would you like to . . ." He cleared his throat and nodded at the dancers.

Fran threw a nervous glance at the dancers and shook her head. "No. No, I don't know this dance."

"Neither do I," I said. "Come on, it'll be fun."

"I could teach you," Fred offered, but Fran shook her head and started playing with her fingernails. "Fran—"

"I said no."

* * *

"Okay, okay. Maybe the next one?" I suggested, but Fran was just staring at the floor as if she wanted to burrow into it. "You." I turned to Fred, who still had that blank, stunned look of retreat, and held out my arm; he grinned and hooked his arm through mine. "Let's do this thing." I tugged him toward the dance floor.

The tune was bright and lively, the kind that pricked up every cord of your body until it was clamoring to move. Fred took my hands and swung me into the dance. Hop—Skip—Clap—Twirl. Fred was good, or at least he was good at pretending he knew what to do.

Twirl—Skip—Skip—Change partners. I had no idea what I was doing, and it didn't seem to matter much. The steps kept repeating, but my new partner made up half of it, twirling and turning me out of sequence.

Skip—Skip—Skip—Clap—Change partners. The air was hot and heavy and clear. My new partner nudged me into the right place with a smile. Twirl—Turn. The girl next to me winked and said, "No, the other way." Clap—Change partners again.

Peter was my partner this time, face flushed, eyes bright as we messed up each other's moves. I stepped on his foot, he limped (or faked it) through the next steps. I laughed an apology. Clap—Skip—Spin—Spin. And I leaned back, giving in to the momentum.

It wasn't until we heard the students clapping that we realized the dance was over. We smashed into each other, trying to stop, and Peter was smiling—actually smiling—and I couldn't breathe for laughing. The musicians waved off the applause and started right up again. Faster.

I grinned. "Go again?"

He took my hands.

CHAPTER 11

Nate didn't lie. They did feed us well. Breakfast was as impressive as dinner. For the first time ever, the scrambled eggs didn't need salt. They didn't need anything; they were savory, and so smooth they were like custard. There was a plate of thickly sliced bacon, still sizzling, and a basketful of golden, pillowy biscuits with little pots of butter and jam. Kids at the other tables kept their servers running as they cleared their plates and asked for more. At our table, the only ones who managed to eat were Peter and the thin boy (whose name, I learned, was Cesar—and I had to ask Becky for it). I forced down a couple of bites—it was so tasty, it seemed a shame to not eat it—but my stomach was so busy twisting and churning with nerves, there wasn't any room for food.

"What do you think they're going to teach us?" Fred had just about reduced his biscuit to crumbs, smearing and resmearing it with strawberry preserves, until Peter reached over and pried the jam pot out of his hands.

"This is a school, right. So school stuff," I said, trying to convince myself.

"Isn't your sister . . . Doesn't she run this school? Didn't she tell you anything?" Fred asked.

"No. She just said this was a school for ords." And I hadn't asked her about anything else, I hadn't *cared*, because I thought if Alexa was in charge, then nothing bad could happen. Now I wished I had. "We'll learn ord stuff, I guess. Like . . ." What did ords do, besides get kidnapped by adventurers? "Camping."

"Or how to escape from a camp," Fred joked.

And Peter suggested, "The proper way to get captured."

On the other side of the table, Cesar's eyes flicked up briefly from his plate, and then he went back to shoving bacon in his mouth.

"Maybe this is just a normal school," Frances whispered, barely loud enough for us to hear over the breakfast buzz. "Maybe the only thing different about here is that they let ords in."

I turned to the Majid sisters. They were seated at the far side of the table, chairs edged together and heads bowed. They'd been chatting to themselves and ignoring us since we sat down. I asked, "What do you guys think?" And then I felt silly, because what if they didn't even speak Westren?

They stopped talking and stared me down. After an endless moment one said, "They will teach us what we need to know."

"That's really helpful," Peter remarked.

"What *you* need to know," the other said. "We have no reason to be here. Maj take care of our own," she finished imperiously.

Peter snorted and said what we were all thinking. "Even ords?"

"Maj take care of family. All family. It is their duty."

"Then why are you here?" he demanded.

Before they could answer, there was a chime and the servers raced through, snatching our plates off the table, even if there was still food on them. Cesar grabbed the last three biscuits out of the basket—so fast you'd miss it if you blinked—and stuffed them in his pockets.

Mr. O'Hara appeared next to our table as the rest of the students began to file out. "Good morning. I hope you ate well. It's going to be a long day."

• • •

Fran was right; it was just a normal school. Sort of. At first.

We were prepared for weird. You can't be an ord headed to an ord school without expecting weird, especially after a summer of people telling you "you are different" and that your life is never going to be the same. Which is why it was so unnerving at first, because our morning classes weren't weird at all. It was the stuff everybody learns—you know, math and history and reading (which Mr. O'Hara called literature). Stuff you would learn in any school, no matter what kind of kid you were. In those classes, things almost seemed normal.

First period was Mr. O'Hara's literature class. He led us up the stairs and down a hall to a fresh-scrubbed classroom with desks and chairs that had to be pulled out by hand—no magic here—and a wall of windows that overlooked the courtyard. We sat in uneasy silence as he tried to get us talking about the last thing we had learned in our other schools, and when had we gotten kicked out, and what books we liked, and what we "expected to get out of this class." Nobody said anything, but he just kept asking questions, long after other teachers would have broken down and started lecturing about what *they* expected us to get out of class to save everyone the trouble of answering. After ten minutes of keeping silent, I finally raised my hand and told Mr. O'Hara I loved Miranda Blythe's romance novels, and I decided I liked him immediately when he didn't laugh or reassure me that we'd be reading *real* books. Like Mrs. Andrews had last year.

He did say, "I'm afraid Ms. Blythe is not on the curriculum this semester. We'll be starting your education here with the epic poets—boring, I know, but necessary building blocks. However, an extra-credit book report is always welcome, and you're free to choose whatever topic you like."

Then Mr. O'Hara added, "I think Ms. Blythe's works would be a particularly interesting topic for a report. In fact, if you want an example of the archetypal hero journey—"

"Wait, wait, wait." Fred raised his hand. "You read romance novels?"

"My dear boy," Mr. O'Hara replied, "I read everything."

We stayed in the same classroom for languages. That class was a little weird, I'll admit. I mean, a couple of language classes are required at every school. I don't know why; you usually don't learn more than how to say "Where is the bathroom?" and "I'd like a cheeseburger." (Or, in Olivia's case, "Oh my, a button has popped off!") Olivia and Gil said if I had a choice, I should take

Astrin, which is supposed to be the easiest because it's so close to Westren, and Jeremy insisted it'd look better on my transcript if I took Svar, because it's the hardest. But they all agreed that language is usually two semesters, over and done with. It's a token class.

That was not the case at the Margaret Green School. Here it was required. We were going to learn a different language each year, and in order to graduate to the next grade we'd have to be what Mr. O'Hara called "functionally fluent."

"Why? So we're ready to be bought and sold?" Peter muttered under his breath.

"In case you're bought and sold," Mr. O'Hara answered so everyone could hear. "I think you'll find escape much easier if you know the local language." And then he spent the rest of the class introducing us to Astrin and teaching us the tourist basics, like *hello, good-bye, please, thank you,* and *help, I'm being kidnapped!*

Every now and again I'd glance out the large windows and watch Becky holding her class down in the courtyard. I wasn't sure what she was doing, but it looked like she had the older students and was making them run around a lot and dig into the ground.

Midmorning was Ms. Macartney for math and history. Unlike Mr. O'Hara, Ms. Macartney didn't seem interested in what we'd done in our other schools or in getting us to talk. She barely talked herself. She took roll by waiting for everyone to sit down and stop talking (something about her calm, watchful expression made it a short wait) and then checked our names off a list. She walked up and down the rows, handing out quizzes, and took a seat behind her desk as we spent the better part of the class filling them out. The quiz was basic math—adding, subtracting, multiplication, some division, and a little geometry. I guess to figure out how much we knew. The instructions said to try every problem, even if we didn't know the answer, and to show our work.

Class was almost over by the time we finished; Ms. Macartney stood and gathered the papers herself, though it would have been easier to just poof them over to her desk.

When she spoke, I realized it was the first time I'd heard her voice, because I wasn't expecting that slow, seaside drawl. It sounded at odds with her cool-eyed stare and every-hair-in-place bun. "The life of an ord is hard," she began, taking us in kid by kid, "and it starts here. I do not give out As in this class, or Bs or Cs. You are all old enough to know your alphabet by now. You either pass or you fail. If you fail"—and she somehow made *if* sound like *when*—"you will be required to repeat this class and this Year until you pass. Judging from this attempt"—she paged through our quizzes—"some of you have a lot of work ahead of you."

History was the same, except with more names and fewer numbers. Ms. Macartney didn't give her speech about the alphabet or our grades again, but it was understood.

As we left, I looked out into the courtyard again. Down on the grass, students were paired up and spaced out, sparring. It took me a second to realize they weren't just attacking each other, they were taking turns, all moving the same way. Becky let out a piercing whistle and they stopped. She pulled an older boy to the front where everyone could see and, moving like she was in a dance, tackled him to the ground.

The bell rang for lunch, but Becky held up three fingers and her students went at each other again. We plastered ourselves to the windows and watched until Ms. Macartney icily ordered us along.

. . .

"Finally, we're getting to the good stuff," Fred started. We were clustered around our table in the dining hall, leaning in like we'd discovered some big secret, and loading up on chunky vegetable soup and grilled cheese. I was hungry now that I knew what was coming. Or, at least, I knew that something was coming. Something ord. The dining hall was buzzing with kids shouting and stuffing their faces. I caught a couple of older students watching us and snickering. "Fighting I can do," Fred continued with exaggerated casualness. For the first time that day he looked relaxed. "I've got—I had—I grew up with three brothers."

"I didn't know we would have to fight." Fran was wringing her hands. Her face was so pale it looked like she was going to faint. "I don't know how to fight."

"That's why we're going to class," I told her. "They're going to teach us."

"And if you stink at fighting I'm sure they'll teach you the right way to stand on the auction block," Peter added, eyes in his book.

One of the Maj girls snickered. I chucked a roll at Peter. He looked up, surprised, when it bounced off his head. "That's mean. Don't be mean."

Peter glanced at Fran, and pointedly stuck his head back in his book, scraping his pencil against it with a vengeance.

"Oh, please, she needs to learn how to take it," one of the Maj girls was saying—Naija, I think, though I couldn't be sure. They liked to switch back and forth.

"Abby." It was Nate, his thin mouth twisted into an irritated scowl. "You're late."

"I am?" I asked.

"Just come with me." He turned and charged through the double doors. I shrugged at the table full of curious glances and hurried after him. Inside the kitchen it was as hot as I recelled but not quite as crazy as the night before.

Cook Bella was at the stove. "Is that Abigail?"

"Yes, Chef." Nate shoved me over to her, then hurried to the sink.

I edged toward Cook Bella, feeling suddenly nervous. Her focus was on a large black skillet that was hissing with hot butter. "Last night you said you wanted to help."

I glanced around, confused. All of the other kids were busy. "Yeah."

"Did you think we only needed help the one night?"

"Uh, no?" I said, feeling like I was taking a test and failing.

"Do you think dishes only get dirty one meal out of the year?"

"No," then I added, "Chef."

"Has your offer of help been rescinded?"

"No."

Finally Cook Bella looked over at me, like she was measuring me up for a recipe. Then she gave a brisk nod toward the sink. "Then go help. And tie back your hair."

I jogged to the sink, braiding my hair as fast as I could. Nate tossed me the sponge, but I missed and it squashed wetly on my arm. He smirked. "Don't be late for dinner."

· · ·

Becky was waiting for me in the empty dining hall after lunch. She took in my splattered skirt and pruney hands with one quick look. "You're late."

"I know, I'm sorry, I—"

She charged past me into the kitchen before I could finish. The door swung wide, and I caught a low, firm "I'll thank you not to wear out my students before my class, Arabella."

"The girl offered to help," Cook Bella tossed back. "If she gets worn out washing a few dishes—"

But Becky was already striding back into the dining room. "And keep your eye on the clock next time!" She took my arm and steered me outside without missing a beat.

The rest of the class was out in the courtyard—Fred shifting back and forth on his feet, darting glances around at everyone, while Fran tucked into herself like a turtle again. I don't think Peter was even paying attention. To the side stood Mrs. Murphy and Dimitrios. "Sorry about the delay," said Becky. "I needed a minute to go over class schedules with our esteemed cook."

"You really should be nicer to the woman who prepares your food," Mrs. Murphy remarked.

"And she really should be more careful about when I need my students. Okay," Becky announced, rubbing her hands together, "don't you all look bored. Just like real students. We give you the regular stuff first on purpose; it's supposed to give you 'a sense of normalcy.'" She grinned at Mrs. Murphy. "You ready to wake them up a bit?"

Mrs. Murphy cracked her knuckles. Dimitrios rolled his shoulders back, stretching. Above us, classroom windows swung open and kids leaned out, shoving each other aside to get a good view. Becky ignored all of it. "Now, we won't be getting to this for a while yet, but I find it helps with motivation if you get a preview of what you can do. Call it a practical demonstration. Boys and girls, you are all going to need to back up a bit." We took a couple steps back; Becky waved at us and we took a couple more steps, until she gave a thumbs-up.

Behind Becky, Mrs. Murphy suddenly burst into flame, so smooth and professional she had to be a Six at least—and a Six who'd obviously had a lot of schooling. Usually people had to call and cast; it took serious training to flick a spell on like a lamp. Red and orange waves of magic twisted around her like a torch, and she held her hands out, palms up, focusing the fire, feeding it until it grew too bright to look at.

"You all know by now that being an ord means you can't do magic. That's the easy answer, the one everybody knows. But it's only half of it." Becky stopped and smiled at us. "What's the other half, you might ask."

Mrs. Murphy blasted Becky.

Fran screamed. Fred cursed really, really loudly. Mrs. Murphy *tsk*ed. "Language, Mr. Randalls." My first thought—other than it really does feel like your heart is leaping up into your throat— was to run over and shove Becky into a stop, drop, and roll, which is standard procedure for underage kids who can't be extinguished. But Peter grabbed my arm and held me back. Her eyes bright with amusement, Mrs. Murphy kept blasting away at Becky until flames billowed up around her, almost reaching the third story. It took a second to realize the pounding in my ears was cheering from the students leaning out the windows.

Mrs. Murphy called the flames back and Becky stepped out. It took a few seconds for what she was saying to register through that instant, thrumming panic. "Ords can't do magic. And magic can't really do ords either."

She was still on fire, except that she wasn't. Her clothes were on fire—sleeves smoldering and ashing away—but Becky was fine. It was strange to see the flames twisting around her legs, lapping at her hair, and not having any effect. She combed a hand through her hair, sending fiery bits of magic showering to the ground, and stepped toward us. I was so close to the flames now, my damp skirt started to steam, but . . . I didn't feel the heat. I could smell the singed fabric of Becky's shirt, but I didn't feel anything. Strange.

"Lesson number one," Becky said. She was still on fire and Dimitrios was laughing at this point. "Invest in magical cloth-ing. It's expensive but durable, and as long as you have cash, most stores don't care who they sell to. I promise, it'll save you money in the long run."

"That's lesson number one?" Mrs. Murphy remarked.

"Lesson number two," Becky continued. "There's a difference between magic not affecting you, and not affecting the things *around* you. Or on you, as the case may be." She swatted at the flames still eating at her shirt. "There is a big difference between magic fire, which won't affect us, and magic that starts a fire, which'll burn you just the same as everything else. Between the magic that'll choke the air out of your lungs and the kind that'll suck the air out of a room." Mrs. Murphy dismissed the fire, and there was a low, grumbling sound, like an ogre shifting, and the ground began to shake. "Part of this class"—Becky raised her voice to be heard over the rumbling as we struggled to stay upright—"is about learning to tell the difference."

She nodded to Mrs. Murphy and the earth stilled.

"Why is that, you might ask," Becky continued when Peter raised his hand. "Work. You are *all* going to grow up, and that means getting jobs and being responsible adults. Believe it or not, there are places out there that need people who don't get messed up by magic. Museums, guilds—maybe even a private collector—looking for someone who won't become sick sorting magic inventory. That line of work means being around a lot of artifacts, a lot of powerful magic in an enclosed space, which can make it really dangerous for normal folk."

Dimitrios tossed her a towel, and Becky scrubbed the soot off her face and hands. "Thanks. There are also adventurers,

* * *

as I know all of you are aware. There are some out there—not a lot, but some—who are willing to hire an ord, give them a share. There's money to be made in adventuring, if you're willing to take the risk. So we're going to be learning about the different types of magic and how to identify them. Things like, what's the difference between charms and enchantments? Or, how do you identify a warding sequence so you know where to break through without sounding an alarm?

"Some adventurers, however, don't want to pay anything for an ord. They don't think they should have to invest in them, not when they used to be 'free to a good home' before King Steve took the throne. And they don't take no for an answer. Many won't even give you a choice in the matter." (The kids hanging out the windows started shouting, "Get her, Dimitrios!" and "Five on Becky!") "When that happens"—Dimitrios snorted and scraped his hooves against the ground—"well, you're just going to have to know how to defend yourselves. Which leads me to the next part of our class—"

Dimitrios charged, but Becky was already moving, whipping her belt free as she leaped out of the way at the last second. Her wrist flicked, almost lazily, and her belt flashed out, spinning around Dimitrios's ankle. Frost started climbing up from the black links wrapped around his leg, and his breath puffed out in cold white clouds. Mrs. Murphy appeared behind us and gathered us back a few steps just as Becky yanked *hard*—hard enough to jerk his foot out from under him but not quite hard enough to make him fall. Dimitrios winked at Becky and yanked his foot back. Laughing, she held on and let the momentum carry her forward, rolling under his arms, out of his reach, and started running. Dimitrios tugged the chain off, ignored the icicles forming in his hair, and thundered after her. The ground shook under his hooves. He was fast, but Becky could run, her long legs eating up the ground, not even breathing hard. She charged flat out at the building, springing up at the last second to kick off of the wall, the force of it twirling her around in time to grab Dimitrios's horns. She latched on to his back, but only for a second because he flailed, strong enough that I was surprised she didn't go flying. She held on to his horns as he flung her, twisting his head to the side and bringing them both to the ground. She had counted on his trying to get rid of her, and she used it to bring him down.

They sprawled on the grass, laughing. Becky held out her hand as he stood. "I win."

Dimitrios yanked her to her feet, brushed the grass off her shoulders. "No, I let you look good in front of the newbies. Plus you still owe me from last time. I'll take it off your tab."

Becky shoved him and turned to us. "Self-defense," she announced, back in teacher mode. "Yes, you will be learning how to fight and to defend yourselves. But first things first. We're going to go over simple maneuvers, escape techniques, what to do if you are captured. We're not going to be getting to that stuff"—she nodded at Dimitrios—"for a little while yet. Not until I get to know you all a little better. Not until I trust that you won't act out.

"Which leads us to the next part of our class." Becky whistled and the kids in the windows quieted down. It was strange

* * *

how the courtyard went from pep-rally loud to dead silent so quickly. "And this is the most important part, boys and girls. Using your knowledge responsibly."

Becky stared at us. "Protection spells don't work on us, or wards or charms. We can walk right into a bank vault, into someone's home. Being an ord means more than just magic not working on us. It means you can steal—you can hurt—and you cannot be punished. Normal jails? Can't hold us. We can cross back over enchants borders. We cannot be Banished. Right now people are afraid of you, and they should be because you can't control yourselves. And that is what ultimately makes you dangerous."

There was nothing amused or playful in her face right now. It was so hard and fierce, a thread of fear crept down my spine. "Now, I hope you learn something in this class. I hope you enjoy it, but—Mark. Me. Well. This is not a place for messing around. What you do reflects on every other ord out there. If I catch you doing anything I don't like, you're out. The school will still take care of you, feed you, help you find a place if you like, but your days as a student are over. You got that?"

We got it.

"Good." Becky smiled. "Now, who wants to hop on inside a fireball?"

CHAPTER 12

The beginning of the school year was a busy blur—all movement and new stuff and us new kids panting to keep up.

It was tough at first, because we were always moving. Morning classes were quiet and normal and stationary, but once we got to Becky's class, forget about it. Mondays, Wednesdays, and Fridays were self-defense days, days when we never stopped running, jumping, running, dodging, and more running, until our legs felt like they were going to fall off. Even when we were just studying, Becky tried to keep us moving. She couldn't just describe breaking through a barrier, we had to run through one to see for ourselves. She wouldn't tell us what different ward stones meant, she'd toss five different heat-based ones around the courtyard and tell us to hunt for the one that had smoke magic. We knew it was bad when we started joking that history with Ms. Macartney was a vacation.

Eila, the other Majid sister, finally broke down during a Saturday class—yeah, that's right, we had Becky every single day including weekends—and demanded to know "*why* do we have to do so much *running?*"

"What else are you going to do if someone tries to snatch you?" Becky asked. "You're too little to fight back, even if you knew how."

The trickiest part about self-defense was that Becky would demonstrate a move with Dimitrios and then pair us up to try and attack each other. It sounds fun and exciting, and to be honest we weren't at the point where we could hurt each other. That is, unless you were paired with Cesar. *Nobody* wanted to be paired with Cesar. Usually there was a rush to find a partner, any partner, that wasn't Cesar. The first two classes the Majid sisters tried to bully Fran into taking one for the team, which got Becky mad and earned all of us extra laps for not "sticking up for one of our own." Then she paired both of the sisters with Cesar, which he totally had no problem with, by the way.

The rest of us were pretty much on an even playing field. The Majid sisters liked to mock people into submission, which, though never fun to endure, was also not what Becky called "an effective fighting strategy." Fred never hit girls, and Fran couldn't be counted on to hit anything at all. The best thing I had going for me was endurance. We all thought Peter would be tough, because of the general bitterness that seemed to absorb his every waking moment. And he would hit you, but never hard. It was always just enough to let you know he'd won. Instead he preferred to point out your weaknesses and tell you how he was going to take advantage of them. Granted, this provided an opportunity for the less scrupulous among us—if, say, you *deliberately* made a mistake and then used the time when Peter stopped and snarked at you to tackle him to the ground.

The problem with Cesar was that Cesar fought dirty. Biting, pulling hair, twisting fingers, there was nothing he wouldn't do to win, which meant he *always* won, which led to a very informative lesson on how to treat a human bite wound.

It was early on still, and Becky had been teaching us how to twist out of somebody's hold. She was correcting one of the Majid sisters' postures when suddenly Fran cried out. Cesar had gotten her on the ground and it wasn't practice anymore, it wasn't fun, because he was hurting her. I charged Cesar and tackled him—I was actually pretty good at tackling people; turns out most of it is about where you hit them—and we went rolling. And then Cesar went crazy. Kicking and scratching, he grabbed my hair and twisted so hard I cried out. I heard Fred pleading, "Come on, stop it, you guys," and Peter jumped in, and there was a full-on fight for about half a second before Becky lifted Cesar up by the scruff of his neck. She carted him over to a corner of the courtyard and reamed him out. I only caught the words "Alexa Hale" and "funding" and "disciplinary action."

Fred hurried over and helped me up. "Abby, are you okay?"

"Is Fran okay?" I asked.

Fran was still on the ground, squashed up in a bundle, her fingers wrapped in her hair. "I'm fine," she said, not looking at us. "I was fine. You didn't have to . . ." Her voice faded away and she turned pink.

"No, you didn't," Peter agreed, getting up off the ground. "That was really stupid. Fight your own battles, Hale."

* * *

"He was *hurting* her!"

Peter rolled his eyes so hard I was surprised he didn't strain something. I would have smacked them straight out of his head except Fred latched on to my arms.

"Enough." Becky's voice was a sharp, cold slap. She swung over to snatch up the first-aid kit, then bore down on us. "Everyone. Sit." We dropped, and Becky waved a hand at Peter. "No, no, not you—you come here." She positioned him in front of us, and I saw that his arm was bloody.

Becky stripped his sleeve back with practiced efficiency, while she lectured us about bacteria and the importance of cleanliness and the damage a bite could do. Fran raised her hand, dropped it, then raised it again.

"Miss Rose?" Becky called, her attention still on cleaning the raw, red circle of holes in Peter's arm.

"Isn't that . . . what Cesar did? I mean, isn't that cheating?"

"Yes."

"He cheats a lot," Fran said after a moment. When Becky didn't respond, she continued, "Isn't that *wrong?*"

"No." Becky looped a fresh white bandage around Peter's arm, not missing a beat as she finally looked over at us. "Not when it matters. Not when it's the auction block if you lose—or a back-alley deal with a rope around your ankle to keep you from running. Not that I approve of teeth marks in my students, Cesar, and don't you think that you and I are done having words about this. But you don't fight fair when it's your life on the line. *They* won't. You can trust me on that."

Becky tied off Peter's bandage and came over to Fran, looked

* * *

her straight in the eyes. Her voice was low, but we were listening. "We play it safe here, I know, but you need to know that we're not *playing*. This is your life. And you need to choose—right now, while you're warm and safe, while there are no chains on your wrists and you have a meal in your belly and you know where the next one's coming from. You have to decide what you're willing to do to keep it that way. You have to decide now, before something happens. Because when it does, you won't have time to wonder about it. You just have to know. Consider it homework." Becky stood and raised her voice. "For all of you."

After that, Cesar was only ever partnered with Becky.

• • •

Our last class of the day was zoology, with Dimitrios. When we were done running or fighting, or we were just too exhausted to move, he would appear from somewhere and herd us down to the dark cave of the Public Safety office. It was our favorite, and easiest, class by far, because Dimitrios didn't assign homework or schedule tests. In fact, he didn't ask us to do anything more than sit down and listen. It turns out there was yet another fun part of being an ord—there was no shortage of magical creatures that were a lot more dangerous to us than they were to normal folk.

We started off with goblins, because they're basic and easy and everybody knows about them. At least, that's what I thought until class started, because it turns out there were actually tons of different goblins; some good, some that'll give you nightmares.

Along with all that, I was expected to be in the kitchen, at the sink and at the ready, for every meal. I'd get a chance to eat something quick while everyone else was working, and I was usually scrubbing and scraping while they clustered around the island to eat. I didn't know how they had so many dishes, or where they stored them all, and sometimes I wondered if it was all a big practical joke and someone was magic and they'd enchanted a never-ending pile of dishes.

"Are you sure about this?" Alexa asked when she discovered I'd been helping out in the kitchen. "You don't have to work there."

"I want to," I said. "It's fun." She lifted her eyebrows at *fun*. "I said I would."

"As long as it's *fun*. But if it's ever not fun anymore, you let me know. Cook Bella can be a little difficult."

I wanted to say, *uh, yeah*, but I didn't want to tell Alexa just how difficult Cook Bella had been toward me. So I blinked up at her and gave her my most innocent "baby of the family" look and said, "Oh really?" and "How interesting" and "I hadn't noticed that," which Alexa didn't believe for a second but at least she didn't go marching into the kitchen and start a scene.

Because the truth was, it *was* fun in a strange, exhausting way. I was getting used to the kids laughing at me for being new and not knowing anything. Oddly enough, the kitchen was the only place I saw kids smile. Really smile. Like they enjoyed being around each other. And the kitchen was always hot and noisy and busy, and the air tasted like tomatoes, garlic, onions, and olive oil. It wasn't like Mom's bakery, but it was close enough—and close enough was everything in those first weeks.

• • •

Now, you might think with all the washing and running and the schoolwork on top of that—because clearly it wasn't a school if they didn't pile you with homework—I'd be completely exhausted. And I was, but being tired and going to sleep are two different things. Every night at lights-out, we had to check in with Becky and shut our doors and pretend to go to bed. Alexa had arranged for me to have a private room, and I know this'll sound stupid and spoiled of me, but I didn't like it. I didn't like being alone, and I didn't like the quiet. Not that it's ever totally quiet in Rothermere, but after a while you just forget about the street noises and the sirens and all that and it seems quiet. When I did sleep it was in fits and starts, waking suddenly in a panic that I'd heard something, only to realize it was what I *hadn't* heard, the sounds that were supposed to be there. Like the shower running and the soft, padding footsteps as Mom got ready to leave for the bakery in the dark hours of the morning. Like Dad humming as he started a new project, and Gil muttering to himself as he wrote, testing out dialogue, and Jeremy's aggravated cry of *Mom!* whenever he needed her to settle an argument, and the clink of Olivia's hairpins on her dresser as she put her hair back down after a date. I missed those noises so much my stomach burned.

Of course, it wasn't just that I went to school and that was it, that was the end of family. I talked to them all the time. Mom and Dad called, like, every day, and Olivia and Gil sent care packages, and Jeremy sent textbooks, and not a day went by when I didn't see Alexa. My family does not know how to leave people alone.

121

* * *

But they also got me in trouble.

It was early on, and I was hanging out in the lounge with Fred after dinner, picking apart an epic poem fragment for Lit. I discovered the lounge on my second day, and it quickly became one of my favorite places at school. Like everywhere else on campus, the floors were clean and the walls freshly painted, but it had a little more of a lived in feeling. The chairs were banged up around the edges, and there were a few scuffs under the floor polish. The only untouched thing was the crystal ball in the corner; it looked like it was fresh out of the packaging. Kids would crowd in come the evenings, and the noise and people made me feel a little less homesick. I liked Fred, too, because he'd talk to a person, at least, if you started talking to him first, and he was about as good as I was at picking out the author's intended theme.

An older girl plunked down on the seat next to me, smiling as she tucked her legs under her. "You don't have to wear it anymore, you know."

"Wear what?" I asked.

"The collar," she said, nodding to my necklace. "I had one too. I know, you forget it's there after a while. But you can take it off. It only feels weird not having it for, like, a day."

My hand automatically went to the charm Alexa had given me. "It's not a collar," I said.

"I know, it helps to think like that." The girl leaned forward for a closer look. "It's a nice one, I'll give you that. You must have been owned by someone swanky. Adventurers, right? My guild had me for a while. The Guild never pays out for anything half this nice. I can take it off you, if you want. I had to get someone else to help me with mine. My hands were shaking so bad I couldn't undo the knots." Her smile was reassuring. "Don't be scared."

I shook my head. "No. I mean, my sister gave it to me. In case I got in trouble."

Another kid laughed. "You need to study up on your charms, Em. You should know protection magic when you see it by now."

"Yeah, that's Alexa *Hale's* sister," a boy said in a bitter voice. "The one with the family."

The smile dropped off the girl's face. "Oh. Sorry. I didn't mean . . . to be rude."

"That's okay," I said, but she'd already gotten up and moved back to her friends.

I looked over at Fred, who was staring at the charm around my neck and looking really sad about it too. That is, until I caught him watching, and he shoved his head back in his notes.

The next day, Dimitrios set me up in front of the crystal ball in a corner of the lounge and cast a call to my parents. The kids in the lounge kept talking in that way people do when they don't want you to know they're listening to all the exchanges of *how are you* and *I miss you* and *I love you*. After we hung up, I could feel the whispers about *family* pelting my back, and for a brief second I was in Lennox again and it was the day after my Judging. Fred gave me a sympathetic shrug and asked me at the top of his lungs what I thought of our math homework.

· · ·

123

After the third quiz came back from Ms. Macartney with a big fat Fail, I knew I was in trouble. I'm an average student, I fully admit that. I think it's because Jeremy came right ahead of me in birth order and sucked up all the brains, so there was nothing left for me. And since my parents aren't known for their reasonable attitudes when it came to my grades, I had to take drastic action.

Fred and I had gotten in the habit of doing our homework together. It wasn't too hard to talk Fran into joining us, and between the three of us there was usually somebody who knew the answer to whatever question we had.

The problem was that if we came right out and asked Fred what he got, he would just hold up his hands and apologize and say, "We're at school, you know, to learn. What would you learn if I just told you the answers?"

"That you're nice," Fran said.

"I am nice," Fred said.

"You're the best," I agreed. "How about this? I got 'the Battle of Trivore' under 'Ethelred the Observant.'"

"Let's put it this way," Fred said, grinning, "that would be an error about Trivore."

"Which part is the error?" Fran insisted.

But Fred would just shake his head, and we'd have to go back over our books and figure it out ourselves, and all because he had a sense of fair play.

Peter, though? Peter barely even looked up during class. He acted annoyed when teachers asked him a question, but he always knew the answer. And, most important, Peter didn't seem to know what fair was. I'd invited him to join us a couple times, but he always went back to his room after dinner and did his home-work alone.

But three Fails in math *plus* an essay on the great poet Damokles for Lit meant I needed help. After beating our heads against the poem for almost an hour—seriously, it didn't even have any carpet chases or kissing or *anything*. How are you sup-posed to stay interested in something like that?—I slammed my book closed and stood up.

"What are you doing?" Fred asked, worried.

"What has to be done." I marched out of the lounge and down the hallway. I could hear Fred chasing after me.

"Abby, Abby, Abby—" Fred tried to block me, but Becky'd been teaching us evasion, and after a couple of tries I managed to twist under his arms and keep going. He ran ahead of me and plastered himself in front of Peter's door. Technically it's Fred's door, too, though he never goes in it except to sleep. "Think, Abby. You"—he tried to grab my hands as I reached around him and banged on the door—"you don't want to do this."

"Why not?" I asked.

"'Cause he's scary."

"He is not. Okay, he is," I admitted at Fred's look of utter surprise. "But he's just a kid like us."

"No, no, no, Peter's *not* a kid, he's, like, a golem. He wasn't born, he was activated."

The door swung open then. I think part of Peter's scary problem is that he's so tall. A lot taller than any twelve-year-old has a right to be. And he's got his mom's coloring—the dark curls, the thick dark eyelashes—and these pale gray eyes, and the whole thing can just be really intimidating.

Fred pointed at me. "She did it." I elbowed him, which was a mistake because then he elbowed me back. Fred has the sharpest elbows in the world.

Peter shifted his eyes to me.

"It's about the Damokles essay. We need help," I said. "Come to the lounge and help us with our Lit and we will be forever grateful."

"Forever?" Fred repeated.

"For a really long time. The rest of the year, at least. You can blame Jeremy."

Peter glanced back and forth between us, but his "Who?" was just as deadpan as everything else.

"My brother Jeremy," I said. "He's the smart one, and I have been asking him questions—homework questions— but he says he's not going to answer any more because that's cheating. It's *not* cheating, it's helping, but he wants to be a teacher, so he says he has to be strict about these things. Of course, Olivia—she's my big sister, well, my younger big sister—"

"You know, I don't actually care."

"Don't be mean. We need your help with homework," I pressed.

"No. Go ask Cesar or Fran or, I don't care, anybody else," Peter huffed. I was starting to agree with Fred. Peter has two modes: annoyed and golem.

* * *

I began listing reasons on my fingers. "Fran is already help-ing us out; Cesar's actually worse than I am at, you know, normal classes; the Maj girls don't open their door; and you are the smartest kid in class. Why wouldn't I come to you?"

Peter smiled at that. Just a quick little flash, gone as soon as it came, but he actually looked nice when he smiled.

"Just get your homework and come to the lounge," I said, and I planted myself in the doorway to make sure he did. "Please?"

"You're very pushy."

"I know, right? Olivia says it's because I'm the baby of the family, and I always get my own way. So you should just give up and do what I say. It'll make everything a lot easier. And I did say please," I reminded him, looking to Fred for confirma-tion. He nodded.

Peter's fingers strained against the wood of the door. "It's not my problem. It's your homework; do it yourself."

"Um, yeah, it is your problem. You're supposed to help your friends."

That shut him up. Just for three seconds, but still—it was nice to see him absolutely flabbergasted.

Then it was gone, and Peter was back. "We're not friends."

"Okay, we're not, but only because you're super-mean. But you know who are friends? Your mom and my mom." Okay, that was a little bit of a stretch. It'd be more accurate to say that Mom and Ms. Whittleby were friendly, because Ms. Whittleby was nice and didn't mind if Mom called her up three and four times a week to ask about raising an ord. But still. "What do you think is going to happen if my mom finds out that you wouldn't even help me with one little homework assignment?"

Peter's eyes narrowed, then he smirked. "Now you're being mean."

"I know. I'm sorry. I feel totally bad about it."

He grabbed the heap of papers off his bed. "This doesn't mean we're friends."

"Oh no, absolutely," I agreed, nodding.

"I still don't like you."

"A lot of people don't like me." I was getting used to it. I wasn't sure why Peter didn't like me, though. It wasn't the family thing, because Ms. Whittleby straight out adored him and called just about every other day. And it couldn't be school jealousy, because Peter was the only one Ms. Macartney praised. "I don't like you either, so that makes us even."

Peter slammed his door shut and headed down to the lounge.

* * *

CHAPTER
13

About a month after school started, the first out-of-season kid turned up. He climbed over the gates at night (which meant he had to be an ord to get past them) and almost got attacked by the minotaurs. He was in the kitchen when I headed down for breakfast duty early the next morning, shoveling ham and eggs into his mouth as fast as Cook Bella could fill his plate.

Two more kids arrived a couple weeks after that, and then another about a month later. Sometimes they only hung around long enough to get a good meal and a nap and a change of clothes. The teachers would load them up and try to talk them into sticking around for their safety. And some of them did decide to stay. When that happened, they had a little chat with the teachers and were quietly placed in the proper Year.

So at first when I saw eyes glowing in the dark through my window, I thought it might be another kid. It wasn't.

I was grumpy that night. I was sick of trying to read myself to sleep, sick of being tired, sick of the bruises and the leg aches and the stupid stories that were no fun at all to read and the math problems that made no sense and that we'd probably never use anyway. I turned off the lights and crawled up on my desk to look out the window for a while. Inside the school might have been dark and quiet, but outside was all lights and people and movement. Traffic hurried and paused and hurried again. Women raced by in spangly dresses. A loud, laughing group of guys ran down the middle of street, dodging around carpets, instead of chancing the sidewalk in front of the school. Lights glowed in the windows across the streets, and I could see shadows moving around inside.

Maybe it would have been easier, better, if we were allowed out. The older kids went off campus sometimes as a treat, but we younger students were stuck inside because it was danger-ous, what with the adventurers and all that. Also, we were dangerous, because we didn't exactly know what we were doing. What good was living in Rothermere if you only ever saw one building?

I leaned closer to the window. On the roof of one of the build-ings, in the dark, I saw a small, huddled shape. A shadow that didn't fit with the others. Then there was a flicker, like a dragon's eyes, or a cat's, the way they cut through the shadows. Gil told us stories of things that lurked in dark alleys in Rothermere, wait-ing for a poor sap to wander down so they could relieve him of his money or his organs. Of course, Gil had a tendency to improve on the truth if he didn't like the way it turned out.

But then there was another gleam, another set of eyes, peering out from an alley. Peering at the school. Watching.

* * *

I knew I was safe in here, behind the thick walls and the cold iron bars. But it was hard to remember that when I eased back and both sets of eyes snapped to my window, searching.

I scrambled back, almost falling off the desk. Heart pounding, I backed up to the door, out into the hallway, and followed the sound of laughter and talking to Becky's room at the end of the hall.

Becky always kept the door open. Inside, she and Dimitrios were drinking coffee, Dimitrios propped on the edge of a chair, Becky sitting on the floor. He saw me first and grinned. "Somebody's going to get in trouble. You're not supposed to sneak out of bed after—"

I cut him off in a nervous rush. "This is going to sound crazy . . ."

Becky and Dimitrios put down their coffee cups and stood in the same movement. "What is it?" He wasn't grinning anymore.

"I saw something. Across the street. There were . . . eyes in the dark." Okay, it sounded stupid out loud. "It was like they were watching the school. I thought it was a kid, but it's not, I don't think it was. Kids' eyes don't look like these eyes—"

"Show us," Becky said. Dimitrios picked up his spear as Becky put her hand on the back of my neck and steered me out into the hallway. Dimitrios whispered a shadowed word and the lights winked out. A few seconds later Fran's door opened and she peeked her head out in the darkness. Becky pointed at her and told her, "Get back inside, young lady"; her tone didn't leave room for argument. Not that Fran would have argued.

✶ ✶ ✶

They hesitated outside my door, Becky tucking me close as Dimitrios cast a wide-arced shield, big enough to cover all three of us. "Don't step out of this, or they'll see you," Dimitrios said.

"Who'll see me?"

He didn't answer. We crossed my room carefully, an inch at a time, with Becky's iron fingers digging into my shoulder until it felt like she was grinding the bones together. When we stopped in front of the window, Becky took in the street in one quick glance. "Alleyway, seven o'clock."

"There was also one on the roof—" I began.

Dimitrios cut me off. "Rooftop. Second building to the right. Two o'clock."

"Garbage can, alley, five o'clock."

"Bookstore alley, ten o'clock."

"That's four," Becky said. Her fingers wound around her belt, but Dimitrios put his hand over hers with a pointed look. "All right, all right," she said. "But I could take care of this now."

"That I do not doubt. You could clean out the entire city if you had a week and no other responsibilities."

Becky eyed him down, and then sighed and nodded. She and Dimitrios all but carried me out of the room. My door safely shut, Dimitrios dropped the shield and winked the lights back on. "I'll sound the alert. You grab the Year Ones?" Becky gave a sulky nod, and he laughed. "Sorry, Beck. No killing tonight."

"Darn," she muttered, but she was smiling.

Dimitrios ran off, the tile floor shuddering with each hoof-beat. "What's happening? Where are we going?" I asked.

Becky stopped by her room first. "Dimitrios has to report

it to Public Safety. You and I are going to get the other Firsties, and we'll all sleep in the lounge tonight."

"Why?"

Becky buckled on a holstered belt with two sheathed daggers, taking care it didn't cover her chain. "Those things you saw, they're red caps."

"Red cap." The words tasted cold and prickly. We'd heard about them in zoology—but we hadn't learned much because we were still working our way through "nice" goblins.

"They're always waiting, you know." She looked down at me sympathetically. "You need to know that. This is our life. Come on, and let's keep the red cap bit to ourselves for now."

Becky took me by the arm and dragged me down the hall. She stopped at the first door and knocked, three harsh solid cracks that had the door rattling on its hinges. One of the Maj girls answered, rumpled and sleepy-eyed. Becky streamed out something in their language and moved on to the next door, not waiting for an answer.

When we'd gathered everyone, half-asleep and grouchy, we headed back to the lounge, clutching pillows and blankets. Fred, hair a mess and tripping over his feet, grinned at all of us. "Slumber party?"

"If it helps to think of it like that. Let's push all this furniture out of the way," Becky announced, and she wouldn't answer any questions about what was going on or why we were in the lounge.

Dimitrios was back before we finished clearing the floor. "Nic'll be up in a second," he said, taking a seat by the door and leaning his spear against his shoulder. "Murphy wants to double up protection for the newbies."

" 'Course she does. Is she in her office?"

He shook his head. "Ours."

"Good. I'll check in with her before I start rounds," Becky said, and helped us fold our blankets into makeshift sleeping mats. "Bedtime, everyone."

I lay awake after lights-out until my eyes adjusted to the dark, until everyone else was asleep. Becky headed off, disappearing for long stretches, but she always came back for a few minutes at the door with Dimitrios before heading out again.

"They're early this year," he said quietly.

Becky nodded and started playing with a dagger.

"A lot of them this year too."

"Fewer than last year."

Dimitrios snorted. "Of course. After the beating Steve gave them last year, I'm surprised they're willing to risk it, actually."

"Guess that means they're hungry," Becky said, twirling the dagger in her fingers. The blade was a dull glint in the shadows. I watched her carefully flip the dagger back and forth one handed, until I drifted off to the steady, soothing movement.

• • •

I slept better that night than I had since I'd started school, and woke up in a panic that I was late for the kitchen. I only just made it, but Cook Bella didn't have any sharp words that morning. During class, Mr. O'Hara kept the humorous asides to a minimum, and Ms. Macartney was quieter than usual, if that's possible.

When I ran into the courtyard after lunch (after that first day, Cook Bella was very good about getting me out in time), Becky and Dimitrios were talking to Mrs. Murphy off to the side. It was a quiet, serious discussion, with lots of quiet, serious, grown-up looks. Finally Mrs. Murphy nodded and headed back inside.

That day Becky didn't have us run. She sat us down and looked at us, hard. "You're probably wondering about last night. Why we slept in the lounge." Becky cleared her throat. "This morning, just after midnight, red caps were spotted outside the school. Nothing happened, thankfully"—Dimitrios muttered what sounded like a prayer—"but red caps aren't something you want to take chances with."

Fred raised his hand. "Red caps?"

"A goblin. A kind of goblin," Dimitrios corrected himself. "This is my fault. We should have gone over this in class straightaway, but I . . . wanted to stick to the lesson plan. And I hoped we'd have more time. We don't, and I'm sorry for it."

"They're nasty little buggers," Becky interrupted. "They're a problem for us, and they are a very big reason why you're here, right now, in this class."

"What do they want?" Frances asked.

An undercurrent passed between Becky and Dimitrios as they looked at each other. "To eat us," she answered. "And dip their caps in our blood."

"Don't you scare them," Dimitrios said.

"They should be scared," Becky shot back, eyeing him down. You might not think a twentysomething woman could stare down a minotaur, but she held her own. "They like it. They could go vegetarian, get donor blood, animal blood. They like . . ." Still staring at Dimitrios, Becky seemed to struggle for words, before settling on, "Going after people. Problem is," she continued, turning back to us, "most people out there are magic. They have spells and shields and such to protect them, so goblins—"

"Red caps," Dimitrios interrupted, holding up his hands. "Let's not go stereotyping all goblins."

"Red caps," Becky corrected with a gracious nod. "They can't get to regular folk. Not without a mess, or cops, or someone caring. Lucky for *them*," she sneered, "here's a whole group of weaker, unprotected targets. People who don't have magic, or who don't have people who will care if they go missing."

"Becky . . . ," Dimitrios started.

"They should know what they're in for."

"Lucky for *us*," Dimitrios said, cutting over her, "red caps tend to stalk their prey, so five times out of seven we catch them watching us before anything happens. Just keep your eyes open. King Steve has a contract with you, to protect you. There's not a red cap or dragon or any creature with a working brain that'll shrug that off."

"And we are not without our own protection," Becky said, standing and hooking a finger through a loop in her belt. One quick flick, and she pulled the belt free. The movement was smooth and fast and perfect—perfected, I guessed, through repetition.

"What is it?" I asked.

"Cold iron. Master of them all." She handed it to Fred, so he could take a look at it and pass it around. "Best weapon we have against red caps. And fae, for that matter, unicorns, mermaids—oh, a whole lot of things, but it's mainly for red caps."

"Where did you get it?"

"I bought it off a metallurgist my very first Fall Fest here. The reds got sixteen that year," she told us, and it was awful because her voice was so calm and casual, though her eyes went distant for half a moment. "We lost five before the caps went underground for the season, and another eleven when they came out of hibernation. I almost had to auction myself to get that"—she nodded at Fran, who was staring down at the chain-link belt soberly—"but it's saved my skin more times than there are links in the chain."

Frances passed the belt to me. The metal was rough and prickly, as if it hadn't been filed down after it was carved into links, and it was a lot heavier than I expected. The cold of it frosted the air around my hands and made my breath fog. Only an ord could have worn it every day; it would have frozen a regular person solid.

Fran said what everyone else was thinking. "I want one."

"I don't doubt it," Becky said, taking the belt back once it made the rounds. "And if you have a mind to and the means, you can get one of your own one day. But not yet. You don't know how to use it, and that's just as dangerous as knowing how. More dangerous, maybe. Instead, today we're going to teach you a couple of tricks to get away if you can, and fight back if you can't. It's all about the soft spots. Eyes, ears, cap," she said, tapping each. She clapped her hands. "All right, partner up and remember, this is just practice, so no real power behind your punches. Anybody who forgets that gets punched back."

CHAPTER 14

Being part of the kitchen meant a lot of early mornings and late evenings, and it also meant I was usually the last one to escape.

One night in October, the kitchen was nearly empty. Most of the kids had already finished up their dinners and headed back to the dorms. Usually I gave a hand to whoever was helping dry, and we went back to the dorms together, as the school frowned on kids going anywhere or doing anything alone. My partner was an older girl. She wasn't mean, not really, but I still wasn't "one of them," so it was hard to get her to talk.

We had put the last of the dishes away and wiped down the sink, but Cook Bella stopped us when we headed toward the door. "You can go, Sarah. Abby isn't done yet."

Sarah and I glanced at each other. "I'm not?" I asked.

Cook Bella shook her head, taking a bucket and a bristly wooden brush out of a bottom cabinet. "The floor needs a good scrub. Don't just stand there," she said, waving the bucket at me. "Fill this up, soap and water."

There was a moment as Cook Bella stared at me, and Sarah stared at the floor, and then I swallowed a sigh and went over and took the bucket. I set it filling with hot water (of course it had to be hot water, it always had to be hot) and hunted under the sink for soap.

Sarah hesitated in the doorway, then came over and helped me lift the full, heavy bucket out of the sink. "It'll get easier as you get stronger," she said in a low voice as we set the bucket down. Water sloshed over the edge onto the tile floor.

"What am I supposed to do?" I asked. I knew the floor got cleaned every day—I always had to move out of the way for the kid with the bucket—but I had been paying attention to the dishes. That'd teach me to be more observant.

"It's easy. Soap goes in here—"

Cook Bella cleared her throat and Sarah stopped dead. Cook Bella went to the door and held it open. "Good night, Sarah. Don't forget your leftovers."

"I . . . can help."

Cook Bella nodded, as if she was sure Sarah could, and then nodded toward the door. Sarah rubbed her hands on her skirt and hurried out. "Good work tonight," Cook Bella murmured as she passed by.

The door swung closed with a muffled *thwack*. Steam rolled up from the bucket. I sat back on my heels, hating to ask, but knowing I'd hate it more if Cook Bella came down on me for doing something wrong. "What—"

"Figure it out," Cook Bella said, pulling the chalkboard off the back wall and carrying it to the island. "You're not stupid, Abigail, so you don't get to act like you are."

Turns out scrubbing a floor is just like scrubbing a dish. A really big dish that you have to wash on your hands and knees, with nooks and corners and the space under the island that you have to lie down on your belly to get to properly. It's hot, sweaty work, with my sleeves sticky and too tight after ten, then twenty minutes. But it's not that bad, especially when compared with having to look Cook Bella in the eye and tell her I couldn't figure it out or I wasn't able to do it.

It was almost lights-out when I finished. Cook Bella set aside her cookbooks and chalk, and, after pointing out one or two corners I needed to do over, walked me across the courtyard to the dorm.

After that it became a routine; I'd stay behind after dinner was done and scrub the floor. There were a few questioning glances thrown around the kitchen when Cook Bella remarked, "Abby will take care of the floor from now on," since most of the kitchen jobs were rotated. But I don't think anyone missed scrubbing the floor that much.

• • •

Third week in, fatigue was a living thing. It wasn't bad, but it was always there, gray and fuzzy at the edge of my eyes. I figured with all the extra work I'd be tired enough to fall asleep, but . . . yeah, that didn't happen.

I felt myself getting angry at people—over stupid, little stuff—and wanting to snap at them. And then I'd get angry at myself, because that was mean, and I knew there was no reason for it. I tried to keep quiet about it, until the third time in a row I was late for study group in the lounge, and Peter called me on it. I got so mad I threw my book down on the table—which made Fran jump—and told him I had work to do, and they didn't have to wait for me if I was holding them up.

"You're not. I'm done." Peter gestured to the neat, perfect pile of homework in front of him. I bet it was finished, every single page of it. I yanked a seat out, and Fran jumped again.

"Somebody's in a bad mood," Fred teased nervously.

"Somebody's *tired*—got homework to do," I amended quickly. "Sorry, Fran." She nodded, a soft little bobble.

"Hey, here's an idea," Fred offered. "You could stop." He was only half joking.

"Homework? I'd fail." I flipped through my notes, the pages blurring before my eyes. If I slowed down and concentrated, they came into focus.

"I meant the kitchen. You're there all the time, it seems. And I was wondering if, maybe, you don't have to? Because Nate says you're not even a real mouse."

"Rat," I corrected him.

"Whatever, still gross. Can't you be the kitchen 'cleanly animals'?" Fred asked.

"Cats," Fran suggested, her dimples appearing with a small smile. "Cats are very clean."

It worked. I smiled. "All right, all right." I took a couple deep, gulping breaths; trying to calm myself felt like trying to let go of the scrub brush after a long night, when my fingers were so stiff and cramped from holding on that it actually hurt to relax. "Where are we?" I asked, waving a hand over my Lit book.

" 'The Most Tragyc Saga uf the Warryur Hynrulf.' We have to answer the questions on page forty-eight. And *he* gets to sit there and do . . . whatever he does with that thing, because he's already done," Fred said, pointing at Peter and his little blue book.

"Good. Great. What's Hynrulf up to?"

"Still stuck in the lake," Fred said. "What I don't get is, he's magic, right? So why doesn't he just freeze the water, pop out like a Popsicle, and get the leviathan's mother that way?"

I shrugged. " 'Cause that would make too much sense?" I noticed Peter staring at me. "What?"

"You do look tired," he said.

"Thanks."

"I didn't say you looked bad, just tired. But you do look bad."

"You can't tell a girl she looks bad," Fred warned him.

"But she does."

"Yeah, but you can't say that. Girls won't like you."

"Abby doesn't like me anyway," Peter said.

"I do too!" I protested. "Sometimes."

Peter was still staring at me. I looked away, down at my book, flipping the pages without really paying attention to what was on them and, without really planning to say anything, said, "I can't sleep. It's—it's too quiet."

Fred laughed. "It's never quiet here. And you have your own room," he insisted when I didn't answer. The longing was palpable in his voice. "I'd kill for my own room. Not really," he added to Peter.

"I am relieved," Peter replied. "Don't you three have home-work to finish?"

• • •

That night as I was getting into bed, Peter knocked on the door. Now, lights-out means in your room until morning roll call, but Peter just shrugged when I told him that and closed the door behind him. He was in his pj's and carrying a pillow. "Just as long as I'm back in my room for roll call," he said. "It's not like they can use magic to track us."

"But Public Safety patrols the hallways."

"But they don't go in the rooms unless they hear something. Like us talking," he finished in a whisper. He nodded to the spare bed. "You got extra sheets for this thing?"

I was still standing by the door. "You're going to stay with me?"

He shrugged and sat down on the bare bed. It squeaked. That seemed to be answer enough. I was dimly aware that I was grinning like an idiot.

So I got out my extra sheets and we made up the other bed without talking. Then I got in my bed and he got in the other one, and we still didn't talk, but I was grinning the whole time, grinning until my cheeks hurt.

Peter shook his head and smiled. "Okay. What?"

"We're friends."

The smile dropped away like a stone. "We're not."

"Yeah, we are. You like me."

144

"I don't."

I rolled onto my stomach, tucking my pillow under me. "Then why'd you come here?" I teased.

"Pity." There was light from the streetlamps through the windows, just enough to make his eyes gleam like a cat's in the dark. "Maybe I'm just a nice person."

"You're not nice."

"Goes to show how much you know. I'm the third-nicest person I know."

"You punched Fred in the face this afternoon." Granted, it was during Becky's class, and mostly because Fred had been too busy trying to block Peter with humor to remember to block his face.

"I don't like Fred either," Peter tossed back. "He's a fake."

"He is not, *he's* nice. And you're just mean. That's okay, though," I reassured him, because at some point this teasing thing had become fun. "I'll still be your friend."

Peter sat up. "If you're going to be this annoying, I'll leave."

"No, you won't," I said, swallowing my laughter.

Peter glared at me for a full minute before he sniffed and defiantly lay back down, pulling the covers up around his shoulders. I waited until the quiet seeped back in, until he'd feel safe, then whispered quickly, "It's because we're friends."

He groaned and shoved the pillow over his head. "Abby! Go to sleep!"

With him there, I did.

* * *

CHAPTER 15

The Fall Festival was still a few weeks away, but Ms. Macartney roped several of the First Years into decorating the dining hall, stringing garlands and wreaths made out of pinecones and fallen leaves. Carving jack-o'-lanterns and setting up the remembrance table (as a treat for the souls who'd pass through on the hunt for good parties) was later on, not until the week before the fest. (Plus cutting pumpkins meant knives, and we weren't allowed to handle anything like that until we were Third Years.)

Peter and Fred and I were pinning up garlands around the windows when the doors flung open and the rest of the school was herded in by the teachers. Ms. Macartney, if possible, went more tight-lipped and rigid than usual. Becky had that "straight as an arrow, walking on the balls of her feet" stance that she used for the *really* dangerous demonstrations. Even Mrs. Murphy looked more formal. Only Mr. O'Hara looked completely relaxed, but then, I couldn't think of a time when he didn't look completely relaxed.

"Everyone, please take a seat. Students, please sit with your own Year." Mrs. Murphy's voice rang out, loud and clear, above the scuffing footsteps and the low, edgy hum of chatter. "I know I can trust all of you to be on your very best behavior."

Kids hurried to their places, and Mrs. Murphy stepped forward and cleared her throat to silence us. "We have just received word that His Majesty, King Stephen, and several members of his court will be gracing us with their esteemed presence tonight for an inspection." She paused, waiting until the exclamations died down to a low buzz before she continued. "Here are the rules, which you will not under any circumstances break unless you want me to break you. One: you will not speak unless spoken to. Two: if you are spoken to, you will give a short, polite answer. Three: if you are speaking to our esteemed patron, His Royal Majesty, King Stephen, you will refer to him by his proper title, and with the proper amount of respect—so help me, Eric, you wipe that look off your face. The same goes for his court. Four: you will be on your best and most proper behavior tonight, and you will make them all believe that we know what we're doing, or I will murder you. Do you understand?"

We understood.

She nodded. "Take this time to straighten yourselves up as best you can. Aprons off, laces tied. Girls with long hair, pin it up. Let's pretend you really are well-behaved children."

Mrs. Murphy and the other teachers talked quietly for a moment, then moved through the room just under marathon speed, tucking away half-hung decorations, making sure everything was orderly.

* * *

One of the older girls was showing us how to twist up our hair and pin it in place with a pencil when *they* arrived. It took my brain a moment to process what it was seeing. Spots on the walls, ceiling, and floor warped into faces, and ten—twenty—a *lot* of men in official-looking uniforms poured out, as if they simply stepped into being. It was like they were both part of bricks and separate from them. It was like those creatures in the Black Forest that splooge over their victims and absorb them whole.

One man dropped down from the ceiling and landed on our table. Frances gasped, and Fred and I started back in surprise. He stepped down off our table with an amused look on his face, like Gil when he played a trick on someone. But he was clearly a normal guy, and he never would have gotten into campus unless he was allowed in. And the only people the school was allowing in tonight were King Steve's men. You didn't have to be a Level Ten mage to figure out he was a Kingsman. Also, the uniform with the royal crest was a big clue.

Kingsmen aren't just regular guards who stand watch over the castle. Kingsmen are special. It's not just the training (with its rumored ninety-seven percent washout rate); they have to put themselves through experiments, push themselves to become something more. Kingsmen aren't quite human, not anymore, and they go into it willingly and with eyes open. They sign away their lives to the throne, and it makes them really intense, and I think that's why there are so many romance novels that feature them. (Like *Married to a Kingsman* or *The Kingsman's Secret Baby* or *Kissing the Kingsman*, which is the best one, actually.)

* * *

The Kingsmen took their position all around the room, stiff and formal, and then the door opened. Alexa entered, her hair done up and wearing the royal colors. Following her were four or five people, in much more expensive outfits and elaborate hairstyles, who glanced over us and made sure to keep a wide berth. They had to be the king's court. And then came two Kingsmen in more complicated uniforms, showy ones with heavy belts that had powerful magic stuck all over them.

And then came King Steve.

I recognized him from the papers. (He's in there a lot and, besides, he was the one wearing a crown.) He didn't look very much like his pictures. Oh, he looked enough like that you'd recognize him if you passed by him on the street. But he looked—geekier, if you can imagine. He was tall and lanky, with a long thin face; the papers didn't catch how thin it was, or how ordinary. And he did look ordinary. He looked like anybody else, which kings really aren't supposed to do. He glanced at Alexa as he entered, and smiled. It made him look human, and not one bit majestic. Then he went over to the teachers, received their bows and curtseys and welcome with a regal nod.

I have never, ever heard the dining hall that quiet, not before or since. Nobody moved. I'm not sure if anybody breathed. We all just sat there, quiet and still, as if we really were nice, obedient children.

King Steve spoke to Mrs. Murphy briefly—he had one of those rounded, clear voices, kind of like announcers on game shows but less annoying—then Mrs. Murphy stepped forward and said a few words. It was everything you'd expect a teacher to say if the king came: how glad we were that King Steve honored us with his presence, and how hard everyone worked to earn his patronage, and how we all wanted to show the king how much we deserved his trust.

Then she stepped back and King Steve stepped forward, and he said a few words. It was a lot of his usual stuff too. Mostly that he knew his faith and trust in us was justified, and that he was proud to serve us, and that we had to keep strong and keep going on—that kind of thing. "We hold no illusions as to what life is like for an ord," he concluded, "even, unfortunately, in our kingdom. We hope that this place will provide a measure of comfort, safety, and support for you all."

Mrs. Murphy thanked him, and I thought that they were going to talk to us—ask us how we were doing, or if we liked the school. Maybe even ask for a demonstration of what we had learned so far. But King Steve and his council left then, with the teachers and Alexa and about half of the Kingsmen, for a tour of the school. It took a while, and all during that time we had to sit quietly and not move. At one point I could see them through the windows, slowly circling the courtyard, testing all the bars on the windows and the locks on the doors.

When they finally returned, there were a couple more talks. King Steve thanked us for our hospitality, and Mrs. Murphy thanked him for stopping by, and then Mrs. Murphy excused all the students except us First Years, because there was still decorating to do. King Steve stood by the door smiling at the students as they passed, while Alexa stopped everyone to shake hands and say a few words. Then he and Alexa said good-bye to the teachers. I climbed up on my chair to wave to Alexa, but she signaled for me to follow. I glanced at Mrs. Murphy, but she nodded and I ran after my sister.

Alexa was waiting for me by the door. She slung an arm around my shoulders and leaned down to whisper, "Best behavior."

"I'm always on my best behavior," I protested.

"I'm serious, Abby."

"You're *always* serious."

She shook her head and led me out to the courtyard, where King Steve was waiting. The court was gone, and most of the Kingsmen too. But King Steve was there—waiting for us.

Alexa had to more or less push me toward him. "This is Abby."

I curtseyed as best I could. "Your Majesty."

He held out a hand and, surprised, I shook it. (The Kingsmen inched forward at that, and King Steve gave them all a smile, like *hey, just friends here*, with a touch of *I'm your boss*, and a little *so relax*.) "Hello, Abby. Alexa talks about you non-stop."

"Just the bad stuff," Alexa reassured me.

"Okay," I squeaked. Not my cleverest response, but I was still trying to process that I was really standing there chatting with King Steve. Really.

"How do you like the school?" King Steve asked.

Tell him it's nice, my brain commanded. "It's nice."

"Nice," King Steve echoed.

"Yes." I glanced at Alexa, who was looking at me with the "you can do better than that" look. Okay, if they wanted more . . . "And it's tough. And weird. It's not even like a real school at all. I mean, we do have regular classes, like history, and I'm going to be honest, I'm sure your great-grandparents were nice people and all, but I have no idea why we have to learn what year they came to the throne—"

"They were horrible people," King Steve corrected me, his eyes bright.

"Oh. And it's scary," I continued, encouraged. He wasn't smiling, but I heard it in his voice.

"Yes, they were."

"No, I mean the school. And just being an ord. I didn't even know how scary until I came here. Three nights so far they made us sleep in the lounge because there were red caps watching the building, but I'm sure Alexa told you that because she says her job is to tell you everything. And Becky's teaching us about ward stones but it's mostly recognizing magic and it's a lot of research but apparently people are actually going to pay us to do that when we get older, like real money, like give us jobs, and—they know I can see them, right?" I glanced around at the Kingsmen, but they were maintaining an air of professional detachment. And invisibility—the blurry, fudged lines around them were unmistakable. "We all can, we're ords. Why go invisible at an ord school?"

King Steve glanced at Alexa and then smiled, a quick,

genuine flash. "To show off. Kingsmen are terribly conceited, you know. It's in the job description."

One of the Kingsmen cleared his throat. I wondered if that was weird for other people, normal people, who couldn't see them, who'd just hear a cough come out of nowhere.

"Alexa tells me," King Steve continued as if no one had cleared anything, "that you had a very close call this summer. A pair of adventurers who harassed you and your classmates."

"Yes, Your Majesty."

"I would have liked to have some private conversation with them, but it seems they have disappeared. Pity, but I have let it be known that I'd very much like to meet them, whenever they turn up."

"You think they're going to turn up?" I asked.

"They might. Alexa tells me they were rather desperate for an ord, and where better to find one than—" He gestured to the school. "I think it wise for you and your classmates to keep close to the school."

"That's not a problem. They don't ever let us out." Although Alexa had promised to get me special permission to escape during Fall Fest.

A Kingsman spoke up. "Your Majesty."

"Our cue," King Steve said. "And yours, Miss Hale," he said to Alexa. He held out his hand again, and I shook it. "You must come to the castle sometime and take tea with us. We should be glad to know you better."

"Seriously?" I asked.

"We are always serious, Miss Abigail. It is the primary defect in our character. Pleasure meeting you."

I curtseyed again, a little better this time. "Really nice to meet you, Your Majesty."

"Let me walk her back in, Your Majesty," Alexa said, and aimed me toward the dining hall.

King Steve put a hand on her arm. "That pleasure must be mine." And he took my hand and led me to the door, like a gentleman leading a lady out of a dance. The Kingsmen crept close enough to practically meld into my dress, but King Steve ignored them, so I did too. Alexa tagged along next to me, and King Steve watched with this funny little look on his face, when she scooped me up for a hug and kiss good night. And they left.

"What was *that*?" Fred burst out the second I walked in.

"Oh, you know," I said, flipping my hair over my shoulders. "Just chatting with King Steve. He asked me about school and everything. He even invited me to tea."

Peter chucked an apron at me. "You are so full of it, Hale."

CHAPTER 16

Fall Fest in the city is sunshine, mellow as butter, and leaves in a dozen shades of gold and orange swirling through the air. It's the smell of cinnamon and apples and roasting meat mixing with the cool, clean fall air. It's jack-o'-lanterns clustered in shop windows and piled up by the doorways, and trailing along down the streets so the flickering lights can lead you to the party. It's people dressed like fire, in shimmery, gauzy skirts and beaded vests, and jingly belts dripping with gleaming gold charms.

I'd been to the Fall Fest in Rothermere once before, when I was six, and I mostly remember how loud and huge everything seemed. Somebody (popular vote had it as Mrs. Murphy) realized that keeping us locked up when there was a huge party going on right at our doorstep constituted cruel and unusual punishment, so the school was actually letting us outside. Though for safety purposes we had to be in groups, those groups had to have grown-ups in them, and we had to wear our school colors.

Apparently there was an ongoing debate whether or not we Greens should be required to wear our greens at official stuff— outside the school, that is. The pro side said it was a scary world out there for an ord, and wearing official colors made it easier for everyone to keep an eye on us. The con side said, yes, that was the problem. See, until King Steve came to the throne half a dozen years ago and made it not okay to buy and sell children just because they couldn't do magic, Rothermere had been the place to buy and sell ords. Becky (and Alexa and Mrs. Murphy and just about everyone else in the school) had warned us repeatedly that it took some people a while to get the message. There weren't any sales, at least not obvious ones, but some people still came looking, and bright green tends to stick out.

But the totally awesome part was that my whole family was coming up. I mean, I knew they were going to for weeks now, because it was a planned event, but the closer it got the more exciting it became. I hadn't seen anyone, except Alexa, live and in person since school started. We were even going to celebrate Alexa's birthday. It'd be a week early, but we'd all be together, which Mom said was more important than timing. The excitement made it hard to keep still—well, everywhere except Ms. Macartney's class, because she didn't care if your leg was being chewed off by a red cap, you were going to sit still and be quiet. I didn't even care that the whispers of *family* and *parents* started up again, loud enough that they weren't actually whispers.

Becky and Ms. Macartney offered to escort me and Peter to the festival and make sure we met up with our parents (Ms. Whittleby had hitched a ride with Mom and Dad), and Fred and Fran were along for the day, too, since Fred's father couldn't come up to Rothermere because he was hosting a company picnic, and Fran's parents, who were here for the fest, weren't, as Fran said, up here for *fun*, they were here on *business*, they wouldn't be able to see *anything*, which included their daughter.

We'd arranged to meet my family and Ms. Whittleby early in order to get a full day in, so we left before breakfast. It was a cool morning, with the promise of the winter not far behind it. The sky still had that new-day pink, but the streets were already clogged. The school's right on West Avenue, one of the four major streets that cut straight to the palace, and for the festival it's blocked off to traffic so people can set up booths along the sidewalks and everybody else can stroll straight down the middle. Usually there's a trolley at the end of the block, but today we had to walk all the way to the Palace Plaza, the huge circular courtyard around the castle where the main fairgrounds are set up.

The vendors were already out when we left, dragging tables and merchandise into the streets, and musicians tuning up and dancers stretching at the small stages set up every so often. We passed a couple of dinky kids' rides, the ones for babies and under-twelves, you know, the kids who hadn't been Judged yet, and so couldn't ride the real stuff. Fred started cracking jokes about them until Peter cut in that the baby rides were the only ones that we could go on. The biggest, fastest, showiest rides— the ones with loops and drops and swirls and all that stuff—use magic, not just to run but to secure people in.

As we got closer to the main fairgrounds, everything got

bigger, flashier, and more elaborate. The prices at the vendors' booths went up, the rides had more lights and dips and twirls, costumes got a lot costumier. Even air seemed to get in the mood and warmed up a bit. A couple of shows started, hawkers shouting out "Amazing Feats!" and "Wonders in Store!" and "Come Check It Out!"

Here's what I learned about being an ord—you get really good at hearing that word, no matter where you are, no matter what the circumstances. I heard it tossed around behind my back a lot in Lennox, but after weeks of being shut up in the school, I'd almost forgotten how it sounded: Ord. It's like there's something deep down under your skin that flares up whenever someone says it, so it's not so much hearing the word as it is feeling it.

Of course, it's just as much hearing as feeling when the word is sung out, bright and loud, by a caller looking to lure people into his show. Along with a "Deadly Leviathan, the Scourge of the Southern Sea!" and "Bloodthirsty Red Cap, Come and See but Don't Get Too Close!" he promised a "Genuine Ord, One Hundred Percent Tame! Step Right Up and Give It Your Best Shot!"

Hearing that, Becky came to a dead stop, so sudden that Fred walked straight into her. She stood there for a moment, hands clenched into fists, wound so tightly it was like a touch might shatter her. The only movement was her eyes flicking over to Ms. Macartney.

We were in front of a tent, a long, winding one, that snaked its way through the crowd. It was so ornate I wondered if whoever designed it had wanted it to look silly on purpose. It was probably the same person who had drowned the whole thing in fairy dust; under the sun the shimmer made my eyes hurt.

The caller cast out some chimes and started his routine over again. "The Mermaid Melusine, Enchantress of the Deep! Beware Her Siren Song, Lest It Bewitch You!"

Shivers crept over me like spiders on my skin.

"You take them on," Becky told Ms. Macartney, indicating us. "I'll catch up."

"They're old enough to see," Ms. Macartney replied, without a drop of sympathy. "Besides, if all else fails, I have some money."

Becky's smile was a horrible thing. "Oh, I doubt we'll make it as far as money, Caroline."

"What is it?" I asked. "What are you going to do?"

Ms. Macartney and Becky exchanged a glance. "What do you think?" Becky asked. Her eyes were cool, and she added, "Do you want to see the ord?"

"No," Fran said.

"Yes," I said.

"Yes," Fred echoed.

"All right, come on. You too," Becky said, putting an arm around Frances's shoulders. "Don't worry. If they have the kid as a showpiece, then they're going to treat him well."

Ms. Macartney went over to the caller and bought tickets, which was a very weird moment because, first, we'd spent months at a place where everybody said we were just as good as everybody else, and treated us that way. And now we were paying real money to see a kid just like us. It kind of warped your view of things. And, second, because when the caller was

159

* * *

tallying up the ticket price, he looked down at the four of us in our attention-grabbing school colors, and was like, "Oh, you're Greenies?" And when we told him yeah, he only charged Ms. Macartney for two tickets, saying that kids got in for free.

"I thought kids are half-price," Peter said, nodding to a sign shimmering by the entrance.

The caller glanced over at the sign. "Suggested donation," he said smoothly. "Always read the invisible ink, kid."

"There is no invisible ink," Peter pointed out, because we could have read it even if there was.

"Look, who's in charge here, you or me?"

"You're in charge?" Ms. Macartney asked.

The man looked at her. "Yup."

Ms. Macartney nodded. "Good to know."

Inside, they'd clearly had the same decorator as whoever did the outside of the tent. It was just as *much*. They'd gone for dim and mystical—you know, atmosphere. The sunlight was muted as it tried to push its way through the tent walls, and a few fog charms swirled up a thick white blanket for us to walk through. It billowed around our feet when we moved. Lanterns hovered in the air, glowing spots of color in the mist, but they were so dim it was obviously more for effect than light. The glow inside the fogged glass flickered oddly, showing tiny little arms and legs. Pixies, or something like them—which meant it was fake, because pixies get ticked off when you capture them, and an aggravated pixie's the last thing you want at a professional show. As Dimitrios often warned us, imprisoned didn't necessarily mean powerless. And pixies have short tempers and long memories.

Every now and again there was a shimmer of something out of the corner of our eyes, spiraling in the right direction, leading us on. It took us through a long hallway, which opened every now and then into an exhibit room, I guess you'd call it.

They had a pretty good collection, but it was clear straight off that the exhibits were as fake as the pixies. They'd probably look good if you didn't know any better, but—okay, for instance, the mermaid. She looked exactly like you'd think a mermaid would: seated on a mossy rock by a water-lily pool, her tail flicking in and out of the glistening water, combing out her streaming hair as she sang a lullaby that was cool and sad as the salt air. Except it was all a glamour. A professional one but still just a spell, and our ord eyes could see through that to her two normal legs. Besides, Ms. Macartney informed us, the setting was a dead giveaway since mermaids are saltwater creatures; you'd never find one at a freshwater pond. She didn't sound happy about it either, because I think the teacher in her takes it as a personal affront when people don't do their research.

It was like that for all of them. Even the ones that were real weren't real. The basilisk was a cockatrice (but Ms. Macartney said people get those two mixed up a lot, though I don't know how because one is a poisonous snake and the other is a poisonous chicken). The phoenix was a regular Svar firebird, which is not quite as bright or flammable, but I have to admit, it did a pretty impressive death scene. To Becky's visible relief, the red

* * *

cap turned out to be just a brownie with a red hat. I'd never seen a real red cap up close, but even I could tell he was all wrong. His claws seemed too short and the red of his hat was a shade too bright and cheerful. Plus, Becky said, it didn't smell right—meaning the hat. Fred started to ask her how it should smell when Peter elbowed him in the stomach.

By the time he recovered we'd already moved on to the leviathan room. It was a real, honest-to-goodness water dragon, slick and slithery, with long fanlike fins instead of proper arms and legs and wings. But it was a miniature one, barely as big as Becky. It was in a huge tank with lots of waving, underwater fronds, and it came right up to the glass and stared at us with its huge, black, unblinking eyes. Then the crest around its face flared out, and it seemed to pose, as if for pictures. Ms. Macartney pegged it as a cold-water, lake-dwelling breed that could be tamed if you kept them in warm water. Besides, we knew from Dimitrios that it was stupid to be scared of something just because it was big and strong and had tons of sharp, glistening teeth. Like most creatures, leviathans were perfectly chill if they were well fed and not poked at too much.

So hopes were that the "ord" would turn out to be just a normal kid with an impressive shield. Or maybe there were some tricks set up around the room to block magic.

He wasn't. It wasn't. The kid, at least, was real.

Compared to the other rooms, this one was plain. It was reasonably well lit, with no fog or shimmers or anything to distract you. Just a kid in a cage.

I say *kid*, but he wasn't really; he looked like a teenager, around Jeremy's age. He was stocky, with a thick neck and smooshed-in features, like a bulldog. And he was just sitting there, on a stool, in the cage. When we came in, he was reading a splashy romance novel; he carefully marked his place, stood up and moved a couple steps closer, and waited.

"Hello," Becky began, but by that point he'd gotten a good look at us and something in him shifted, relaxed. He came up, leaned against the front bars. "How are you guys doing, you having fun so far?"

Confused, we nodded.

"This is my third year at the fest. King Steve, he always throws a good party. I'm not going to get to see any of it until five, though, when we shut down, because Frank, he doesn't like me going around on my own, you know how it is. Hey, I'm sorry, you want to have a go?" he asked Ms. Macartney.

"No. Thank you." She seemed to rally herself and asked, "What's your name?"

"Dave. Just Dave, not David or Davey or any of that. When there's a line, we set a limit of three spells per customer, but I don't think we're going to get crowded for another hour at least. You want a go?" he asked her again. "Just, uh, wait, hold on." Dave scooped up his book and tucked it in a corner, then jogged back. "Okay, shoot."

"That won't be necessary," said Ms. Macartney "Are you . . . being treated well?"

"Yeah, I'm good," Dave answered cheerfully. "Ever since King Steve passed that law, it's like 'you're free, do you know you're free, because you're free.' Okay, look." He took a deep breath and recited, "Frank is not my *owner*, he's my boss. This is my job, and I get paid for it, and I'm not forced to do anything I don't want to do, except maybe eat carrots, which are disgusting but Frank's a stickler about eating your veggies before you get dessert."

"You're in a cage," Peter pointed out.

"That so, Ace? How's this?" Dave waved us closer. He fished a key out of his pocket, unlocked the padlock, and swung the front section of the cage open.

"Did I just blow your mind, or what?" he asked, locking everything back up. "I'm an ord who chooses to work in a cage! I appreciate the concern, but seriously, I'm cool."

"So you sit in this cage by yourself all day?" I asked.

"Yeah, pretty much. I mean, I get breaks and all that, and during slow times I can read. And"—he glanced at Ms. Macartney and lowered his voice—"I know this isn't nice, but it can be pretty funny messing with the normals."

Becky and Ms. Macartney looked at each other. "It appears we were mistaken," Ms. Macartney said slowly. "I apologize for disturbing you."

Dave shrugged. "No problem. I get it, you know? There are worse things than folks being worried about you. And it's always nice to meet a couple of fellow ords. Stop by again and say hi."

He shook our hands and waved after us as we left.

164

* * *

CHAPTER 17

What happened next was my fault. I just want to say that straight out. I know Olivia blamed Peter, and Alexa blamed, you know, the actual people responsible, but I should have known better. I mean, how many times has Becky told us *not* to go off on our own? She practically had it tattooed onto our foreheads.

Outside the tent, the world was normal. There were shouts and jostling and colors whipping in the wind and the smells of meat sizzling and hot cider simmering.

"Well." Becky's lips twitched. "That was not what I was expecting."

"I want to talk to this Frank," Ms. Macartney said. "The boy seems well enough, but still, I'd like to talk to him."

Frank the Non-Owner was at the entrance, so we had to go back to the front, and by this time it was even more crowded, to the point where we were squeezing through people. I wasn't sure how long we'd been in the tent, but the sun was higher and the cool of the morning was already starting to give way to autumn heat.

We heard Frank before we saw him. He sounded angry. "I said *no* and I mean it! What don't you get about that?"

I only half heard the reply; I didn't catch the words, but the voice, that harsh tone, I'd recognize that in the middle of a rock concert. Panic flashed into my chest. I glanced around at my friends, to see if anyone else had noticed, but Fred had paused to let Fran squeeze by first, and Becky and Ms. Macartney hadn't been in Lennox or Thorten, so they wouldn't know their voices. Peter, though, was already pushing forward. We squeezed past a family, and there was Frank the caller guy, jabbing a finger at a couple wearing cloaks. Though their backs were to us, I had no doubt who they were.

"You're threatening me? How 'bout I call the cops over here, let them know you two are trying to buy one of my kids?"

Barbarian Mike—and it had to be, only one person in the world was that big—held up his hands. They were covered by the thin, shimmery fizz of a glamour. "Hey, no worries. We were just asking. She didn't mean any harm. Got a bit of a temper, right, babe?"

Frank seemed calmer but no less angry. "Fine. You were just asking. Now you can just be leaving," he said, jerking his thumb at the road.

The big one started in on *no problem, no problem*, and he and his companion moved away. I tried to catch Becky's eye, but she was still back with the others trying to make her way through the crowd. Peter went for the more direct approach, however. He ran at them. I wasn't sure what he was going to do, but the way he looked, he could have done anything.

I should have waited for Becky and Ms. Macartney and told them what was going on, or what I thought was going on since voices and somebody with a glamour don't prove anything.

I should have at least checked with Fred and Fran to make sure I wasn't going crazy. But I didn't. I guess when you're scared or excited enough your brain shuts off and you do the first thing that occurs to you. And that was plunging into the crowd after Peter.

But the crowd was so crowded that I couldn't see him anymore. Not really—there was just a glimpse of dark curls and a flash of green in the throng of people in front of me. I shoved through after him. People muttered angrily, and sometimes shouted and shoved back, until it got harder and harder to keep my eyes on that dark hair. I lost sight of him once, twice, and then completely. By that time, I wasn't sure that the hair had been Peter's, or if I was even moving in the right direction. The street was a sea of red and gold, and everything looked the same. I jumped up and down, trying to see something, shouting Peter's name. And when that didn't work, I figured maybe if I cut around to the space behind the vendors, where there weren't as many people, I could get a better view.

I skirted behind a bakery stand with a tower of apple tarts and a steaming vat of cider, and I was right—the way was a little clearer. The only problem was, which way had Peter gone? Which way would Barbarian Mike and Trixie have gone? They probably would have wanted to blend in with the crowd, right?

✳ ✳ ✳

That's when a big, meaty hand clapped over my mouth and nose and yanked me back into an alley.

I had a moment of total and complete surprise—I caught muscles, giant sword, dark-red hair, impressive angry eyebrows— and then my surprise raced into fear. I twisted and kicked, but Barbarian Mike lifted me up by the back of my dress and flipped me over his shoulder. I started screaming, frantic high-pitched shrieks. "Let me go! *Let me go!* LET ME GO!" It was hard to hear anything, but there were people everywhere, the city, the festival, someone *had* to hear something. A few people looked over; I don't know what they saw or what they thought was happening, but they didn't *do* anything. Barbarian Mike ran with me through the alleys.

I kept shrieking—*LEMMEGOLEMMEGOLEMMEGO*— over and over again, until it wasn't even words. Just panic and desperation. I grabbed at buildings, poles, anything we passed, and how could this mountain not notice when I kicked him in the face? When Barbarian Mike jogged past an open Dumpster, I latched on to it, not screaming words anymore, just *screaming*, and he had to stop to pry my fingers free. I kicked and scratched and twisted and grabbed a hunk of his hair. He hissed in pain and a protection shield sizzled into place around him, but my hands passed through it like the film of a bubble, and I yanked and yanked and yanked until I ripped a whole chunk of hair out of his head. Barbarian Mike cursed, then stopped again and shifted me so he could clamp a hand over my face. "Enough with the screaming, okay? You're not helping the situation."

168

* * *

So I bit his hand—hard. As hard as I could, hard enough to taste blood. He jumped, enough that I could wrench away. I fell to the ground and, scrambling to my feet, I *ran*. I didn't know where I was going—it was all dark alleys, twists, and turns. Something snatched at my hair, I couldn't tell what. I kept running as fast as I could, and I tried very hard not to think about how my twelve-year-old-girl legs would measure up to grown-up-adult legs. I looked for streets, carpets, people, *anything*. I wasn't picky, I didn't care who I found, *but please, let me find someone*.

I slammed into something then—right across my middle. It hooked me into the air and my stomach practically flipped inside out. I focused on not throwing up on Trixie's leather boots. "Not so fast. Did you lose something?" she teased as Barbarian Mike jogged over.

"Thanks, babe." He wasn't even breathing hard. She tossed me over to him, and he caught me with one arm like I was a package.

Stomach still lurching, hate making my chest burn, I sucked in a deep breath, and screamed as loud as I could. I tried to sound like the girls in horror movies. Trixie jabbed an angry finger in my face. "Quiet, you, or I'll quiet you myself." I snapped at her finger, and she snatched it back. Barbarian Mike took the opportunity to tie something thick around my mouth and nose.

CHAPTER 18

I realized later that I should have been counting the streets. You know, counted the turns, tried to keep track of where they took me. But by the time I thought of it, we didn't have much farther to go.

We were in an abandoned building, something suitably dark and ramshackle that even the homeless probably avoided. The light outside the windows was turning into a rosy pink sunset. Inside, it was all dusty shadows and broken boards. A space had been cleared in a corner, where rubble and broken stones had fallen away to form a sort of alcove. Two worn travel packs were slumped against the wall, and there was a scorch mark in the middle of the floor.

I expected them to grab the packs and go, expected that I'd have to scream and strain to catch someone's attention, or hope someone noticed them carrying me over their shoulder like a rolled-up carpet. But they stopped inside the alcove and set a shield sizzling. With a pained "you have the boniest knees,"

Barbarian Mike let me drop to the floor; I tugged off the gag and started yelling. I tried to run, too, but Barbarian Mike caught me—he barely had to move, he just reached over and snagged me—and then held me down while Trixie roped my wrists and ankles together. Magic rope, which slid in and out of loops like a snake, but it felt strong enough. There was a devilish little smile on Trixie's face as she guided the knots tight. I wanted to tell her it wouldn't work on me, at least the magic part, but I didn't think she would care.

Trixie went to throw a loop around my neck . . . and then paused and crouched down in front of me. She slung the rope over her shoulder. "What's this, then?" Her fingers brushed Alexa's charm. I felt it weighing down my neck like a boulder. "Looks like a collar."

No. No-no-no-no.

She closed a hand over my mouth when I tried to scream again, her focus still on the charm. "And here I thought your family was the one so against selling their darling baby child." Trixie snorted.

"What is it, babe?"

"This ord's collared."

Barbarian Mike cast his glamour off, shaking free the last clinging traces of magic. "Get out. Isn't this the one from Lennox? Where they put up that huge fuss?"

"The one that should have been ours in the first place? Yup." I smelled an acidic flash of magic, and felt the chain disintegrate against my skin. "Guess we just didn't offer enough," Trixie said, tossing Barbarian Mike the charm. "Take a look at that."

Barbarian Mike held it up to catch the faint streetlights coming through the dirty windows. "Looks pretty sophisticated. Must have sold her someplace nice. Should we break it?"

Trixie eyed the iridescent glint of the shield arcing over us. There was a muted buzz where it touched the ground and it gave off a cool scented sting, like the soap we used to scrub the kitchen floor. I knew it would cover up everything inside the shield—all of the sights and sounds. All of the magic, too, so that anyone walking by could never guess that there were people hiding there.

She shook her head. "Nah. Better not take any chances. We'll sell it off down the road. That looks like a pretty fancy piece of casting, which means whoever had her first is going to be on the lookout. It'll be safer to get it out of our hands. Let some other sap deal with it."

Clapping the last traces of magic off her hands, Trixie edged away to the scorch mark on the floor and cast up a small fireball, just enough to keep us warm. Barbarian Mike pulled his pack over and started methodically checking his gear. So there was time, then. Time to think and figure something out, or try to. Time for my family to tear the city apart. I thought about that moment when Becky and the others would have had to go meet up with my family and tell them what happened. My mom would storm every police station in town, and throw such a fuss she'd have every detective in the city looking for me by now. My dad would—he'd get on a carpet, I decided. He'd fly up and down every single street looking for me. I tried not to think about how many blocks, how many buildings. Jeremy would have to stick

* * *

with the parents, probably Mom, because he was good at reports and organization and stuff like that. But Gil and Olivia were old enough to go off on their own. And Alexa. She would head straight to King Steve, because he was her friend and friends helped each other, and he would get all of his people out there. It was only a matter of time. They were coming, they would find me, and every second they got closer. I would remember that.

So I screamed. Or I tried screaming. I tried to make it solid and shrill and shrieking, the kind of scream that you can't *not* hear, that could in no way be a happy scream, that could only ever mean *help me*.

And as I screamed I strained against the ropes. Of course, if I got free, then there was still the problem of two big adventurers who'd chase me down, but first things first. From what I learned in school, adventurers' ropes were either enchanted to make you go numb or zapped you with an increasing pulse each time you tried to unknot them—not that those spells would work on me, but the ropes were still tight enough that every twist was like fire around my wrists. They'd had ords before; I guess they had practice with imprisonment.

At first the adventurers ignored me. They were probably used to the whole "screaming in terror" thing. Barbarian Mike calmly polished the runes on his sword, and Trixie paced back and forth in our little protective bubble. It was like she couldn't stand still. She'd take a few quick strides, then abruptly turn back and head the other way, her movements jerky and impatient. Every now and again, Barbarian Mike would glance at her when her back was to us.

Trixie turned on me, so abrupt and fierce my next scream squeaked to death in my throat. Her hand blurred with movement, and I felt the sting before I realized she'd chucked a stone at me. "Stop that," she hissed, and turned on Mike. "Where's the gag? Why did you take it off her?"

"Relax, babe. Nobody can hear her." He paused in his polishing and tossed a glance around the shield. Then shrugged. "Probably."

"Don't call me *babe*," Trixie bit off. "She's giving me a headache." She crouched down in front of the fireball, and a second later popped back up and started pacing again.

I sucked in a deep breath and let out another one. My lungs were starting to burn with the effort; I wasn't sure how many I had left.

"Hey, hey." Barbarian Mike snapped his fingers at me. "Chill out. No use screaming your head off. Nobody can hear you. Nobody's coming for you."

"My parents are," I croaked. "And when they find you they're going to obliterate you. And then Alexa, she's going to piece you back together so that Olivia and Gil and Jeremy can do it all over again."

"No, they're not," Trixie purred. "And no, they won't."

I'd never hated anyone as much as I hated her in that moment. If I were free—well, I wouldn't be able to do anything, because I was twelve, and she was bigger than me, which meant that she would win.

"Listen . . . what's your name again?" Barbarian Mike asked.

"Abby," I said.

"Really?" His eyebrows quirked, making him look serious and thoughtful for a second. "You don't look like an Abby. Julie, or, I don't know, Zoe maybe," he decided.

Trixie scoffed. "She's not a Julie."

"What do you want to call her, then?"

"Call her ord. That's what she is."

Barbarian Mike shrugged. "Listen, Zoe, don't be scared. We aren't kidnapping you. We're recruiting you for a noble quest. For the good of mankind."

"And womankind," Trixie snapped.

"And womankind," Barbarian Mike echoed. "And also other-species-kind."

"I'm not going to help you with anything," I said, pulling at my bound wrists. The rope held as fast as cold iron. I ordered myself to calm down and remember what Becky had taught us. These weren't anything special. For me they were just ropes, and ropes I could deal with. If I could get them loose enough, maybe I could get a hand free or reach the knots to pick them apart.

"Don't be so selfish," Trixie said. She watched me struggle for a minute and sighed. "Oh, training this one is going to be a joy."

"Training doesn't worry me," Barbarian Mike said. "There's plenty of time for training later. We should be grateful we got one."

"We should have gotten two," Trixie corrected him. "We should have waited until that other one circled back."

Other one. "Who?" I demanded, even though I knew.

Barbarian Mike lifted his eyebrows, surprised. "Is that what's freakin' you out?" He grinned at Trixie. "And you say ords don't get attached." To me: "We doubled back to try and grab him, but you showed up first. Don't look a genie in the bottle, right? Too bad, though. It might have been nice for her to have a friend, eh, Trix?"

"Ords don't have friends." Trixie dropped into a sitting position next to Barbarian Mike, her shoulders slumped. "I can't believe we're even talking about this, like it's a *person*. Six years ago—" She stopped.

"You want to leave?" he asked.

"What?" Trixie seemed to snap back and shot up, away from him.

"Do you wanna leave? Now? Not wait for sunup. We can do that."

She hesitated before tossing back, "That would be stupid. We should wait, and leave with the rest of the tourists. It'll be . . . easy."

"What if someone is coming—"

"No one's coming," Trixie said.

"Someone might," Barbarian Mike said, sorting the potion bottles in front of him. "You know how valuable they are. Collar like that, somebody's not messing around. The longer we wait, the more time they have to find us."

"No one is coming!"

Barbarian Mike waited until her shriek died away. "The festival's still going on, so it's still crazy out there. We don't need to wait for cover."

Trixie shook her head. "The festival's at the palace. Everywhere else'll be quiet. We'll stick out."

"We've got everything we need to recharge the glamour right here, babe."

"A good glamour takes time, *babe*. A rush job'll just get us more attention. People will think we're trying to rob a bank. No, we stick to the plan. We'll wait until all those tourists finish brunch and start clogging the streets, and then we just stroll out. Even if someone is looking for us, they wouldn't be able to find a hungry red cap in that exodus."

I stopped at those words; I stopped moving, maybe stopped breathing. If they wanted to sneak out in the crowd—if Mom and Dad didn't find me first, I reminded myself—then maybe that was my best chance. Getting away on the road would be harder. They'd know the road better. I didn't know how well they knew the city, or even how well I knew the city since I'd been stuck in school the entire time. But a crowd would give me a chance. If I could get away, I might be able to hide in the crowd. If they'd let me walk. They'd have to let me walk; they couldn't very well head out with me slung over their shoulders like a carpet, could they? That would get attention. I wouldn't even have to get my hands free. I'd just run. *Because running worked so well last time.* And I told my brain be quiet, be quiet, *be quiet.*

"If you say wait, we'll wait. I trust you." Barbarian Mike stood and set his pack against the wall. "But you're still nervous, and that ain't like you, Trix."

She didn't answer for a minute. When she did, her voice was quiet and her eyes flickered everywhere except at him. "We had to steal an ord, Michael. *Steal* one. Because we couldn't beg, or buy, or borrow." She jabbed a finger at me. "Look at her. Defiant ones always burn out the fastest. We'll get a year out of her, at the most—and that's if I don't push her off a cliff first. What happens when she wears out?" Trixie stopped pacing and looked at Mike, and for once she didn't look angry. "Then what are we going to do?"

"Whatever happens, we'll deal with it," Barbarian Mike told her. "Together."

Trixie looked over at him, startled naked emotion on her face. Then she turned away, and Barbarian Mike cleared his throat.

"I think you should leave now," I said. They both looked at me, heads snapping over in unison. "King Steve. He's my friend. Alexa's friend—my friend too. He likes me, and he is going to be *so* angry—"

Trixie looked angry, and Barbarian Mike looked amused, but underneath that they both looked worried. "Lesson number one," Trixie said, picking up a rock and tossing it in her hand, "never lie to your mistress."

"I'm not lying. My mom taught me not to lie." Exaggerating was completely different. "So you'd better leave now. Get out while you can. If you run fast, he might not catch you. Because if he catches you—"

Barbarian Mike gagged me.

CHAPTER
19

It was only one night, but it didn't feel like that. To be honest, it didn't feel like anything. There wasn't any time there, just tiredness pulling at me like an undertow, with me fighting it every second because I had work to do. There was twisting at the ropes until my wrists were on fire, then more twisting until they finally went numb. There was my stomach gnawing at me because Trixie demanded a "please, mistress" and "thank you, mistress" for every bite and I couldn't, I wouldn't say it.

There was no hope of escape during the night. Barbarian Mike and Trixie were up for hours, measuring and casting, reinforcing the thin, clinging coats of magic in their glamours that would conceal their identities.

It was very late (or very early) when they finished up and did a test run. It was good work—clean, simple—but it didn't cheat ord eyes. Satisfied, they double-checked their equipment and settled down on either side of the fireball, Barbarian Mike offering to take the first watch. It took Trixie time to calm down enough to sleep, though, and for a long while they sat in silence, watching the flames.

In the dark and the quiet, Barbarian Mike said, "I want you to promise—"

"Don't."

He kept his eyes on the flames. "I want you to promise me, if anything happens—"

"I can't believe you're letting it scare you."

"If it gets messy," he continued doggedly, "you'll get away."

"If you're afraid—"

"I am. For you."

Trixie stared at the floor. "I can take care of myself."

◆ ◆ ◆

At some point the ropes slacked enough that I could reach the knots and start to pick at them with my fingernails.

Toward the morning, when light started to smudge the shadows at the window, I thought about their previous ord, who didn't have friends and family coming for him (mine *were* coming) and I thought, he hadn't fallen.

◆ ◆ ◆

Trixie shook Barbarian Mike awake, and the two of them had a quick, cold breakfast. It was mostly quiet, except for when Mike nodded at me and asked, "What about her?"

Trixie tossed a strip of meat more like leather in my lap with a smirk. That earned her an exasperated "*babe.*" "Oh, I'll help her eat," Trixie replied. "When she asks nicely."

They cleaned up and cast their glamour, and Trixie undid

the ropes around my ankles and jerked me to my feet. My legs had fallen asleep during the night; I stumbled and fell a bit before they woke up and remembered how to walk straight.

"All right, since we're so worried about *damaged goods*, let's patch you up proper." She pinched the fabric of my sleeve, rubbing it between her fingers, and the green coloring seeped out of my dress, puddling on the floor and leaving the fabric a generic yellow. She rubbed my face clean and raked a comb through my hair, then spun me around. "My, my, haven't we been busy. Here, let me get that for you." Trixie slipped a finger under the ropes at my wrists and the knots fell away. For a second the feeling rushed back into my hands and I almost cried out. And then she yanked the ropes tight, and knotted them again. "There, that's better."

Trixie jerked a cloak over my shoulders, long enough to reach the ground. It had a hood that she pulled low over my face.

"I can still see the gag," Barbarian Mike said. "We should take it off. Gags get attention."

"If we take it off, she's going to scream."

"Then we'll just have to convince her not to."

"I could break her jaw . . . ," Trixie offered.

"Um, no. That'd get attention too." Barbarian Mike pulled the gag off, clapping a hand over my mouth before I could make a sound. "People worry when they see a kid with bruises."

"Bruises won't show up for hours."

"Trixie, *enough*. Okay, here's the deal, Zoe. We're not going to gag you. We're going to be nice, but in return you've got to be nice and not scream or nothing. You scream, you're going to make Trixie angry. I have seen Trixie angry and you don't want that. Understand?"

I nodded. And when Barbarian Mike slipped the gag off, I played nice.

Outside, the sky was cloudy and the city was quiet. With Barbarian Mike on one side of me and Trixie on the other, they guided me out of the alley to the street. We headed left, then right, then straight, then left again. This time I paid attention, looking at street signs to try and figure out where I was, but the city was a sea to me. I tried to spot some cops or, even better, Kingsmen. I hoped I would at least see some people, because if I was going to run and have a chance, I'd need a crowd to hide in. But normal eyes are a lot better than ord eyes, and if you have spells, you can sense stuff too. Barbarian Mike and Trixie would suddenly turn and head another way, as if they knew something was there. They even switched directions once because of a postal carrier delivering a package. I don't know if Trixie suspected I might try to signal for help, but her fingers slowly tightened until they felt like they were digging straight through my shoulder.

If we would only hit a big road, a major road, but Barbarian Mike and Trixie kept to the side streets, strolling along unhurriedly and taking turns seemingly at random. Above us, brightly colored taxi carpets zipped in and out of traffic like dragonflies. We passed a restaurant, where a few people sat, sipping their morning coffee, so relaxed it made my stomach churn. How could everyone be so calm? Did they ever even look out the windows? Why wouldn't someone just look over and *see* me and *help* me? Horrible, selfish people. I hated them, *I hated them*, and I didn't even know I was crying until Trixie shook me and told me to *hush up*. I heard Barbarian Mike saying I was fine, I'd just had too much fun at the fest, then Trixie said, so help me, I was going to *regret it*—

Why are you waiting for THEM? my brain suddenly shouted at me. *Why aren't YOU doing anything? DO SOMETHING!*

And I launched myself at Trixie with the only thing I had— my teeth. I latched on to her wrist and bit and bit and bit. She howled like a wounded animal and tried to wrench me away, and we fell together on the pavement, tumbling over the stones and slamming hard into a vendor's cart. Potion bottles shattered down around us. Then there was a loud *pop* and Trixie started yelling, hot shrieks of blind pain. Strong arms wrapped around my waist, and Barbarian Mike lifted me up bodily. I was twisting and kicking like a wild animal, and for one split second I twisted the right way, and he lost his grip and dropped me.

With my hands still tied behind my back, I landed awkwardly, the impact stunning me. But my body was beyond needing my brain at this point, and it scrambled to my feet even as my mind merry-go-rounded out of control. Barbarian Mike was there trying to latch on to my cloak. Behind me Trixie was still screaming awful curses, and in between that "My knee! My knee!"

There were pounding footsteps behind me but I didn't look back. I was running—down the sidewalk, shoving between people, and corkscrewing through the crowds. If they caught me, I'd know it soon enough. I shoved past the wrong person and they shoved back, and I fell forward into the street, scraping along the cobblestones.

"Ord!" Two people. One lurching. I rolled onto my butt and managed to squeeze my legs through the loop of my arms to get my hands in front of me. Pushing up, I dashed into the street. There were angry shouts, and carpets and people whizzed around me, lurched over me, just missing me and barely missing each other. Too fast for me to grab any, to hop on. I pushed forward, across the street, to the opposite sidewalk, all the while ripping my eyes up and down, looking for police, a Kingsman, anyone. My chest was so tight it felt like it might shatter. They were coming, I wouldn't get very far, I needed, I needed—

There. An alleyway between two buildings where the wind blew leaves up against nothing, as if there were an invisible wall. Right in front was a sign: ONE WAY: NO ENTRY. I raced for it, heart hammering, and sprinted into the cool dark of the alley as the adventurers caught up. Trixie was limping badly, and her knee had swollen up to the size of a dragon's egg. Her mouth tightened as she looked me over. "I'll handle this," she said to Barbarian Mike.

Trixie studied the barrier and tried to grab the sign. It gave her a nasty, crackling shock. She let go and carefully flexed her fingers, then leaned forward and knocked against the barrier with one knuckle. "Little pig, little pig, let us in."

* * *

Behind her, people were starting to gather. It looked like our run across the street had caused a carpet accident; nothing bad, just a little roll-up. But an accident meant an ambulance and officials—it meant *police*. Or it should. Eventually.

I couldn't wait for eventually. "Somebody help me! Call the police!" What did Becky say? Be specific. "You!" I pointed to a guy in the gathering crowd. He flinched but he looked at me. "Call the police! Call the Kingsmen! Call Alexa Hale at the palace! Do something! *Why are you just* watching?"

Barbarian Mike was obviously thinking the same thing. "We should get out of here—"

"Just a second!"

"And there are witnesses." He nodded to the gathering crowd.

"*I can get her!*"

"Trixie, come on!" he shouted. "We can get another one. There's rug burn in the road. Somebody's got to have called the cops. We've got to go."

Somebody had. There were sirens in the distance; I held on to the sound like an incantation. Barbarian Mike grabbed Trixie's arm, but she ignored him. "The longer you draw this out," she said to me, "the more it's going to hurt."

I didn't care anymore. All I cared about was holding on a few more minutes as the sirens steadily got louder. Trixie blasted the barrier, but it bounced back, scattering over the crowd. There were shouts of outrage, and one guy charged up to Trixie, exclaiming, "Hey, that was my wife you got there!" She ignored him. Barbarian Mike wrapped his arms around Trixie's waist and hefted her up, preparing (I hoped) to carry her out of there.

"What's going on here?" The two men pushing through the crowd wore the deep, dull crimson of the police. Relief left my legs shaky, and I sagged against the brick wall.

"Nothing," Trixie said, "nothing. Put me *down*, Michael!" He did and she landed on her bad leg, wincing.

"We didn't mean any harm, officer," Barbarian Mike intervened. "We were just trying to get our . . . child. She's had a little too much excitement this weekend, and got mad at us, and ran away."

"They *kidnapped* me!" I screeched. "They kidnapped me yesterday and they were trying to sneak me out of here and you have to arrest them!"

"It's only an ord," Trixie said, her tone like honey. The cops looked at me very closely, and for a second no one moved. Then one cop looked at the other cop, and he started waving the crowd away, and talking quietly in his crystal. In the distance, there were more sirens. The other cop removed a length of gold chain from his belt and asked the two adventurers to lie down on the ground and put their hands behind their heads.

Instead, Barbarian Mike shoved Trixie behind him and . . . it happened so fast, I'm still not clear on what happened. Barbarian Mike shouted, and then the world exploded into lights and magic and noise. So bright, so *loud*, I flinched and clapped my hands over my ears. There were more police, there were—Kingsmen? Melting into being out of thin air, and somebody must have done something to the crowd because they vanished and the street was empty except for us. There was so much noise and shouting, and I thought I heard Barbarian Mike's voice, bellowing for Trixie to "Run, *now*, RUN!" She looked at me, agonized, but she did, her body turning into flame as she streaked away. Kingsmen flashed after her, and Barbarian Mike charged them, looking a hundred times more terrifying and heroic than in the stories. The air shook as he started summoning magic . . . a lot of magic. Trees bowed toward him, branches snapped off and swirled. Cobblestones cracked in half and lifted up from the pavement. Magic swirled around, through me, and it was strange how I could stand there, shaky but more or less steady, in the midst of magic while the sheer force of it ripped awnings up the middle and twisted street signs into loops.

Then there were arms around me and at first I kicked away, panicking—but it was all right because I *knew* those arms, and it was like the string that was holding me up snapped. My knees went to water, but it didn't matter because Alexa was holding me tight, and everything was okay. Then we were moving. She was hurrying me somewhere, I didn't know where, I just knew it was away. I couldn't tell anything for the relief crashing over me. Alexa was *here*. She'd come for me. "Finally," I murmured, and started laughing.

"Are you okay?" Alexa asked, her voice ragged. "You look okay. Are you okay?" Murmuring soft, broken nothings, she cast away the ropes around my wrists. The second they fell free I latched on to her.

I think I nodded. I know I asked her about Peter. "They didn't find him," I said. "He wasn't there. He ran off."

"He's at the school, he's fine. The police found him inside of an hour."

I'm pretty sure I nodded again, but my head felt weird and bobbly and Alexa had to help me climb up on something—a carpet—and we lifted into the air. Looking back, I remember how it was quieter by that point. I remember looking down at the street and seeing it streaked with red, and realizing it was uniforms. I also saw the Kingsmen—there were Kingsmen there.

"I told them that you would sic King Steve on them," I gasped, pushing the words out through something more desperate than laughter. "But I thought . . . I was just making it up to scare them."

"You should know me better than that." Her voice was thick, but I could hear the smile. I started laughing so hard I was crying, until everything was mixed up and I wasn't sure what I was doing. I could feel the tiredness of the whole long night racing through me, threatening to pull me down like iron slippers. I wrapped my arms around Alexa's waist and buried my face against her.

• • •

Alexa flew me to the castle so I could make a report and get looked over by a doctor. On the flight there, I felt all the tiredness and the hunger and the hurting that I hadn't had time for until then. But I forgot all about that when I saw the rest of my family waiting in the castle lobby for us. I hadn't thought I could run anymore, but I did. There was an awkward, silly, wonderful moment when everybody tried to hug everybody else all at the same time, and I remember I just kept thinking *this, this, this*. This made everything better.

Of course, then Mom and Dad started yelling at me. But it was the nice kind of yelling where you know it's just because they were worried. There was more hugging and all that lovey-dovey family stuff, which Jeremy usually complains about until Gil demands to know what's wrong with gooey stuff, but neither of them did that this time.

Finally Alexa butted in. "Doctor time."

She took us to what had to be the Official Royal Medical Wing, and a small, fully stocked medical room that felt even smaller once my whole family had piled inside. Dad lifted me up and set me on the high medical table, but I had trouble letting go until Mom hopped up beside me and put her arm around me.

The doctor was really nice, especially about having to work around a bunch of worried grown-ups, and Jeremy, who was actually the worst with his constant questions of *what does that mean?* and *how do you treat that?* and *what are the side effects?*

"*Somebody* has to be interested in Abby's treatment," Jeremy informed him. "How else are we going to track her recovery?"

"We're going to ask her." Gil grinned at me. "You recovered yet, blondie?"

And I nodded.

Actually, other than being kidnapped and running for my life, I made out pretty well. A couple of scrapes, a lot of bruises, wrists rubbed raw, and one cut that didn't even hurt until the doctor pointed it out. But he said it wasn't too bad, considering. Just had to get them cleaned up and bandaged.

The doctor had barely finished when King Steve walked through the door.

Everybody scrambled to their feet, except for Mom, who just sat there, holding on to me. The king stopped them mid-bow/curtsey. "For heaven's sake, none of that. How is our patient doing?"

"Not too badly, under the circumstances," the doctor answered with a deep bow. "The wrists are the worst of it, but even without magic they should heal quickly. All in all, I think what the girl most needs is some rest. I'm going to prescribe a hot bath, a good meal, and a good night's sleep. If she's still feeling shaky in the morning, I'll write her a note for a few days off on classes."

"Thank you, doctor, I'll take it from here."

The doctor hesitated. "I still need to attend to her wrists, Your Majesty."

"That won't be necessary. Thank you," King Steve repeated, and the doctor bowed and ducked out of the room.

Then the king came over and looked at me, and sighed deeply. He looked so worn down that I felt like I needed to say something, so I said, "Sorry I missed your party, Your Majesty."

"Not as sorry as I am," he said, and then smiled. "And not as sorry as *they* will be."

King Steve cast up a tray on the table next to me with a bowl of steaming water, towels, a small jar of salve, and bandages. I reached for the towels, but he gently swatted my hands away, and picked one up and dipped it in the water. Then he began to clean my hands. My wrists had gone numb at some point, but the warm water woke them up, and a tight, scratchy burn flared along the surface. King Steve dabbed my wrists, wet the towel, and dabbed again; slow, methodical, and careful. All around us, the room was very quiet. Everyone was staring at the king (except for Olivia, who was staring at Alexa, and Alexa, who was staring at the floor). And it was a little weird, having a king tend to me. But then, King Steve didn't really seem like a king—he was nice. Like a normal person. With a crown.

The king set the water to the side and dried my hands with a small towel. "There we go. That's none too bad." His long, knobby-knuckled fingers were more gentle than I expected, as he took a salve and started dabbing it on my skin. The salve smelled strong, like mint and rubbing alcohol. Already the itching around my wrists was fading.

"Thanks."

He smiled at me and started wrapping the soft white bandages around my hands. "You're welcome. I'm happy to see you're all right," he said, and he looked up at Alexa, who was still standing quietly in a corner with her eyes on the floor. "Alexa was very worried when we got the call." The smile went away. "I wanted to be the one to tell you. Barbarian Mike is safely in our custody. He has confessed. He says . . . that kidnapping you was his idea. He says that his partner was against it, and that she tried to stop him, and when he wouldn't be stopped she came along to make sure you were taken care of properly. He says that he believes you were able to escape today with her help." King

Steve looked at me, and his eyes were like flint. "If this is true, I might be willing to consider calling off the search for her."

"It's not true, it's a *lie*—" And then my brain caught up with my mouth. "Trixie's still out there?"

King Steve looked me over and then nodded. "We are having some difficulty in locating her. In the meantime," he continued, "you will be escorted back to the school, and until we have the pleasure of Trixie's company, you will promise me not to leave the premises."

"Okay. She was hurt, her knee was hurt. It looked bad."

"And this city has a thousand rat holes. Don't worry. I am certain we will find her quite soon."

CHAPTER 20

We were at the palace for two days. King Steve took the doctor's recommendation that I rest as an order, and wouldn't let me leave until I got back on my feet.

Staying at the palace was a mixed blessing. I mean, I know it *sounds* cool, but I didn't actually see all that much. I spent a lot of the first day just sleeping, usually until Mom or Dad woke me up for a meal, and once when the doctor came to check on me again. And then I'd go back to sleep. I have never been so tired, ever, and it didn't even seem to matter that I was in a strange room and a strange bed.

We didn't do anything the second day, either, except to sit around the guest parlor King Steve had given us, curled up on couches, and watch bad action movies on the crystal. Which is an interactive sport for our family, since Gil likes to groan over the writing and point out the plot twists ahead of time, and Jeremy tears his hair out over the historical inaccuracies, and Dad makes corny jokes, till Mom reminds us, loudly, that *some people* are trying to watch the movie. Then we'll all quiet down for about five minutes, until Olivia remarks that the costume designer should have dressed the star in kitten heels instead, because it's a lot harder to run in stilettos.

That night we crowded around Alexa as she blew out the candles on her birthday cake. We left the parlor for the first time when Mom insisted we go hunt down King Steve so he could have a slice of cake. We made it exactly one hallway before we discovered the library, and Gil refused to leave, even for cake. Fortunately, King Steve heard we were looking for him and appeared just in time to help me pry Gil's fingers off the bookshelves.

It was nice of King Steve to let us stay, but part of me just wanted to get back to school. To see my friends again and make sure Peter was okay. Alexa said they were, that Fred and Fran had been taken back to school right after we disappeared, and that Peter had gotten picked up and was no worse for wear, other than having Ms. Macartney officially reprimand him. And it's not that I didn't believe Alexa, but I wanted to see for myself.

• • •

On the third day, I went back to school. Breakfast was mostly over when I arrived under official royal escort; the front doors swung open and Fred came running out, and then Frances, Mrs. Murphy, and Mr. O'Hara, and Cesar, and a couple of the kitchen rats. A cry of "Abby!" was all the warning I got before Fred yanked me up and spun me around. For a few moments there were just hugs and people laughing and calling my name, and I have never felt as popular as I did at that moment. Mrs.

Murphy—relief mixed with concern on her face—barely had time to say how proud she was, when Cook Bella huffed out into the courtyard and demanded to see "the worst of it."

"Well, I suppose you can't get these wet," she said, her hands surprisingly gentle as she held out my bandaged arms for inspection. "I'll get Sarah to scrub the floors until you're better, but heal up fast, mind. She's not got as deft a hand at it."

In the midst of this, someone was missing; I had to ask Fred where Peter was. "Um, he was at the table with us, so . . ." Fred looked around, blinking in surprise. ". . . still there, I guess? I'm glad you're back," he sighed, and then corrected himself. "I mean, I'm glad you're back, just for *you*, you know, period. But also because Peter's, he's been a lot more *Peter* than usual. Can you please go turn him into a real boy?"

Fred was right. Peter was still sitting at the table, alone, arms crossed and jaw tight. I shoved my way through chairs and just about climbed over a table to launch myself at him with a "You'reokay, you'reokay, you'reokay!" His fingers dug into my shoulders, and it took me a second to realize he was prying me off, and that I was making a fool of myself. "You're okay! Alexa said you were and I knew you had to be and what *happened*—?"

But he pushed himself away and moved around behind his chair. "I don't want to talk about it."

And his voice was so hard, and his face so closed that it cut through my babbling excitement. "What is it, what's wrong?"

"I don't want to talk about it, okay?" he shouted, still not looking at me. "And I don't want to talk to *you*!" Then he grabbed his book and slammed out of the dining hall. I followed

195

* * *

him into the courtyard, calling after him—wanting to know what was *wrong*—but he ran into the dorm and locked himself in his room and stayed there the rest of the day.

• • •

Trixie remained "at large," as the newscasters called it. Nobody saw her either, and I overheard Dimitrios wondering to Becky if anybody would see her.

As you can probably guess, Mom and Dad weren't thrilled with having to head back to Lennox after that. Oh, sure, they ordered Jeremy back to Thorten because he had classes, and Mom packed off Olivia back home because somebody had to run the bakery. But the two of them stuck around for a week, sleeping in Alexa's living room and driving her crazy. Fortunately for her, Yuletide was coming up in a month, and it's a big holiday for bakeries and luxury goods both, which meant they eventually had to leave.

The day before they left, Fred and Fran and I were in the kitchen during our free period, crowded around the island eating cookies. (We'd basically turned into a group of three because Peter was totally avoiding us—okay, me.) Cook Bella had decided she wasn't going to let me be completely lazy while I healed, so she appointed me taste tester. And then Fred managed to talk his way in by convincing Cook Bella she needed a "control group" or something like that, and Fran had gotten to the point where she'd show up for stuff on her own so we wouldn't have to drag her places. We were digging into a new recipe for hazelnut cookies when Alexa appeared, plopping down in the chair next to me. She crossed her arms on the table and plunked her head down. "I tried, Abby, I tried. I promised them that you would call every day, that you would call twice a day—I even offered three times, because Cook Bella has a crystal in the kitchen. But no. They're all 'she's my *daughter*,' and 'she was *kidnapped*,' and 'we're *upset* about it.' Crazy."

"Didn't King Steve say you were freaking out—"

"That's beside the point," Alexa interrupted, her head popping up. "The point is that—ooh, cookies—" She chewed appreciatively for a few seconds before finishing. "Dad is coming to live with me. Just until Yuletide, so he can keep an eye on you, and then we'll all fly down together. Mom would stay too, except she's swamped with all the orders for Yule bread and chocolate logs, which Olivia can't handle alone, praise the heavens on high."

Fred threw his hands in the air. "Hallelujah!"

"Sing it, Randalls." She held out her palm and he slapped it. "Anyway, they're determined to be paranoid."

"But you're here all the time," Fran offered, staring at her cookie.

"But that's cool. Because we like you," Fred added quickly.

"That's what I told them," she said to Fran. "But apparently I'm going to be too busy with work. Which means," she continued to me, "that you need to alert Public Safety about a visiting relative, so make sure you stop by and tell them tonight."

CHAPTER 21

I know I'm going to sound like a total dork for saying this, but it was actually fun having my dad there. He usually came by around dinner, and longer on the weekends, and as per King Steve's orders, we never left campus. He would sit with us, sometimes working off of his belt loom, and want to know how everyone was doing, how our classes were. He even got the Majid sisters to admit, out loud, in front of everyone, that their names were Naija and Eila. It was especially nice to have him around because things got really weird with Peter after the fest.

Actually, it was not so much weird as reversed, as if we'd gone through a time warp and were back at the beginning of the year, when Peter didn't like anybody or anything, except it was worse. He stopped coming to the lounge for homework and he stopped raising his hand in class, until he started getting in trouble for not participating. Fred told us that Peter even stopped snarking about his side of the room, which was freaking Fred out.

"But it's nice, right? Quieter?" Fran asked, twisting her hair through her fingers.

"Oh, yeah. Quieter, sure," Fred agreed. "But not Peter. I can't believe I'm saying this, but I"—he faked forcing the word out—"*liked* normal Peter."

I knew what Fred meant. It was like Peter had turned into that princess in the story whose brothers are cursed and if she says anything to anybody ever, they'll be stuck as blackbirds for the rest of their lives. He just kept his head buried in that little blue book of his, acting like the rest of us didn't exist.

Peter had stopped checking on me at night, too, which was actually kind of a good thing. I didn't want to sleep. When I did I had bad dreams, mostly about Trixie. Mostly that she'd show up, anywhere, everywhere, huge and angry and strong, and sometimes I would run and sometimes I would fight, but whatever I did, it was never enough. A couple of times I woke up, in a panic that someone was holding me down, and then realizing the hands on my arms were real and panicking more. But it was always Becky, who'd heard me and, worried, came to wake me. She'd sit by my bed and murmur defensive techniques until I fell asleep.

• • •

A couple of weeks later, Alexa had finally convinced Dad that I was safe enough at school that they could go to a movie. Everyone was in the dining hall for dinner, and it was one of my last times to sit with my friends and enjoy the meal before I got back into the kitchen. The doctor had stopped by that day to check on me and take my bandages off. Part of me worried I'd have big ugly scars, but my wrists were fine. A little pink, but nothing you'd notice unless you really stared at them. Which Peter did.

Yuletide break was coming up, and Fred and I were talking about the trip home. Or, at least, my trip home and his possible one. Many of the kids would be staying on campus because they didn't have homes to go to. Fred, though, was in a weird situation. He never heard from his parents—or, at least, he never heard from his stepmom, period. And his dad never called, but at the same time he was always sending stuff. Clothes, books, sometimes games, the newest and most expensive kind.

And here's the really cool thing about Fred: he would always share. The books and toys usually ended up in the lounge for everyone to get in on, and it was pretty well known that if you needed a new shirt or socks or something like that, Fred had one to spare. Or he would take a special request, and if Mr. Randalls suspected anything when his kid wrote home asking for three different sizes of pants, he didn't say anything. Probably because that would have meant talking to Fred.

And right before Fall Fest, Fred got a card with a wreath on the cover and *Holiday Wishes from the Randalls Family* on the inside. Apparently this confused Mrs. Murphy enough that she finally pulled Fred aside and asked if he wanted her to check with his family about him going home for break.

Fred said yes.

So there we were, over dinner, and Fred was saying how Mrs. Murphy had called (and called) and had to leave a message at his dad's office, which was really the best way to connect with him.

"They're not going to want me to come. I'm not sure if I even really want to go," Fred told us. "It's a lot of boring stuff, anyway."

"Like what?" Naija asked.

Fred took a deep breath, the humor falling away from his face as his shoulders set tight. "Like my father's office Yuletide party. We're always expected to attend. There are a few charity banquets, too: FeyAid, and"—he glanced around at the minotaurs—"NOMI. Not On My Island," he explained to our blank faces. "It's an Astrin organization, Deeta's really. She's from there. And, of course, the Randalls Family Twelfth Night Party. That's always *really* boring. But it makes up for it by going on forever," he joked.

"My family has one of those," I said. "Not the endlessly boring part, just the Twelfth Night Party, and it is *awesome*. Seriously, years from now Ms. Macartney will be teaching kids about this party instead of horribly boring kings and queens. Your family should come to my family's party," I told him, seizing on the idea.

"I doubt they'd be able to," Fred said. "Deeta's probably been planning the thing for months now."

"Yeah, but if it's not fun, then what's the point?"

"To show off how much money we have?"

That stopped me. I couldn't quite tell if he meant it as a joke. "Really?"

Fred opened his mouth, then stopped and smiled and shrugged. But Fred's usually the first one to crack a smile, which means that when it's not a real smile you notice right away. "Okay, fine, no party. But you should at least come visit us, because you're actually not going to be that far away, and my family—"

"All right, we get it," Frances muttered. We all stopped and looked at her. She sounded . . . grumpy, and it really wasn't like Fran to sound grumpy.

"I'm . . . sorry?" I said.

Fran didn't say anything at first, her jaw working back and forth. Then, louder, "You know, we get it, all right? We get it. You have a fantastic, wonderful family and everybody else's family sucks. We get it. Your family is perfect and they like you. All right? Fine. We don't need to hear it anymore."

I glanced at Fred, who gave me a bewildered look.

"Frances," Fred began carefully.

"What's your problem, Fran?" Peter demanded.

"Don't be a jerk, Peter," Fred rushed in. And I sat there, staring at Peter, somewhere between angry and completely baffled. *He was going to start talking now?*

"I'm not being a jerk, I just want to know what her problem is," he said, not looking at me, just glaring at her.

Fran's chin was trembling. "I don't have a problem."

"Now you're a liar and you have problems."

"Stop it, Peter," she hissed.

"No, you stop. Don't you be a jerk just because Abby has a family that loves her and cares about her and you don't."

First Fran was mad at me, and now Peter—who had been ignoring me and had apparently changed his mind about us being friends—now he was going to lash out at Fran *for no reason?*

202

"I don't like you, Peter," she said. Her voice was close to tears.

"What, are you going to start in on *me* now? 'Cause my mom loves me and doesn't wish I didn't exist?"

"Is there a problem here?" It was Mrs. Murphy, who liked to appear out of nowhere and wait to see how long it took misbehaving students to notice she was there. Only this time I guess she didn't want to wait.

Fred pointed at Peter. "He's being a jerk."

Peter nodded at Frances, a stubborn set to his jaw. "She started it. She was picking on Abby. Because she's jealous. And *pathetic.*"

And now Fran was crying in earnest. And I was so angry it felt like my ribs were made of hot coals. "Not cool, Peter. That is not fair."

"Fair?" he shot back, sounding more surprised than angry. Now he was looking at me.

"Yeah. You shouldn't be so mean to her, she doesn't have anybody!"

"And you shouldn't be nice to her just because she doesn't have anybody!"

I shoved Peter and told him to stop it.

He shoved me back. "*You* stop it! Why do you let her talk to you like that? Stand up for yourself! Fight back! You're too nice, stop being so nice!"

"Nice?" I screeched. "What do you know about being nice?"

"I know enough not to be captured by adventurers!" he shouted back at me. "You got grabbed once already, Abby,

203

and it'll happen again, and next time it'll be all your own fault!"

I went to shove him again, but Mrs. Murphy grabbed my arms, and there was a second when angry mixed with scared— which was silly, because I knew where I was and what was going on. But Mrs. Murphy let me go right away and just patted me on the back, and then said very firmly that she was ashamed of having students behave like this. Ms. Macartney volunteered to take Peter to one of the classrooms and "give him something to do," and Mrs. Murphy suggested that Dimitrios take me down to Public Safety and do the same. But then Cook Bella, who was watching (because *everybody* was watching), said that she was a bit shorthanded in the kitchen, and if Mrs. Murphy didn't mind, ma'am, she'd take charge of me. Which stunk because there's nothing more frustrating than getting into a good argument and not being able to finish it, especially when you know you're right.

Cook Bella set me up in quiet corner in the kitchen. She braided my hair and wrapped a scarf around my head to keep it neat, and got me a cool cloth. I clutched it against my hot face, not wanting to see anybody for a moment, really not wanting them to see me. And then I felt Cook Bella's big, warm hand running back and forth along my shoulders. I choked against the wet cloth, even as I scrambled to pull myself together, because the small, still reasonable part of me recognized that it had gotten way too quiet in the kitchen.

When I had dried my face and felt steadier, Cook Bella let me pound garlic and chop onions and peel and grate potatoes for tomorrow's hash browns until I was too tired to hunt Peter down and shove him in a closet. Nobody talked to me, and for once I didn't want them to. I just concentrated on what I was doing, blinking when the onions stung my eyes.

* * *

CHAPTER 22

I told Dad about the argument—well, the Fred and Fran parts of it—when I saw him the next day, and he got his thinking look on his face. "Wait a minute, baby."

"Why, what are you going to do?"

He gave me a look that said I should wait a minute like he told me, called up Mom, and stepped just out of hearing. I caught something about swapping rooms and calling somebody to get permission. Then Dad hung up and asked me, "Why don't you ask your friends to come spend winter break in Lennox with us?"

"Really?"

"Really. If they want to, Mom'll call Mr. Randalls and Frances's parents for permission."

I threw my arms around his waist. "You are the best dad ever."

"Remember that next time you ask to get your ears pierced." He kissed the top of my head and asked, "Do you want to talk about it?" Because he knew. Of course he knew. Because there were a dozen people here who would have told him—the teachers, probably, or Dimitrios—or maybe he just knew the way dads know things sometimes.

I shook my head, because I didn't, and managed, "He's just *mean*."

Dad sighed.

"Could you—" I leaned back to look at him. "Alexa's going to hear about this, and she's . . . she's not really—"

"I know, I know. She's nosy. I'll talk to her."

It took a little effort to convince Fred and Fran to sign up for the trip—well, none at all for Fred, actually, especially once he'd gotten official word from his dad's secretary that Mr. Randalls regretted to inform him that it would be better if Fred stayed at school during the holidays, as the Randalls family would be traveling out of the country. "That probably means the Astrin Islands," Fred told us. "We, they—there's a vacation house there. My brother, Arthur, really likes it and we went—they *go* there every other Yuletide. We went last year. I guess they decided to switch things up. Have you ever been to the Astrin Islands?" he asked brightly, straightening.

Fran and I shook our heads.

"It's nice. Pretty. Beaches and date trees everywhere. But Father"—he swallowed—"Mr. Randalls is right. It's not a good place for an ord."

Fran, however, needed a good twenty minutes of pleading and repeating that we really did want her to go, that we weren't just being nice, until Fred started shaking her by the shoulders, shouting "Peer pressure! Peer pressure! Give in!" and, laughing, she did.

We never did hear back from the Roses about whether or not Fran could visit, in spite of the fact that Alexa sent them permission forms twice and Mom called no less than four times. Luckily, no one mentioned that Mr. Rose's signature didn't exactly look right when we handed in the permission slips.

It took longer to arrange when we could go down, because while King Steve gave permission for us to leave, he insisted that we travel with proper security. Dad himself wasn't considered enough protection for three ords. Jeremy offered to come up, since Thorten wasn't that far away, but Alexa told him that he wasn't considered any protection at all, and in the end we spent the first part of break up at the school, waiting for Alexa to get off work.

We got the first really good storm of the winter right before we left, which Becky and the older students greeted with outright applause. They'd watched the darkening skies for days, and exclamations of *it looks like rain* and *does it seem more humid to you* ricocheted along the halls. I thought Yuletide might be, like, a depressing time at school, but the students just got more and more cheerful. When the clouds finally opened up and the torrential downpour began, the cheering resulted in a couple of police officers showing up with noise complaints.

"It's because of the red caps," Becky explained when I asked why everyone was excited about the weather. "Rain washes the blood out of their caps. A bad enough storm could decimate a conclave, so with the first really good rain, they head into hibernation. We won't hear from them until spring. What will I do with myself? I'll have nothing to worry about."

"Other than Trixie," I said.

"Yes," Becky said, pressing her lips into a bitter line.

. . .

Flying into Lennox, I was surprised by how small it looked. I mean, it's a nice size as far as towns go, and there always seemed to be people and stuff going on, but after Rothermere it looked so . . . empty. There was so much space, and barely any people. And that scared me. Everyone knows that home is supposed to look different the first time you come back from school. But I didn't want that. I didn't want it to change, I didn't want anything to have changed—I just wanted it to be home.

When we pulled up in front of the house, though, it looked the same. Yellow stucco, red tile roof, and the wide shop windows on the first floor with block letters proclaiming: REX'S TEXTILES, "King of Handmade Carpets!" When we landed, the flowers in the back garden, which had been huddled against the rain, peeked over the fence to see who'd arrived. And then Mom burst out the front door, arms open, bearing down on us like a manticore, and yanked us up into crushing, cake-flour-scented hugs. Fred held out his hand for a proper handshake and let out this little squeak of surprise when Mom wrapped him up in her arms. Gil was at the kitchen table, still in his pj's, though it was getting into the afternoon. He put his muse on hold long enough to help everybody get inside and get settled, and then until Mom marched us down to the bakery to say hi to Olivia. Things were so swamped there that the hi turned into helping box up Yule logs and organizing orders for hot milk cakes. I caught myself glancing up every now and again, wondering if Cook Bella was going to appear.

Since it was just the two extra kids, we didn't have to stretch any rooms. Fran bunked in with me and Olivia, and Fred was in with Gil and Jeremy, and casting up another bed, that's easy. I found out later that Mom had invited over both the Randallses and the Roses—"they should know where their children are"— but of course the Randallses were traveling and the Roses' ball must have been cracked or something. Mom set herself to coddling and catering to Fred and Frances from the moment they stepped into the house. On Twelfth Night, the stack of presents alone for each of them was intimidating, especially considering they'd only had a week to shop, but then, my family likes a challenge.

Mom had also invited Ms. Whittleby and Peter, and they'd politely declined, which I was totally okay with because if he didn't want to be friends, then fine, we wouldn't be friends. But Mom and Ms. Whittleby were friends, which meant they were talking; Ms. Whittleby had a neighbor who let her use their crystal ball. Afterward Mom would always tell me "Peter said this" or "Peter asked his mom to tell you this," which was a lie because Peter never said anything. I knew his mom was probably doing the same thing to him, and I didn't like the idea of unauthorized messages.

"This is ridiculous, Abby," my mom finally burst out. "He's

your friend. If you two have a problem, you should talk to him and deal with it."

"This is a free country," I told her. "King Steve says I don't have to talk to anyone I don't want to talk to."

"Not in my house. Under this roof there is one rule and one rule only, and its name is Mom."

"Sorry, Mom, but I'm with Abby on this one," Olivia said, tossing me a grin. She was at the kitchen table, flipping through a fashion magazine. "Make him suffer, Abs. Boys like it."

"They do?" I asked, even as Mom told me not to listen to her.

Olivia stretched back in her seat with a satisfied, "Oh my goodness, you don't even know."

"But Peter's not suffering, he's just being mean."

Olivia pinched my cheek. "You are so totally cute, I can't even deal."

Mom sighed and shook her head. "I keep telling myself that one of these days you'll find a nice husband and settle down."

"Mom, please, she's *twelve*. Give her some time," Olivia protested. "At least let her graduate first."

"I meant you."

"Mother!" Olivia pretended to be shocked. "You know I don't go for married guys."

Mom pinched the bridge of her nose and started muttering to herself.

· · ·

It was a remembered luxury to sleep in my own bed again, to take a shower in my bathroom and curl up in my corner of the couch, and to eat at the kitchen table with everyone. Though my hands did feel a bit empty and strange when Mom poofed the dishes away after each meal. I finally asked her to cast up a sink and a sponge and some soap. It might be break, but I had to keep in practice.

Every day rain drummed against the roof and spattered on the windowpanes, but there's something about Yuletide that makes it seem cozy, not confining. Maybe it's because it falls so early in the winter. Spending all day inside, sometimes not even changing out of your pj's or having pancakes for dinner, is still nice and new. There's plenty of time to go stir-crazy later, when the wet's dragging on and it seems like you'll never have dry socks again.

Gil rallied Fred and me, the only ones willing to brave the rain, and we tromped outside in the woods and picked through the fallen branches to find the perfect Yule log—a real one, not the chocolate dessert with candy mushrooms. (Though one time Gil tried to trick us by swapping in a real log that he stuck candy mushrooms on, but he didn't get very far because, seriously, wood tastes completely different from chocolate.) We came back, drenched and muddy but triumphant, to the wonderful buttery smell of baking cookies.

Then there was the party.

I didn't lie to Fred when I told him we'd go down in history for this party. Normally, it's crowded and loud and confusing. Normally, the cops stop by to see about the noise, but really it's just an excuse so Olivia can flirt with them while stuffing cake in their mouths. Normally, the living room is so smushed full, Mom and Dad have to stop every hour to stretch it a little more.

But this year, for the first time in Hale history, there was space. The town stayed away. Even some of our family stayed away, which should have bothered me, except it didn't. I guess getting kidnapped and almost forced into service makes some people not wanting to party pale in comparison.

But quiet and empty doesn't necessarily mean boring. Mom put a cauldron of mulled wine on the fire, and spiced and stirred until the whole house was tipsy with the scent of it. We turned off the lights and clustered around the soft, safe glow of the fireplace, sipping from steaming mugs and opening our presents, one by one. We sat around the fireplace until late that night, in a tangle of torn wrapping paper, sometimes talking and sometimes not, but mostly just listening to the Yule log crackle.

The next morning, we left. Alexa got called back to work suddenly, and rather than try to arrange police escorts or minotaurs or whatever they decided was proper for our trip back, she figured it'd be simpler to bring us along with her. Mom and Dad weren't happy, but they agreed to it. However, they both agreed they were coming along, too, so with Jeremy it made for a full carpet, at least until we got to Thorten.

It took the whole carpet ride, though, for Alexa to convince Mom and Dad that they didn't need to stay in Rothermere while I was at school. That I would be fine, that I would be safe, that it would take an army to break into the school, and Trixie did not have an army and even if she did, magic wouldn't work on ords. "Abby will be fine. You two have nothing to worry about," she said.

"I'll have nothing to worry about when that woman is

caught," Mom complained, but in the end, they agreed to go back to Lennox.

"But Abby—" Mom pinned me with one of her looks. "You are going to call me every single day to let me know you're okay. You got that, young lady? Every single day."

"I'll run out of things to talk about," I said.

"I sincerely doubt that," Mom said.

CHAPTER 23

I plopped down in the chair, let my books slide onto the table, and smiled my thanks to Dimitrios before focusing on the crystal ball. "Hey, Mom. Before I forget, everybody says thanks for the lemon squares." (There was a haphazard chorus of *thank yous* behind me.) "They were a big hit."

"How long did they last?" Mom asked.

"I clocked it at just under fifteen minutes. Also, Fred wants me to tell you he likes blackberries."

Mom smiled. "I'll see what I can do. What did you learn in school today?"

I crossed my arms on the table and leaned forward until my nose was almost touching the ball. It felt like Mom was in the room with me. "We're starting a new section in Lit. Mr. O'Hara calls it realism, which apparently is another word for boring."

"I'd like to think it depends on the author."

"All the authors we read are boring. All the stories we read are about people hating each other and being miserable. And there aren't even any carpet chases or magic fights or somebody turning somebody else into a toad. There are no dragons. How realistic can you be without any dragons?"

"Maybe these writers weren't living a glamorous city life like you. Maybe they were out in the middle of nowhere and they never saw dragons."

"That's no excuse. They should imagine some."

"Then it wouldn't be realism."

"Is that Abby? Can I talk to her?" Olivia peeked over Mom's shoulder. "Has Alexa told you about Friday yet?"

"I'm having a conversation with my daughter," Mom said, amused, as Olivia took her place.

"I know, two of them, actually. Friday?" Olivia prompted. I shook my head and she sighed dramatically, adding in a hair flounce for good measure.

"You know that doesn't work on me, I'm not a boy," I told her.

"Please, Abby, I *know* that, but it never hurts to keep in practice. Get yourself pretty, you have a big appointment."

"What appointment?"

"That's for Alexa to tell, and for me to gloat over you not knowing. But it's Friday. And also Gil's coming with her, and you have to be totally nice to him—"

"I'm *always* nice to him."

"—because he's getting called before the editor, who's going to yell at him for missing his deadline."

"They changed it up on me!" Gil called from somewhere in

the house. "They want it *now!* Anyone seen my vest? The blue one with the dragon-scale pattern?"

"Apparently they have been getting a lot of good buzz and want to see about launching it at some book fair. Anyway," Olivia continued, "we're breaking you out of there at three o'clock sharp, right after classes. So be ready."

Gil's frustrated groan cut off whatever Olivia was going to say. "I have *nothing* to wear! How can I have *nothing* to wear? I have to look professional!"

"Calm down," Olivia called, then rolled her eyes at me. "Sorry. Fashion emergencies take priority. Talk later, okay? Don't forget: Friday."

. . .

Alexa appeared beside me the next day with a large envelope in her hand. It had my name on the front in ornate block letters. "Is that what Olivia was talking about?" I asked, reaching for it.

She moved it out of my way, her eyes going wide. "She told you? I swear, that girl couldn't keep her mouth closed if you bound it shut with cold iron braces."

"What is it?" I asked, grabbing for the envelope again.

"Just tea with King Steve. No big deal. And—" Her expression turned serious. "Barbarian Mike is being sentenced this week."

"That was fast," I said. They'd told us ten months, maybe, for the case to work its way to the top of the list.

"His Majesty has decided to take this case on personally, so it has been accelerated," she explained. "Sentencing is next

Monday. He'd like you to come to the castle Friday after classes for tea and to talk about the incident."

"Again? What about all those reports we filled out?" I asked.

"His Majesty has read the reports, but it is his esteemed pleasure to host Miss Hale for the afternoon so as to hear her side of the story personally," she said, handing me the envelope. It was smooth as cream and ten times as fancy, wrapped with a velvet ribbon and sealed with the ornate royal crest. Alexa tapped the seal. "Come on, you know it's her." With a faint huff, the seal lifted, the ribbon unfurled, and, with great ceremonial dignity, the letter opened up in front of me. "You'll have to excuse them. The king's personal invitations don't get sent out that often, so they get a little stuffy sometimes."

The thick black script gleamed like liquid silk. "What's he going to do to him?" I asked, scanning the words.

Alexa gave me a veiled look. "I don't know," she said, and I was reminded that my big sister is a very good liar. "But His Majesty does not believe in light sentences for kidnappers."

• • •

"I hear you're getting away from us this week," Becky said the next day as she walked us down to Public Safety after her class.

I nodded. "By order of the king. Also, my brother has a meeting in town."

"I know Alexa's going with you, but all the same I'd like you to come by whenever you have a free moment to get some extra training in. Especially after what happened."

"Sure."

And then Becky asked what kind of meeting, and after I explained she asked, "So which brother is the author? Jeremy or . . . Gilbert?"

"Gil, but he doesn't write under his own name because his editor said he'd get better sales if he had a fake lady's name. So he writes romance novels as Miranda Blythe."

"Miranda Blythe?" Becky grabbed my arm; she'd gone pale, and her eyes were very wide.

I nodded. "He has a new one coming out next fall, called *Race Against the Wind* or *Racing the Wind*, I forget which."

Her fingers tightened on my arm. "*Race the Wind?*" she asked breathlessly.

"Yeah, that's it. How did you know?"

"She announced it on her fan channel. Dimitrios hooks me up on the ball at least once a week so I can check in. I have been waiting for over a year—your *brother* is *Miranda Blythe?*" The hallway outside the Public Safety office was completely empty now, but we were past caring. "I *love* those books! I remember stealing the first one from my owner's nightstand and . . . that is—" Becky stopped, and the color rushed back into her face as she muttered something about another lifetime.

And I wanted to ask, *Owner?* Except I didn't need to ask, not really. Not with that look on her face. So instead I asked, "Aren't they the best books ever? Which one's your favorite?" And we completely ignored Dimitrios when he stuck his head out into the hallway and pointedly cleared his throat. "Mine's *Rules of Passion*," I said, "but that's just me preferring Rafe to Enrique."

"Oh, absolutely. Enrique's way too moody," Becky said. "My favorite is an old one. You probably wouldn't know it."

"Yes, I would. I've read every single one of them, but don't tell my parents because I wasn't supposed to because of all the kissing and stuff."

Becky smiled at that. "There is some 'stuff.'"

"Rebecca . . . ," Dimitrios said, then cleared his throat again to get her attention.

"So which book? I'll keep annoying you until you tell me," I told Becky.

"You know I have been standing right here," Dimitrios said. "I have heard every word of your discussion."

Becky finally turned to him. "Yes, thank you, I see you. But we are having an important teacher-student discussion at the moment. I'll send her in when we're finished. It's one of his first ones," she told me. "A contemporary."

That was easy. Gil had only written one contemporary before switching over to historical, which is where Mom says his strength is. "*Kissing the Kingsman?*"

"All right, all right." Dimitrios held up his hands. "But don't go biting Bella's head off the next time she delays Abby from *your* class."

Becky clenched her hands into fists and took a long exaggerated breath. "Fine. We will continue this discussion later, Abby."

Later turned out to be an hour later. We were gathering up our books, trying to figure out which creature we were going to pick for our essay (undead vs. enchanted, pick any two creatures and compare/contrast strengths and weaknesses) when Dimitrios's crystal chimed. "Wait a minute, Abby," he called as the class shuffled out. "I have been asked to run you up to Ms. Macartney's classroom. She wants to speak to you."

"I didn't do anything."

He grinned. "Why don't any of you kids look that worried when you're sent to see me? We're the law around here."

There's something about Ms. Macartney's classroom that always makes it look like it's got a tint of cool-blue shadows, even with the afternoon sun coming full on through the windows. She was sitting there, poised and perfect, her pencil making precise little marks as she graded her way through a neat stack of papers. Becky was there too, which I hadn't expected, leaning against a corner of the desk.

"Here's Miss Abby, ma'am," Dimitrios announced, still grinning, and Ms. Macartney said *thank you, that will be all,* without looking up. He ducked out; I felt the click of the door as it closed.

"Did I do something?" I asked carefully.

"Not that I'm aware of, yet." Ms. Macartney set down her pencil and looked up at me. "I understand we are expecting a visit from your brother at the end of the week."

"Yeah, I—" I stopped. "Seriously?"

"We were wondering," she continued, turning her attention to tidying up her perfectly neat desk, "if we provided you with personal copies, if you could have your brother sign them."

"Really? Gil would completely love that. He's never had a

real book signing before, which I guess is just as well because he can't exactly show up as a guy when everyone's expecting Miranda."

"Yes, I can see how that would cause some problems. Thank you. Becky, you'll have to remember to return the copy of *The Rules of Passion* I lent you," Ms. Macartney said. "I'd love to have him autograph the full set."

CHAPTER 24

At three o'clock sharp on Friday afternoon, Becky walked me out to the main gate, her fingers white-knuckled on a small stack of books. My brother and sisters were waiting with a private carpet, courtesy of King Steve. Gil was off it the moment he saw us, giving me a speedy pat on the head as he raced over to Becky. It was a little funny watching them, Becky so spine-straight and formal, calling him "sir," which had Olivia snorting with laughter, and Gil gushing and excited as he gleefully signed his way through a small stack of books, exclaiming, "This is what authors do!"

"I thought authors *wrote*," Alexa called from the carpet.

"Writers write," Gil returned. "Authors get book signings."

They stood there, talking about how Rafe was so much cooler than Enrique, and was he ever going to get to Jamie's story, until Olivia started to glance around and wonder loudly didn't some of us have an appointment with someone important, and wasn't there a madwoman still on the loose? That made Alexa laugh. "You really think it's just the five of us out here? And that we're going to fly on down to the castle all by our lonesome? That's cute."

"I can point out the hidden Kingsmen if you want," I offered.

"Later," said Olivia. "Time, Abby." Gil and I climbed on the carpet and waved good-bye to Becky as we sped off.

"All right." Alexa rubbed her hands together. "We have five minutes for endearing family chat. How is everyone doing? What's new? What have I missed?"

"I'm not doing too bad, but Olivia's only had three dates this week," Gil said. "She's hoping we'll drop her off at the nearest man while we go meet your King Steve."

"I am making a strategic decision to date less," Olivia informed us. "Mom keeps hitting me with the whole 'why don't you find a serious boyfriend and settle down' thing."

"Which means she's going to be coming after me instead, thank you very much," Alexa replied.

Olivia and Gil looked at each other and giggled. "You could try being honest with her," Gil said.

"Because we all know the 'you don't have a boyfriend' thing isn't exactly true, is it?" Olivia finished.

"I have absolutely no idea what you're talking about," said Alexa. "I'm going to ignore you two and talk to my favorite sibling now. How are your classes going?" Alexa asked me.

"Good. Really good. Really, really good."

"Except you're having problems with realism," Gil added.

* * *

"There's no point to realism," I said.

"It's about technique. You have to learn technique if you want to get anywhere," Gil said.

"I don't need technique; I'm never going to write anything."

"You're not supposed to like school," Olivia told me.

"I know, I know, I know," I said at Olivia's expression. "I'm sorry. I promise, O, I promise I'll stop next year. Except I hear Second Year is really boring. Except for self-defense," I added. "All the kids say that next year's self-defense is much more interesting, because we're actually going to learn to flip somebody. Like, over our back. But nobody usually gets hurt. It's all okay."

Gil turned to Alexa. "What are you teaching these children?"

Alexa shrugged. "Hey, we're just trying to train our own child army."

. . .

After dropping Gil off at the publishing house and Olivia off to go shopping, Alexa and I continued on to the palace.

The royal palace is the pearl that makes the rest of the city look like the oyster. Even on an overcast day, it glowed like it was covered in fairy dust—which it probably was. Red banners flapped in the breeze and streamed down the sides. A red carpet led the way to the main entrance, an ornate set of garnet doors larger than most buildings. It was guarded by several very attractive guards in fancy uniforms so deep red they looked black until the light hit them.

The castle is just about the only place in the city where you see red. That shade of deep red is strictly a royal color, so it's all over the castle and nowhere else, except places like museums and libraries that get a lot of royal funding.

We bypassed the main entrance, which Alexa says is for "show and tourists," to a side door, the same color as the castle walls, so that it blended in. Opening it was a complicated procedure involving three keys, two palm prints, a rosemary twig, and exactly one half handful of lavender. And it wasn't so much "opening" the door as making it go all wobbly and stepping through it.

Inside was a discreet hallway and a pair of guards in subdued uniforms. The hallway was small (or at least that's how it was presenting itself) and painted beige, with a plain visible door at the other end, and a handful of invisible openings along the walls.

The guards saluted Alexa with a crisp "Miss Hale," and checked my ID so thoroughly I started to wonder if they were going to let us by. Finally, they stepped aside and Alexa dragged me through the door.

Inside, it was completely dark. It was more than just dark, which would mean that there wasn't a lot of light. There was no light at all.

"Wonderful," Alexa muttered.

"Is this supposed to happen?" I asked.

She sighed. The sound hovered in the air over my head. "Yes. That is, the castle has dark days sometimes."

"Safety procedures?" I guessed.

"Yes. But she never tells us when exactly—here, hold my hand—exactly when she's going dark."

"How do I know this is you?" I asked, tugging on the warm hand in mine.

"It's not me. It's a bloodthirsty *ghooost* . . ." Her voice echoed throughout . . . wherever we were. "But seriously, it's me."

"I figured that one out."

"Actually, there probably is a ghost around here somewhere," Alexa informed me as she dragged me forward, "but my guess is it's just spying on us. Won't turn into corporal form. Too easy to see that way."

"Why spy on us at all? King Steve knows we're coming." Something glinted oddly in the dark, and I realized those were her eyes.

"Well, it might not be us. It could be someone enchanted to look like us. Best to keep an eye on us just in case."

I clutched Alexa's hand and tried to keep track of where we were going, but it was no use. She led me left and right and left and around to a set of the steepest set of stairs I'd ever skidded down. The air felt cool and misty around us, like fog clinging to my ankles, and Alexa's footsteps slowed, as if she were fighting against something. We passed by a clacking, skittering on the right; Alexa jerked me away and hissed something that made the scuttling move in the opposite direction.

Not long after, the air changed. It grew warmer and lighter. I could feel the mist around our ankles dissipate, and I could hear Alexa start to move easier. She stopped and said, "Close your eyes."

I did, not that there was much difference from having my eyes open. There was some scratching and a big heavy *clunk*, then the squeaky screech of a door opening. I sensed light on my face. After a moment Alexa led me forward. "Careful, Abby. Your eyes will need time to adjust."

We weren't in an office. I'd expected an office. Maybe some official waiting room. Instead, we were in a small sitting room, with a lot of latticed windows, through which daylight streamed in. A couch, a couple of comfortable-looking chairs, and a low polished coffee table were clustered around a big fireplace—much bigger than me, and almost as big as Alexa. The couch cushions were ornately embroidered, and the coffee table was heavy and beautifully carved. There were stacks of books towering against all available wall space, a to-do list tacked up on the back of the door, and a burdened coat rack (holding, among other things, a bathrobe, a long heavily embroidered cloak, and a ruby-studded crown). The whole room smelled faintly of tea and firewood.

King Steve was sitting in a tall-backed chair, reading the entertainment section of a newspaper. He had his shoes off and looked about as relaxed as a king probably ever gets. He didn't look up as we came in, but Alexa didn't seem to mind, or notice. "Help yourselves," he said, "I'll be done in a second."

A tea service set itself out on the coffee table, and there was also one of those tiered trays of sweets. Mostly cookies, and mostly the ones half-dipped in chocolate that Alexa likes, but there were also the golden, buttery kind filled with little pockets of jam. The pot poured out two cups and then hovered impatiently over a third until I said, "Oh, yes, thank you." The cups are supposed to come to you, but this one floated to a spot on the couch, then jiggled until I got the hint and hurried over to sit down. A tiny spoon dipped into the sugar bowl and paused, like a question mark. I held out my cup and said, "Three, please," but it only gave me two, and when I tried to grab it to get another it flew away and hid in a cupboard.

"You have to be firm with her," King Steve said, setting aside his paper. "She's been hearing too much about the evils of refined sugar, and"—he raised his voice—"not enough about minding her own business." There was an angry scratching from deep in the cupboard, but the spoon didn't come out.

"I have this for you." I reached in my pocket, and the walls rippled at me as three Kingsmen started to shift into view. I froze. "It's a card."

"A card. Thank you." King Steve held out his hand. He didn't even glance at his guards.

"Exactly. I mean, it's a thank-you card." I maneuvered the bright purple card out of my pocket and handed it over—slowly. "It's my mom's idea. I mean, you can thank me all you want, but Mom suggested it. For taking this on yourself."

"Alexa asked me to." King Steve paused. "She is my . . . close friend. And my situation is not one that promotes friendships." (Alexa shook her head and muttered something about *sappy*.)

King Steve helped me to the sweets himself, which was only partly his being nice and partly because whenever I moved, the Kingsmen would start fading into being. One stationed himself right by me, and another behind King Steve's chair, so it was better if I just sat still and didn't make any abrupt gestures. He handed me a loaded plate, and I pulled one cookie apart slowly, hoping for strawberry, knowing I'd still have to eat it if it was apricot.

They were all strawberry.

King Steve set his cup down and said, "Abby, you know why I asked you to come here."

"Alexa said you were going to sentence Barbarian Mike," I said.

He nodded. "Quite harshly too. Before I close the case, I'd like to hear your version of events."

"I'm not sure if there's anything left to tell that I haven't told everybody already."

"Still, I would appreciate it if you refreshed my memory."

So I told him about how we stopped at the sideshow and saw the nice ord who was employed, not imprisoned, and how Peter and I had recognized Barbarian Mike and his girlfriend, and Peter ran off and I followed. I told him about the old building where we sat all night while Trixie chucked rocks at me. And that the next day I tried to get away again and this time it worked.

I told him about all the other stuff, too, like how everyone was super-careful around me for a while after that but eventually they went back to normal, thank goodness, except for Peter, but I didn't tell him about that. And then Alexa said that Becky told her she had to come wake me up every now and again because I was having nightmares. I told Alexa that was supposed to be *private* (because who wants to seem like a baby who gets bad dreams in front of the king?) and besides, it's not like I could sue Barbarian Mike and Trixie for lack of sleep or anything like that.

King Steve said, "Technically, you could file a complaint for personal suffering due to actions taken therein, et cetera. Personally, I'm willing to stack on as many claims as possible, even if they were to be brought into effect retroactively." He smiled at Alexa. She eyed him back pointedly, somewhere between glaring and smiling. "Any other aches or pains?" he continued, turning back to me. "Splinters?"

"No splinters. I don't even have any scars—look." I held my arms out for inspection. Jeremy was still baffled at how it managed to heal up so clean and neat without a single drop of magic. "I . . . had a sore throat for a little bit because I screamed a lot."

"Wonderful. Sore throats carry a very serious penalty."

"Seriously?"

"Very serious," King Steve informed me. "I think that would fall under the heading of emotional distress. And it's more a matter of the judge determining if the complaint is valid. Fortunately for you, I am the judge in this case, and I'm in a humor to determine that any complaint you make is valid."

"Is that fair?" I asked.

Alexa choked on her tea. "Fair?"

King Steve shrugged. "I am not overly concerned with fairness where kidnappers are concerned."

We had to go over everything a couple of times to get it all straight. The king asked us to stay for dinner, but by the time we finished I had to head back to school to get in by curfew. King Steve walked us to the door of his private quarters and paused. "I have to invite you to witness the sentence carried out," he began. "It's standard practice, and as the victim you have a right to be there. So, Miss Abigail Hale, you are hereby formally invited to see the sentence carried out against one Barbarian Mike. But I'm asking you not to come. It's not a pleasant thing to witness, even if you have seen it a hundred times. It's not the sort of thing a little girl should ever have to see."

"I won't," I promised.

"Thank you. Just know that he will never bother you or anyone else again."

"What's going to happen to him?" I asked, thinking about Peter's hatred for Barbarian Mike.

"Well, the sentence is severe when you're dealing with treason."

"Treason?"

King Steve looked at Alexa. Alexa looked at King Steve. "Yes," she finally said. "Treason."

"But I thought that's only for the most serious crimes." I gaped. "Betraying the country. Attacks against the royal family."

"It is applicable to a certain number of other charges," King Steve answered. "And kidnapping an ord is one of then."

"So what are you going to do to him?" I asked.

"I'm going to Banish him." I could hear the capital letter when he said it. "And you promised you weren't going to come."

"No, I don't want to come." Nobody in their right mind wants to see that. Banishment isn't a simple "get out of here, we never want to see you again." It's a nasty business, and you end up in a nasty place, and even those who eventually return are shattered, broken shadows, jumping at birdsong and quaking in

232

the corners. "Can I see him?" I asked suddenly. "I'd like to . . . if that's okay. Before it happens."

King Steve lifted his eyebrows, but he said, "Yes, of course. If you wish it. He's been staying with us here at the palace. We could go right now, if you like."

CHAPTER 25

Barbarian Mike was vacationing in the palace dungeons, which were, as King Steve explained, reserved for his most exclusive guests. So it was a simple matter of finding the right staircase—there were several, mostly real but a few of them illusions, and all of them enchanted—and then heading down. (It was a simple matter, actually, for an ord.)

The stairs curled downward, below the wide windows and rich beauty of the palace, to where heavy dark stonework closed in around us. Past the afternoon light and the humid patter of rain on the paving stones to someplace dim and chilly, where the air began to condense on my skin.

The staircase, when we finally found the right one and it stopped shifting directions on us, leveled off into a small, narrow hallway, lined every now and then with dimly flickering torches. After I almost walked into a wall, King Steve offered me his arm. "This is, alas, one circumstance in which we have the advantage, my girl," he said, his eyes gleaming with a night-vision spell. And he was right. Down in the dungeons, it was barely light enough to see where you were going.

"You could always turn up the lights," I suggested as King Steve tugged me out of the way of something.

"I could." His voice was thoughtful. "The old king redecorated this place around the time my elder brother was born. I suppose he thought it wasn't intimidating enough, and, to be fair, my warden tells me that proper atmosphere does half his work for him. Don't worry, your eyes will adjust shortly. Everyone duck!" he called out cheerfully, putting a hand on my back and pushing me down. Something long and thin whistled as it sliced through the air right above our heads, glinting faintly. "Everyone still have their heads?"

"You're enjoying this, aren't you?" Alexa asked, and I could hear the suppressed laughter.

"Not in the least." King Steve guided me to the far edge of the hallway, the floor under our feet narrowing until we had to inch along with our backs to the wall. I could see well enough to make out the huge gaping darkness in the middle of the floor. An impatient, brassy hooting came from inside it. "Whose turn is it to feed the manticore?" King Steve asked.

The dungeons were mostly empty. It was a slow time of year, the king explained, when even criminal masterminds preferred to stay inside and plot as they waited for the end of the wet season. "We'll fill up again as soon as spring comes, but at the moment Mr. . . . Barbarian is our only guest. Isn't that so, Michael?" He came to a stop in front of a cell, thick black bars crossing between us and—*him*.

My eyes had adjusted, and I could see now. Well, I could see enough. The bars continued on every side of the cell, and I could make out the frost mottled along the jagged metalwork. Barbarian Mike was stretched out on a cot in the direct middle of the cell, as far away from any metal as he could get. No wonder; the cold and the damp together must have really stunk. His hair was matted, and he was wearing loose prison clothing—long sleeves and actual pants that covered up his muscles and made him seem smaller. He looked . . . It wasn't that he was cut up or beaten or anything like that. It was just that he looked like how I felt that one night.

One of the Kingsmen materialized enough to bang on Mike's cell and tell him to get up, he had a visitor. Barbarian Mike rolled his head to the side to look at us, sneered when he saw the king. It dropped away when he saw me. "Zo?" And he rushed over, bare feet on cold iron, to the front of the cell, crouching down to look me in the eye. "You're here, you came!"

"I came," I said.

"Trix—" Barbarian Mike gripped the bars, though that had to hurt. "Do you know what happened to Trixie? Nobody will tell me," he said, his voice ragged.

"I don't know."

"Where is she? No, don't, never mind," he said quickly, glancing at King Steve. "Don't tell me that." The frost had started to eat its way up his fingers, freezing the fists clenched around the bars. "Last time I saw her, she was running—trying, anyway. Her knee looked like it hurt pretty bad. She's probably seeing red over that. You tell her—when you see her again, you tell her from *me*—not to break anything, okay?" His grin was a white flash in the dim light. "Not that she ever listens to me anyway. "Do you at least know if she's okay?" Barbarian Mike continued.

"No one does. She disappeared," I told him, because it seemed like he should be told.

He rested his head against his hands, and it took a second to realize he was chuckling. "She always was one for running and hiding. No, you won't see her again, not for a long time, not if you looked for a hundred years."

"I came to tell the king what you did to me," I said.

He nodded. His sleeves had gone stiff as ice, and his skin was starting to look off. Gray. "She's the clever one. She'll have found a way out of this place, got low, and she'll stay there until you stop looking for her and she can get on with her life."

"They're going to Banish you," I said.

Barbarian Mike went quiet, and his grin faded. "When?"

"I don't know."

"Soon enough," King Steve supplied. "We have some minor details to take care of first."

"Do it now," Barbarian Mike said. "Get it over with."

King Steve *tsked*. "Now, now, Michael. When you say things like that it makes us feel as though you do not appreciate our hospitality."

Barbarian Mike looked up at the king through his matted

hair and sighed, wheezing a little because his chest was going to ice. "She's just . . . an ord. No . . . offense, Zo."

When someone says *no offense* you're supposed to say *none taken* or something like that, even when some is taken, just to be polite. But polite or not, the words weren't there, and I didn't want them anyway. "My name is Abby."

"Sure, sure. I still say you look like a Zoe," he said. Kindly. Teasing. And he *winked* at me. As if it were a private joke between us. I wondered, if I hit him, would he shatter into a thousand pieces? I felt Alexa's arm go around my shoulders.

I wish I hadn't gone down there. I wish he hadn't kidnapped me. Except that wasn't really true. If they hadn't gotten me, they would have gotten someone else. I couldn't wish away what happened; I wouldn't, even if I wanted to. But looking at him, I felt sorry. I just wasn't sure for who.

"Are you satisfied?" King Steve asked me, and I said yes, even though I wasn't, and didn't know if I ever could be. I wanted to go home.

CHAPTER 26

Sentencing criminals is a matter of public record, or so Alexa told me. I guess that's how word got out. When people learned that the king was going to Banish a regular, magical, human person (with an attractive headshot) because he tried to kidnap one ord, they weren't happy. I wasn't sure how unhappy, since tucked inside the school, we only heard about it from Alexa. I tried to nose around, but my family wouldn't tell me anything. Mr. O'Hara was willing to help out by casting up old newspapers, and I found a lot of angry letters to the editor. Some half-finished graffiti—words I was really glad hadn't been finished—showed up on the wall outside the school. Becky and Cook Bella took turns going out with a bucket to scrub them off. And Mrs. Murphy admitted that there'd been a few "unpleasant" letters sent to the school. She wouldn't tell me what was in them.

But as the days passed, the anger died down. King Steve is the law, and the law is absolute, so if you're angry the only thing you can do is get over it.

Or you can do something about it. You can try, at least. That's what Trixie decided to do.

◆ ◆ ◆

It was a dark and stormy night, and Becky had headed out with one or two of her best students to Haven Park, up on Ninety-Sixth. Occasionally the older kids were hired out on a job, a win-win situation for everyone because sometimes there were problems a magic person couldn't deal with, and it gave us a little real-world experience and a couple of bucks. This time someone had tossed a bunch of nasty charms around the park, probably as a joke. Because killing plants, driving birds crazy, and making every park sanitation worker retch violently is apparently *hysterical*.

We were still in the dining hall when the two students returned, dirty and wild eyed. It was only when Dimitrios lifted one of the kids in the air by his shirt and growled, "Where is she?" that we noticed Becky was not with them.

"Seventy-Second Street," the boy choked out. "Red caps. Becky put us on a carpet and went after them."

Mrs. Murphy put a hand on Dimitrios's arm and helped him slowly lower the boy to the ground. "Thank you, Mr. Parris. Dimitrios, if you would go look for her."

Dimitrios called to another minotaur, and the two of them charged out.

As soon as they were gone, Mrs. Murphy demanded to know what had happened. The two kids looked at each other, until one shrugged and started to explain. "The job went fine, right? A couple of hours picking up charms, no problem. We're heading back, and all of the trolleys are full or else they're not letting Greenies on, so Becky tells us we're going to walk instead."

"And?" Mrs. Murphy prompted when he paused.

"And we're about halfway when Becky sees the red caps watching us."

There was a sudden, icy silence, and then a frightened murmur passed through the room. The rain had been slacking off with the arrival of spring, but it wasn't finished yet. It wasn't dry. We were supposed to have some time.

"And there's this taxi carpet coming by, and Becky shoves us on it and heads after the caps herself."

Mrs. Murphy thanked the boy and let him leave to clean up. Mr. O'Hara and Ms. Macartney joined Mrs. Murphy, close enough for our table to overhear. Mr. O'Hara muttered, "Red caps. Already. I'll contact Alexa." Mrs. Murphy nodded, and he made his way toward the door.

"This is out of the ordinary," Ms. Macartney remarked. She kept her voice low, but the dining hall was quiet enough that we could hear her. "They should still be hibernating. It's far too early for them to be out and about."

"Unfortunately we are well aware how difficult hibernation is for them if they haven't eaten enough. Considering our king's numerous restrictions, it wouldn't be surprising if hunger woke them early," Mrs. Murphy replied.

"Hungry enough to approach us openly?" Ms. Marcartney shook her head. "What if someone saw them? What—" She dropped her voice. "If there was a death. Their entire conclave would be threatened by retaliation. They cannot be that stupid, to risk that. There has to be something else going on."

"Maybe. Then again, starvation makes people, and creatures, do foolish things."

"We had such a good fall," Ms. Macartney said, her voice a low ache. "We didn't lose anyone last year."

"Cheer up, Caroline," Mrs. Murphy said. "We still haven't lost anyone."

"You are such a comfort," Ms. Macartney replied.

Becky wasn't back by lights-out, so the Teaching Trio took over the final check-in, assuring us all that if there was anyone to *not* be worried about, it was Becky. She and Dimitrios were more than capable of handling a couple of goblins. Still, I kept waking up, hoping to hear Dimitrios's hooves in the hallway, the jingle of Becky's belt as she went into her room. But I never heard anything.

The third or fourth time I woke up, I was certain that I'd heard something. But what it was escaped me—until something scraped at the window. I pushed back the covers and the bed squeaked as I stood; the scratching paused. It was a clear night, and moonlight flooded through my window. The sound had definitely come from the right window. My window.

I took a step toward it—or I was about to—when I saw something near the latch.

The latch. *There were scratches in the glass by the latch.*

I was at the door when the window crashed inward. I ran out and slammed the door behind me, but it didn't lock on the

242

outside. There was a sound, high pitched and keening, and the scratch of something sharp; I grabbed for the handle, but the door jerked back, torn off its hinges, and I was yanked back inside the room. Something tackled me to the ground.

It was a goblin, a red cap. Smaller than me, but stronger than you'd think, seeing it. There were strange charms dripping off its wrists and ankles, and its hands were so cold they burned against my skin. It started dragging me toward the window and it was *so strong*, but I kicked and wriggled to get free until it had to stop and try to tie my hands together. What did Becky say to do with a red cap? WHAT DID BECKY SAY? And then I remembered and flung myself at it, snatched the cap from its head, and twisted it. I wrung it dry, tried to get out every drop and not think about what exactly those drops were made of. The goblin howled in pain and swatted me back, enough that I could kick myself away and scramble for the door.

The goblin was still braying on the floor when long spindly fingers curled over the broken windowsill and a second one climbed through. I saw it for just an instant and then there was a rush of air as it slammed into me, and we went rolling out into the hallway and smashed into the wall. I could hear screaming, through the doors, from other rooms. I could feel it through the floor. Except it wasn't all screaming—some of it was roaring.

Then the world lurched, and the goblin was torn off me. It was Cesar—skinny little cheating Cesar—tearing into the red cap with a power so fierce it scared me almost as much as the goblins had.

The hallway was alive with the crack of breaking wood and

shattering glass as I raced toward Becky's room. An alarm sounded—shrill and piercing. The door to Eila and Naija's room opened, and they stumbled out, confused, fear quickly erasing their tiredness. Naija shouted something and I ran back and grabbed their hands, dragging them with me.

We reached Fran's room, two doors down from Becky's. The door was broken and I had to drag it aside. Inside, two goblins were struggling to tie Fran's hands and feet, but she was kicking, punching. I ran to her and tried to grab one of the goblins, but Fran kicked out desperately and caught me in the face. I reeled back, pain buzzing through my head. Eila and Naija screamed and, moving together, pounced on the other goblin. It tumbled back and they landed on it, pounding and screeching, until all it could do was try and fight them off. The first goblin, still focused on Fran, tossed her on its shoulders and carried her to the open window. It reached through, clung to the stone outside, and swung out with her. Fran grabbed for the window handle, but it broke off in her hands. I dived for her, grabbed for her wrists, her hands—she was calling *Abby please, Abby please, please, Abby*—but the goblin wrenched, and her fingers slipped through mine, and she disappeared.

Jumping after her wouldn't have done any good, but I was halfway through the window when I froze. What stopped me was the sight of the red caps, dozens of them, skittering their way up the sides of the building. Climbing in and out of windows, handing hollering bundles to other goblins.

I slid off the desk mechanically and grabbed Eila. We had to pry Naija's hands off the goblin and drag her back into the hall.

It felt like we'd been in Fran's room forever, but I realized later it couldn't have been more than a minute. The minotaurs were there when we came out. One charged over to us and I couldn't hear what he was shouting above the alarm, but he was pointing to the doors at the end of the hallway. Naija pulled me toward the stairway. Eila was yelling "Out! Out now!" and I went with them, one sluggish foot in front of the other. But my mind wasn't there with them. It was back in Fran's room, staring out the window.

The minotaur was already running down the hallway, throwing open doors. We ducked out of the way as Mr. O'Hara, magic crackling around him, clambered up the stairs with two other minotaurs. They shouted something to us about the vault, gathering in the vault. "It should be clear by now!" Mr. O'Hara shouted over his shoulder.

He was about to rush down our hallway, but one of the minotaurs stopped him—"Upstairs, they need you upstairs!"—and Mr. O'Hara leaped up, passing through the ceiling with a soft *zuzz*. Naija tugged on my arm, tried to pull me back into the stairway. "Abby, please, please, we must get out of this place."

I shook my head, watching as the minotaurs yelled and went after something in Cesar's room.

"Abby," Eila said. Her voice was hard and hot, like a parent's voice when you did something wrong. "We need to go down the stairs right now." But I started running down the hall. *No . . .* Past the rows of open doors and empty rooms. *No no no no no no.* To Fred and Peter's room.

Inside, the room was torn apart—furniture broken, books

everywhere, the window busted open. In the same moment I spotted a wrinkled red-capped little monster starting to climb out the window, and a stick. A big, heavy stick, like a mage's staff. I think it was a broken part of the bed. I picked it up and ran over, swinging as I ran, and *crack!* The goblin toppled back, and I flung myself on it, not thinking, clawing at its cap. It came free with a little sucking pop. The goblin screeched in pain.

"Not right! Not fair!" it howled. "Give us back our cap! Give it back!" I didn't, and I was afraid of myself in that moment. "We are *sorry!* We didn't mean any harm! We are just so hungry! She said—she said she would help us, and then she doesn't let us eat anything!"

"She?" It took me a second to realize that was my voice.

"She, she!" the goblin agreed. "She take half, we take half. It's not fair, she doesn't need half. She need one, she said she need *one* for dungeon! *I'm so hungry!*" It started scratching at its head, writhing, desperate.

It's funny how you can know something even before your brain completely catches up. Sometimes you don't need the whole puzzle. The *she* and *dungeon* were enough.

Then there was a minotaur, holding the goblin at spear point, and O'Hara's voice, so gentle it didn't seem real, saying, "All right there, Abby. It's all right now. I'll take this, here we go," and he eased my fingers open to take the cap away. "That was very clever of you. You're all right?"

"I'm all right," I echoed.

"Wonderful. Your parents would be very angry with us if we let anything happen to you. Since you're quite all right, I

* * *

think you should go down to the vault now. Everyone's in the vault, it's nice and safe down there. Do you think you can go on your own? The route is safe, but do you want someone to come with you?"

"I can go on my own," I said, and it sounded and felt like my voice. It'd be harder to get away if someone was with me.

Mr. O'Hara nodded, patting my shoulder, and I headed out.

The stairway was quiet, but there was more crashing and yelling on the first floor. I didn't stop to check it out, but I did see a minotaur run at a goblin on all fours, face shining with determination.

Then I was out the front door. The courtyard was lit up, and Mrs. Murphy and Ms. Macartney were herding students to the vault. There was shouting and noise and above it all Mrs. Murphy's voice telling everyone to remain calm, so it really wasn't that hard to slip into the dark shadows of the alcove. The vault would have weapons, but I'd never get back out. Cook Bella had a glittery set of knives in a locked drawer in the kitchen, but even if I could smash it open and get one I wouldn't know what to do with it. I glanced back at the dorm; I could see flashes of light through the windows and dark shapes skittering down the walls.

The main gate opened with a *creak* that I hoped no one heard. I started running.

CHAPTER 27

It had stopped raining at some point. The air was heavy, and warm with the first hint of spring, and the cobblestones were slick with rain under my bare feet—I really should have grabbed some shoes before running out. I heard sirens tearing through the night, caught the flashing lights of police carpets behind me, heading toward the school, but the rest of the streets were dead quiet. It was eerie; Rothermere is supposed to be the city that never sleeps, but at four in the morning, the streets were empty.

Good thing Becky had us run so much. I wasn't even winded when I reached the castle. The plaza circling the castle is wide and open and, at that time of the night, completely abandoned. I didn't see any guards—visible or invisible—but that didn't mean no one was watching, so I kept to the alleys. And I waited.

That was the hardest part. Looking back it felt like one endless moment, eyes and ears open, *willing* her to show up. She had to show up.

And then, wonderfully, from a few alleys away—I heard her voice, yelling at someone. No one else could say *ord* with that level of disgust. I ran over, almost forgetting for a second not to run directly out onto castle grounds.

She was in a dark little corner of a dark little alley. *Trixie.* Worn and pale and ragged and . . . bandaged. Her arms were wrapped up, hand to shoulder, and most of her legs, until she looked like an escaped mummy. She was hissing, "You will listen to me if you want to live," as she struggled with—

"*Peter!*" It came out a lot louder than I intended. He looked rumpled and exhausted and annoyed, but he looked okay, other than the fact that Trixie had his arm twisted so far behind his back that he was on tiptoes. They looked up at my shout, and for a second they both had the exact same surprised expression. And then Peter tried to shove Trixie and get away, yelling "Abby, get out of here!" but she held on, almost absent-mindedly. Because she was looking at me now. Glaring at me.

"You?" Trixie's cry was as hot and harsh as brimstone. "Of course. Of *course* you're alive."

"Are you okay?" I ran toward Peter, but he pushed me away one-armed and yelled for me to go *away*, go *away* as Trixie started cursing about me turning up more times than an enchanted ring. "Fred—Fran—they took Fran, and the goblin said something about . . . divvying them up."

Trixie was still spitting like a basilisk. "I *told* those goblins—and when they didn't come back with you, I *hoped* you were dead."

"She sold them," Peter said, and the anger in his voice almost covered the way it broke. "She gave some to the red caps and she sold the rest."

"S-sold?" The shock made me stumble. "How? To who?"

Trixie gave a patronizingly irritated sigh. "I have had time to think about this. To plan. And, believe me, it's not hard to find buyers, especially with your school cornering the market." She unhooked a pouch from her belt and tossed it at me; it jingled expensively when it hit the pavement. "*That* will give me and Mike the means to go wherever we need to hide from your king, with enough left over for our next six adventures. Almost makes me consider ord dealing professionally."

I stared at the pouch, wondering how much was in it. Then I decided I didn't really care.

"Now, it is so nice seeing you again," Trixie continued, yanking on Peter's arm until he cried out, "but your friend and I have some business to take care of."

"Stop right there." I tried to sound like the heroes in action movies. They always say that stuff to let the bad guys know they mean business, and then the bad guys always have a moment of *oh no* when they realize they're in trouble because the hero is not going to let them get away with it.

Trixie laughed.

"I mean it," I said, pointing my finger at her. "Let him go."

"No," Trixie said, still laughing. Then her face went bitter as she took a step closer to me. "Tell me, little ord. How exactly are you going to stop me?"

"I'm, I'm not," I said, telling myself *don't back up, don't back up* as she took another step. "I'll help you."

* * *

Trixie bore down on me, slow and steady, until we were face to, well, belly button. She cupped my chin with one mummified hand and nudged it up so she could smirk down at me. "Help me. How?"

"Abby, *shut up*," Peter said.

I ignored him. "I'll get Barbarian Mike out. That's why you're here, right?" I rushed on. "To break him out. You can't go in yourself, there are shields and wards and the magic is too strong. That's what you need one of us for. Let Peter and the others go, and I'll do it. I'll do anything you want and afterward, I'll go with you. You guys needed an ord, right? I'll go with you, free of charge." I really hoped I didn't sound as desperate as I thought I did. "Just let him go. That's all. Just let him go."

Trixie wasn't laughing anymore. "How noble. But it didn't work when he tried it"—she gave Peter's arm a sharp jerk—"and I'm certainly not going to listen to the little brat who ruined everything," she finished on a growl.

She started dragging Peter toward the plaza. I raced to block her, arms out. "No, no, no, you want me—*me*, not him, because I've seen him. Barbarian Mike." That stopped her. She was still glaring at me, but her eyes were speculative. "I asked King Steve if I could see him—Mike. I know where his cell is. I know what staircase to use." I jabbed a finger at Peter. "*He* probably doesn't even know about the giant spider."

Trixie arched an eyebrow. "You're making that up."

"I am *not*," I insisted. "And, and, and—you're right. I am the brat who ruined everything. The king likes me. And that's why he came down so hard on Mike. If you had kidnapped anybody else, you wouldn't be here now, and Mike wouldn't be in there. The two of you, you would have gotten a stern talking to and been sent packing. But you didn't."

Trixie's face grew harder and darker as I talked, and I could smell the magic gathering around her, thick and smoldering. "Do you know what they're going to do to him?" Her free hand wrapped around my neck, and I had to force myself not to scream and kick and flail. "Do you know what I had to do to get those goblins on my side?"

Then she took a deep breath and smiled. "All right, then. If you're so eager to repay your debt—"

"Let him go first," I said, nodding toward Peter.

"No. Don't think for one second that I trust you to go off like a good little ord and rescue Mike just because you said you would. You go break Mike out, and I'll use the time to think up all the lovely things I can do to your friend if you don't return. When Mike is standing here before me, safe and sound, then we can reconsider. Oh, and—" She nodded at the money pouch on the ground. "If you wouldn't mind."

I crouched down and carefully picked up the leather bag. Peter watched as I hooked it back on her belt. "Don't do this," he said, staring into me. "Please. Don't go."

"We're not friends," I told him, squeezing my eyes shut. I didn't want to look at him. "I don't have to listen to you."

Trixie twisted a leisurely hand through my hair and pulled me away. She nodded to the castle.

"All right," I said. "Come with me."

CHAPTER 28

The dungeon entrance, like the main doors for the palace, was the sort of thing you couldn't really pass by and not notice. It was a massive set of double doors—huge and heavy and carved with intimidating, eye-catching runes. The doors were bolted shut with an immense bar that, according to the guidebooks, had been forged out of ogre clubs.

I ran straight past it. Like the main entrance, those doors were just for show. I led Trixie (dragging Peter as he tried to dig his heels in) through the shadows to an alley right across from the little hidden door Alexa and I had used the day we'd come for tea. After we'd visited Barbarian Mike, King Steve had brought us up and out through the same door, so I figured I could backtrack my steps.

"Wait here," I told her breathlessly. "I'll be back."

I raced across the wide-open plaza to the castle, hoping somebody would see me. This was the royal palace, after all, they had to have eyes out. The castle itself was probably watching, and if it was watching, it could tell somebody and I'd get some help. Right?

Alexa had needed a good fifteen minutes to open the door the last time we were here. I just had to hold my breath and charge through.

The hallway was the same—short and beige, with an ordinary door at the end and little (in)visible portals all along the walls, and the two guards—*guards*, oh, thank goodness, I knew there had to be somebody. I think I scared them a little, because I basically launched myself at them and started babbling. "Please, please, you have to help me, Trixie's out there and she's got Peter and she's going to hurt him, she already hurt him—"

One of the guards, the older one with the gruff voice and the beard, pried me off, set me on my feet, and demanded that I *calm down*. "What do you think you're doing? How did you get in here?"

But the other guard, the younger one with the serious face and solemn blue eyes, crouched down in front of me. "Are you hurt?"

"What?" I gasped, and it took me a second. Oh. My nightgown. The red caps. *Oh*. "It's a long story, and I don't have *time*—"

He put a hand on my elbow because relief was making me a little shaky. "What's your name?"

"Abby Hale. You have to help me, this is an *emergency!*"

"Tell me," he said.

The older guard scoffed. "Don't bother, Ned. Look, little girl, this is very funny, but it's a little too early for practical jokes."

⁎ ⁎ ⁎

"It's not a joke!" I insisted.

"I don't know how you got in here," he continued, shaking his head, "but this is a dangerous place and you're committing a crime by being here. We're going to have to call the cops."

"Yes, please, call the cops, call *anyone*, but she's out there and someone has to stop her—"

"Tell me," the second guard repeated.

I took a deep breath and tried explaining again. "I'm an ord. Trixie, this woman, she kidnapped a boy from my school, and she said she would hurt him if I didn't come in here and try and get her friend. He's in the dungeon because the two of them tried to kidnap me before except he got caught, and then she set red caps on the school. She said they could take us kids as payment!"

The younger guard looked up at his partner. "I think you'd better wake the king."

"The king's sleeping," the older guard replied.

"That's why I said wake him."

"Over a kid?" The older guard crossed his arms, and I had to fight to keep from bouncing up and down on my feet. Why were they still *talking*?

The younger guard sighed and stood. "I'll wake him. Wait here," he told me, and disappeared.

The remaining guard stared me down a bit before asking, "You really an ord, then?" When I nodded, he pointed to the far end of the hallway and told me to go over there and keep still. He barely looked at me. He didn't even care.

I wanted to wait for the other guard, to see what happened.

To see if he brought help. But then I remembered how Peter screamed when Trixie twisted his arm, and I knew I couldn't wait any longer. I followed my nose to the right portal and sprinted through.

Either the staircase was asleep or it remembered me, because I was able to corkscrew straight down without any shifts or trick steps. It was dim and I was going too fast—taking steps two and three at a time when I could manage it—I slipped a couple times and wrenched my foot, bad enough that I had to run one hand along the wall for support as I hopped down the steps. Fortunately, the wall had cracks and carvings that I could cling to. Unfortunately I ended up grabbing the wrong carving and set off a crisscrossing spiderweb of flames throughout the rest of the stairway. I had a moment of "I'm going to be burned alive" panic, but when I wasn't, it was followed by an "oh thank goodness it's just magical fire" relief. Even so, the sudden, fiery light seared my eyes; I had to squeeze them shut and find the way with my hands until my eyes adjusted.

Another twist in the staircase, and I felt a hint of coolness beyond the fire. I threw myself at it blindly and tumbled out onto the hard, level floor of the dungeon.

Behind me the staircase was still flaming and it was bright enough that I could see where I was going. Maybe I *could* do this. I mean, I'd been here once before—with King Steve. The icy, slicing thing overhead—I remembered to duck . . . except this time it didn't come. And then the manticore pit. *That* was still there. In the light, I could see the illusion of floor covering it, and the dark, gaping space beneath. I plastered myself to the wall as I inched along the narrow ledge. A soft, almost sooth-ing, hooting sound drifted up from the hole in the floor.

Then solid stones stretched out under my feet again, and I scrambled over to Barbarian Mike's cell.

His cell door was barred—*barred*, with one of those sliding-bolt things, not even a proper lock. I jerked the bolt back loudly and dragged the cell door open.

Barbarian Mike looked like he'd been Banished already. He was on his cot, arms and legs shackled (that was new), eyes closed, curled in on himself. *Like Fran*, I thought, and it churned like acid in my stomach. He didn't move when I ran over; I grabbed one of his arms and shook.

He had his fingers around my neck before I realized it. Then he stopped and blinked. "What're—"

"Trixie sent me."

This took a couple seconds to sink in. When it did, he looped his shackled arms around me and crushed me in a hug. I think he might have been crying.

I tried to shove myself free. "We have to hurry. We don't have a lot of time."

He let me go, a wide grin splitting his face. "Anything you say."

I didn't like taking off his shackles, but I didn't think I had a choice if I wanted to get him out. His shackles were secured with a simple toggle latch, although, okay, Barbarian Mike did look unpleasantly gray until I peeled them off, and they left these weird bubbly marks on his skin that he wouldn't stop rubbing.

257
* * *

Barbarian Mike raced out of the cell, then stamped his feet a couple times and started bounding off the way I'd come. And part of me wanted to let him go that way. I really did. Let him drop into the manticore pit, or roast alive in the stairway. Or, even better, help him get through all that and lead him back up to that hallway, where there'd be, hopefully, cops or guards or Kingsmen waiting. I wanted to, but I couldn't; I needed to get him to Trixie, or Peter would suffer.

I grabbed his arm. "Not that way, you can't go that way. It's, uh, on fire. Do you know any other way out? Maybe seen the guards coming and going?"

Barbarian Mike looked around. "This way," he said, nodding in the other direction. "Guards always bring food from over here."

There were a couple of shock traps along the hallway—we hadn't gotten to them in school, but it didn't matter because Barbarian Mike would just grit his teeth and charge through, though a couple of bolts made his hair stand on end. As far as I could tell, that was his strategy for everything. I had to pull him back before he barreled into a loop and got caught running the same three feet of hallway over and over.

But he was right. There was a door. I almost ran straight by it at first, because, for one, it wasn't oozing magic like every other trap and trigger in the place. And, for another, it blended in with the rest of the stone wall. But it was just a little . . . off, the stones a little too regular and even, not quite matching the rest of the wall. I tugged Barbarian Mike to a stop. "Wait, wait, wait. Here."

He looked it over and cursed.

"What? What is it?" I demanded.

"It's a puzzle door. See?" He cast a light, held it up so we could get a better look. "These stones, you slide them around, right?" He shifted a couple of stones; they slid back and forth easily. "You get the right pattern, and the door opens."

"What's the right pattern?"

Barbarian Mike shrugged. "Search me. They're usually easy to figure out. Markings you have to match up, or get the red block from the bottom up to the top, something like that," he added, scanning the door. "Shouldn't be too hard to figure out." He started shifting stones around. "You just have to be careful, though, because if you get the wrong pattern a couple times—"

The sound knocked me back. A screeching, pounding wailing that made the air rattle and the ground throb. It blared up through the floor, jangled out of the walls, until my bones were buzzing with the sound of it. King Steve told me later that they modeled the alarm system on the cries of real-life banshees. Hearing that, you can tell why banshees are so successful; after a few minutes of that screeching, you would do anything just so you don't have to hear it anymore.

I clapped my hands over my ears, almost choking on panic. Could they hear that in the rest of the castle? On the street? Could Trixie hear it? How could anyone *not* hear it?

"Okay, so that's not it!" Barbarian Mike bellowed amicably. "How about you give it a go?" And he looked so calm, so relaxed, I wanted to scream at him—not words, just scream, the way the alarm was screaming.

On the far end of the corridor, on the opposite side of the dungeon, the fire suddenly cut off from the staircase, slamming us into darkness. Then wall torches flared up, turning the hall-way bright as day. Oh, sure, *now* someone was coming.

I turned and ran back to Mike's cell, and yanked the iron bolt out of the door. It slid free easily, which made me think that if I got out of this and saw King Steve again, I was going to make him put actual chains on the actual cell and they were going to have a real, nonmagical lock and it was going to be as big as my head. The bolt was heavy, heavy enough that my arms ached from carrying it by the time I got back to Barbarian Mike.

Anger makes you strong, or at least it makes you able to pretend you are. I swung the bolt back and, with a yell, smashed it into the door. The stones cracked. I swung again and again as stones popped free and went flying and the door crumpled inward.

I could see shadows now on the staircase behind us. Barbar-ian Mike caught my arms just as I was about to swing forward again, and pushed the door open one-handed. It teetered slightly, and crashed against the wall, revealing what appeared to be a small, empty infirmary. Above one length of counter was a win-dow, and the window led to the street.

I scrambled through first, but the window was a little small for Barbarian Mike, and I had to help him, yanking on his arms until he finally popped free. I fell backward on the smooth pavement of the plaza, and he pushed himself up and left me behind, running down the street and bellowing Trixie's name.

And Trixie came right out into the open dragging Peter with

* * *

her. Barbarian Mike's voice broke when he saw her. Peter looked okay. Trixie had him by the hair, and he was cradling his arm, but he looked okay, and the second she saw Mike she let go of Peter and ran. She didn't even look to see if there were any guards coming. She just ran straight for Mike, and took a couple of leaping steps, and they collided. Arms wrapped around each other, faces pressed together, in a clutching, smooshing, desperate kiss. It was like a scene from one of Gil's books.

They really should have paid more attention. Guards streamed out the window, poured around me, heading for them.

I didn't watch. I didn't care. I ran for Peter, which was more of a limp because by that time my ankle seemed to remember twisting on the stairs and wanted to make up for lost time. I grabbed for him, and tripped on the last step. Peter tried to catch me, and we ended up awkwardly half sitting on the ground.

A little ways away, Trixie and Mike battled and blasted at the guards, but they were hampered by the fact that they wouldn't let go of each other.

Peter grinned at me, and it was his first smile in so long it felt like his first smile ever. "You look terrible," he said.

I leaned against him and laughed.

✳ ✳ ✳

CHAPTER 29

It's strange how I remember images, moments most of all. The alarm made everything blur together, but I remember the light shining oddly off Barbarian Mike's and Trixie's clasped hands as they were forced to surrender. I remember the confused look on one Kingsman's face as he tried to cast me and Peter into a containment spell (they didn't realize we were the victims at that point). I remember seeing one Kingsman, crouched down in front of me, seeing his mouth move as he said my name, realizing he *knew* my name, but not hearing it because that awful alarm was still screaming. He'd recognized me and convinced the others to stop trying to put us under arrest. Then he called for help for Peter. They took us into the palace, and I hobbled along until one of the Kingsmen shook his head and swooped me up in his arms. They took us into the small doctor's office, and I remember waiting with Peter under the glaring lights and realizing that the alarms hadn't followed us, that the pounding was coming from my own ears.

We were barely there five minutes when Alexa burst in. She choked something out, I couldn't hear what, and threw her arms around me.

"What do you think," she finally managed, "what do you think I felt like, getting a call in the middle of the night that the school's been attacked, and I show up to find out you're not there?" And she started crying. I'd never seen Alexa cry. Mom and Dad said she hadn't cried since she was sixteen, when she begged them not to send her back to school after summer break. "I found Becky, and we tore through the goblin conclaves—all of them in the city! I didn't wait for permission, I didn't even ask! I threatened—" She put her hands over her mouth and crumbled.

I hugged her; she hugged back until it hurt.

"Did you find the other kids? The ones that were taken?" I asked when she calmed.

Alexa nodded, and I could almost see her pulling herself back together. "Most of them." Then she added, at seeing Peter's blank look of horror, "They're all *alive*. Fred was there. We got him back, he's fine. But . . ." She paused for a very long time. "We're still tracking down some of the other kids. The ones Trixie sold."

"Fran?" I asked.

"Sold," Peter said. He gripped my hand. "She was sold. I saw them take her away."

· · ·

Afterward, Alexa took us back to the school. She guided us past the police barriers, through the courtyard to the dining hall—me on piggyback because the doctor confirmed my ankle was probably sprained and, after wrapping it up, told me to keep off it as much as possible.

Inside the dining hall, all the tables had been pushed aside and there were blankets and pillows and cushions lined up on the floor for everyone to sleep on. It was like that first night with the red caps all over again, when we'd had to stay in the lounge. Except nobody was really sleeping. They lay there, staring at the ceiling, or the windows, or screwed up in their blankets so tight they'd probably have to be cut out. Mr. O'Hara sat in the middle of a circle of kids, reading aloud. It sounded like an adventure novel, something silly and empty and fun, like he never would have taught in class. Ms. Macartney was in a back corner, talking to a group of older students and scouring what looked like a map. And Mrs. Murphy walked up and down the rows, crouching down for a soft word here, a soothing hand there.

And Fred? He was okay. He was scratched up but he was okay, and he was here, and he was safe. He bounded over a couple of curled-up students, and I slid off Alexa's back, and we bounced up and down like idiots. Or tried to, anyway. And we even dragged Peter in, and he let us, because there are some moments when you don't get to be standoffish, when it's just not possible.

* * *

CHAPTER 30

Mom and Dad were really, really, *really* mad at me, by the way. Alexa called them, of course, and they came racing up with Ms. Whittleby to yell at us.

I couldn't blame them. I mean, it was like our lives were stuck in this horrible game of repeat: something bad would happen, and they'd come rushing up to Rothermere in a panic. Mom wanted to know if I was *trying* to give her a heart attack, and I said yes, and she said very funny, young lady, and grounded me for seventy-five years. Dad said I could get time off for good behavior, contingent upon no more middle-of-the-night phone calls to say something bad had happened to their daughter.

"What happened at Fall Fest wasn't the middle of the night," I protested. "It was morning. Like, before noon morning."

He gave me the "you know what I mean" look, and said, "Talking back does not constitute good behavior."

. . .

In the moments right after the attack, it felt like we were never going to smile again, never be happy, never close our eyes without having nightmares. But we did. Time passed, and we did all of those things. Just not right away.

Becky took it harder than any of the other teachers. She was red eyed and quiet for days on end, wandering around the grounds, muttering to herself about what good were safety measures if they could be beaten with enough charms and desperation to withstand the pain. But for Fred, and the other kids who'd been rescued from the goblins' conclave, they treated her with something like devotion. They still hadn't talked about what happened there, or what they'd seen, and I didn't want to pry, but sometimes you'd catch them talking quietly with each other.

Some students left. For the first week after it happened, we'd wake up in the morning to find a cot empty, or a pile of blankets rolled up on the floor. I guess it was all a little too much for some kids to take. Mrs. Murphy would contact the family, if the kid still had one, to see if he'd headed home. Sometimes they did. She didn't force anyone to stay, but she did try to impress on us how we'd be safer sticking together.

We slept in the dining hall at first. It was a matter of safety; the broken windows and busted doors were repairing themselves, but it'd take a couple of days for the building to seal up completely and upgrade the protection. But even if the dorm wasn't messed up, it would have been too hard to go back right away. It was hard enough going back that first morning to get my clothes. There was glass and rubble on the floor, and the furniture was toppled, the books spilled out over the desk and floor.

Only the pictures on the walls were still perfectly straight. I stood there, staring at them, until Fred came to check on me. Then he insisted on helping me pick out my clothes, using himself as a model until I heard myself laughing.

Classes were suspended. There was too much work to do, way too many nights to get through.

To be honest, it *helped* that the school was a mess. It helped to have something to do, to be able to think about something other than that night, to keep moving all day so we were so worn out and fell asleep without panicking too much.

There were scratches on the walls, floors, ceilings. Some, we patched up. Other scratches we left. It was horrible to see them and be reminded. But it was more horrible to cover them up and pretend our friends were just gone, when instead they'd been taken.

The scratches were the first step. Odd as it was, they cut through the fear and shock and found the anger. Someone had *taken* our friends. They'd broken inside our school, which was supposed to keep us safe, and they'd stolen our friends. We'd see the scratches, and we'd forget to be tired.

• • •

The worst part was about a week after the attack. It was dinnertime, and we were all out at the tables. Cook Bella kicked everyone out of the kitchen, and when we protested, she told us she could handle it *herself* and, for heaven's sake, go spend time with friends.

We were at our table, trying to eat, and Fred kept making all of these ridiculously corny jokes that were so stupid you couldn't *not* laugh. So we were—laughing—and I turned, expecting to see Fran. For one second I was confused.

I mean, of course she wasn't there. I knew that. But sometimes, like then, the reality came rushing in.

I didn't cry. I tried to keep talking, and nobody said anything. But I think they knew. Naija glanced over to where Fran should have been, her eyes bright. Then Fred, stumbling over his words, rushed in to ask did we know that with all the donations, Mrs. Macartney said we could send out a scouting party as soon as next week? "Please don't cry, Abby, please don't cry."

Under the table, Peter took my hand. His fingers were warm and steady, and I held on.

. . .

Nobody was looking forward to being allowed back in the dorms, but we couldn't sleep in the dining hall forever. The best we could do was swap rooms, and try to avoid the ones with the most visible scars.

I waited until lights-out, then grabbed my blanket and pillow and snuck down to Fred and Peter's room.

I didn't even have to knock. Peter swung the door open as I limped up, and Fred was setting out an extra mattress on the floor.

Later on, as we fought off sleep, Peter said, "I should have been nicer to her."

The words hung in the air.

And then Fred said, "You're not nice to anybody."

"I know."

"He's nice to me," I said, adding, "Sometimes."

Fred laughed. "Yeah, but that's because—"

Peter chucked a pillow at him before he could finish.

"The point is, you can still be nice," I said. "So when we find her, you just have to tell her that. And that you're sorry."

"If we find her."

This time I threw a pillow, careful to aim for his giant, stubborn head. "*When.*"

"Okay," he said. "When."

CHAPTER
31

Spring came in earnest, full of clear, sunny, mild days, as if the weather wanted to make up for everything we'd been through. Classes started again, and we fell into the routine, thankful for any kind of normalcy.

Of course, this routine included Kingsmen coming by to check the windows before lights-out, and patrolling throughout the night. And Peter struggling to write with his other hand; in the meantime Fred helped him take notes and fill out his homework. There would be nights when Fred started shouting and kicking out in his sleep, and Peter and I would take turns carefully waking him up and reassuring him that he was safe.

King Steve offered Barbarian Mike and Trixie a reduced sentence if they'd tell him where Trixie sold the other kids. It would still mean prison time, for a full century or two, but it wouldn't be Banishment. Nobody at the school was really happy about this, but I think if it came to it, we would have agreed to let them walk if Trixie would just say where our friends were.

They asked for Banishment. King Steve, more than happy to oblige them, performed the ceremony himself. He apologized later for not officially inviting us to watch the sentence carried out the way he was supposed to. I was glad. If it were up to me, I might have wanted to watch, and I'm not sure it would have been a good thing.

Mrs. Murphy refused to have a memorial service for the five missing students, and whenever someone suggested doing something to remember them, she would fire back, "It's not as if they're *dead*." Instead, she and Ms. Macartney (who, it was whispered, had experience with this sort of thing) launched a schoolwide recovery effort.

It was, as Ms. Macartney coolly explained during one tactical meeting, a matter of information and money. We find out where the students were, and we buy them back. If we couldn't buy them, we'd take them. (That got a lot of cheers.) We pasted a huge map on one wall of the dining hall and Ms. Macartney cast up a desk underneath from where she could lead the charge. In a small box, in the corner of her desk, she kept a collection of colored tacks: yellow for leads, red for rumors, blue for sightings, and five green tacks for the missing kids.

We were all assigned jobs—the older students worked with Becky and Dimitrios to train and put together teams to follow up on leads, and us younger kids worked with Mr. O'Hara to contact guilds and get the word out. We made a list of every guild in Rothermere, and visited them one by one, Mr. O'Hara cheerfully leading the way as we tramped all over the city. A couple minotaurs came with us, mostly for protection, but a little for the looks on the mages' faces when we marched through the front door. Rothermere had a *lot* of guilds, but however far we walked, we were never too tired that we couldn't visit one more.

It was Fred who came through on the money front. With black-market prices, the ransom Ms. Macartney was estimating was stomach-churningly high. But right after the first meeting, Fred got Dimitrios to set him up on the crystal ball and he called his family. And he called and he called until his dad picked up in person, at which point Fred blithely talked about summer break coming up, and looking forward to staying in his old room, and didn't Deeta have that charity runway show coming up, he'd *love* to help out, until his dad cast up an obscenely large donation.

The second they hung up, Fred called his dad's friends, one after another, to see what they'd be willing to pay.

"It's mostly good timing," he admitted when Mrs. Murphy stopped him to thank him personally. "Spring and summer is gala season for everyone's charities. All I have to do is threaten to show up."

• • •

We blinked, and the school year was over. The last weeks passed by smooth and quiet, like water over river rocks. None of the teachers mentioned grades, but I heard later that everyone quietly passed except Cesar, who'd been assigned Ms. Macartney as a personal tutor over the summer, to make sure he was ready for next year.

There were the last couple of tests, the last papers to hand in, and the farewell dinner. That night, for the first time in forever, the dining hall was clamoring and noisy. The teachers sat quietly at their table; Mrs. Murphy opted out of a speech, only saying that this once we deserved to get straight to the party.

The teachers purposefully forgot about curfew. I guess they thought we just needed a party. Around two in the morning, the police showed up with complaints about the noise, asking if we could keep it down. Of course we'd keep it down, we said; had they eaten yet? So they took seats in the back to monitor the noise level and tuck into Cook Bella's chocolate cake.

The next day, Mom and Dad came to take us home. Fred was going to spend the summer with my family. While Mom and Dad cast our trunks back home, we hugged . . . well, everyone who was willing to hug. That meant Mrs. Murphy and Ms. Macartney and Mr. O'Hara, and Dimitrios and Naija and Eila. Unless he was fighting, Cesar wasn't comfortable touching anyone, ever, but he came with the others to see us off and nodded good-bye. Becky followed us out to the street and stood there, waving, as we climbed on Dad's carpet and sailed up into the sky. We went up and up and up. Everyone on the street shrank to specks and disappeared, and then the school shrank into a brown square and blended into the city around it.

We landed in Thorten what felt like two seconds later. Ms. Whittleby offered us lunch, and Mom and Dad let her convince us to stay.

Afterward, Peter held me back as the others climbed on the carpet. "You have to visit," he said. "You have to promise me, Hale."

"Don't be silly, Peter. Of course we're going to visit," I said. "And you're going to visit us."

"When?" he demanded.

I thought about it. "My birthday is coming up. You should come then."

"I will."

"Promise," I teased him.

"I promise." And he hugged me.

When I pulled back, I laughed. "I like you a lot better when you're nice."

Peter grinned. "No you don't."

I waved to him as we flew off. I waved as we got farther and farther away and he got harder and harder to see. And I kept on waving, even when we couldn't see him at all.

• • •

After home and hugs, Dad took Fred and me downtown, where we bought a map and a ton of colored tacks. Afterward, we stopped by the Guild to make an appointment with Mr. Graidy for the next day. Mom said they still didn't have an ord, so Fred and I were hoping to hire ourselves out in return for their resources and information.

When we got back, Dad helped us hang the map in the living room, and we divided the tacks into different-colored piles. We could already put up a few red and yellow ones. It was wonderfully satisfying to push them through the paper and into the wall. Red and yellow, and blue soon, and tonight I would dream of green.

In the meantime, I picked out five green tacks and put them

in a small box to carry in my pocket, where they rattled a reminder every time I moved.

That night we circled around the kitchen table, and Olivia cut us slices of strawberry pie as Dad set out our brown clay teapot. I watched the steam curl up into the air as he poured, the delicate scent of mint drifting out of the mugs.

I thought about the school, about Ms. Macartney at her desk in the dining hall, and Mr. O'Hara marching out into the streets every day. I thought about Becky waving good-bye, her belt glinting in the sunlight. There had been talk about improvements, new safety features. I wondered what everything would look like when we got back in the fall, if anything would look different.

Carefully, hopefully, I thought about Fran and the other kids. Not about where they were or what kind of people they'd been sold to, or at least I tried not to, even though it was there all the same. Instead I reminded myself that King Steve was looking for them, Ms. Macartney and the other students were looking, and that we were going to the Guild in the morning to get them to help, one way or another. With so many people looking, they *had* to be found. Sooner or later.

Right now, though, there was dessert. There were my mom and dad beside me, and Gil grumping because he'd only gotten two chapters done before we'd interrupted him, and Olivia talking over him about her last blind date, who was, literally, a troll, but still one of the better setups she'd been on. Fred, at what would very soon become his place at the table, had finished his dessert and was sneaking bites off Jeremy's plate as Jeremy looked up interrogation techniques for us to use on the mages tomorrow.

I kept one hand in my pocket, clutching the box of tacks, as I started in on the pie. The back door was open to let in the night air, but inside the kitchen it was bright and warm.

ACKNOWLEDGMENTS

My profound thanks to my editor, Melanie Cecka, for seeing something there and being willing to take a chance on me, and for being an absolute rock star. Also Lauren Galit, my agent, who was critic, cheerleader, and advocate. Have I mentioned how much I like working for you?

Thanks to my mom and dad, for putting up with me through this whole, *long* process, and Nick for saving this baby when the computer tried to eat it. Also Jenn Rothwell for use of her brain, Diana Evans for being right all along, Marly Rusoff for her help and advice, and Kevin James Kage for his honesty, talent, and insight.

Finally, there is a real Mrs. Murphy, Ms. Macartney, and Mr. O'Hara out there, whom I had the privilege of learning from. Thank you for being my teachers. The great ones stay with you.